LUCAS

by Leah Moyes

ISBN: 9798874432331

Cover Design: Molly Phipps/WGYC Book Design
Publisher: SpuCruiser Media
Editor: Dawne Anderson
Email: Leahmoyesauthor@gmail.com
Website: https://www.leahmoyes.com/
Facebook @BerlinButterfly

Acknowledgments

Thank you, Dawne Anderson, for your ever-watchful eye, catching all of my idiosyncrasies and fixing all of my wayward commas. Your love for the written word has made a world of difference and I appreciate your thorough insight and love for my characters' journeys.

To my amazing critique team with endless patience, supporting me and my stories. I could not do it without you.

As always, I am eternally grateful to my family, especially my husband who stands patiently at my office door waiting for the moment he can interject. Haha, love you, Greg.

And a special heartfelt gratitude goes to the many men and women of the armed forces around the world defending their homes, their freedoms, and their loved ones. Your sacrifice is not forgotten.

To the military men in my life.
My father, Miguel, husband, Greg, and sons, Ryan and Alex

Prologue

February 1812

"To war, gentlemen." Jaxon Gray held up his tumbler of sherry as looks were shared around their usual table at Brooks's. Though the attempt was to make the toast a merry one, solemnity won out. The toast signified their final hour together before they parted ways to begin their prospective military assignments.

The four friends, more like brothers after a decade of association, had survived the halls of Eton together and the challenges of Oxford along with their individual titled households.

Only Lucas Walsh and Zachary Collins had known each other since their days in leading strings, the others had met while learning to navigate the wiles of educational and societal demands.

Hunter Matthews, whose indolent twin brother was the heir to the Duke of Chilton by a mere three minutes, spoke next. "This is one toast I make to you, my brothers… with all my heart, may you serve honorably and return home to this blessed country whole and swiftly in due course."

"Aye, aye." The others joined in.

"Who knew, years ago when Britain entered into the war against Napoleon, that we too would be taking our places amongst the ranks," Lucas added. As the younger son of the Marquess of Granton, he chose his military career from Hunter's lead. Though, unlike the others, Lucas left behind three younger sisters and a heavy heart. "My sisters have not yet ceased their tears since the decree arrived a fortnight ago."

"Your sister, Genevieve, might write to me to pour out her grief with your departure," Zachary chuckled playfully, showing a side of him that the men knew all too well. If it had been anything but jest,

Zachary would face the brunt of the men. They fiercely protected each other's feminine interests, especially sisters.

Lucas shot him a teasing look. "Heaven forbid, man," he said. "She will never get wrapped up in your rumors or scandals, I can assure you that."

"Scandals?" Zachary scoffed. "You all know with a certainty that Miss Burton withdrew her accusations when presented with the facts. I am an innocent man…" Then he mumbled, "Most of the time."

The group laughed loudly if only to release some of that pent up tension lying low beneath the surface from their pending orders to ship out. They all knew Zachary's reputation to be puffed up and harmless, he would sooner hurt *anything* over a woman's reputation, but a flirt he was, no doubt.

As glasses were raised once more and clinked together in one final acknowledgement, additional glances were passed silently from one man to another. *Would they all come home… whole and in their right minds?*

The underlying fear of going to war was mixed with the pride of fighting for one's King and Country and, while they all knew their duty as younger sons of the peerage, they also knew they were made of flesh and bone like any other man who felt the responsibility to do one's duty… and they would answer the call, nonetheless.

Chapter One

Lucas

March 1812

"Do not humiliate me, Son."

The words spun wildly in my head as I leaned against the railing of the ship, overlooking the expansive ocean. Each roll of the blue-gray waves rippled against my chest and etched my father's last words deep within before I boarded the ship bound for Spain barely a day ago. The exact location of my destination currently remained a mystery. Though I would have gone wherever my command sent me, I was silently grateful my cavalry commission entailed a duty against Napoleon's troops and not the American's. That, and the addition of my valet turned batman. Giles had seen action of his own a decade ago before he came into my family's service. His presence, and my proximity to Britain, brought some ease to my sisters' fragile hearts.

7

Brushing a piece of lint off my scarlet uniform sleeve, I replayed my father's parting words once more. This was not the first time he had demanded that I avoid humiliating him. In fact, those words had been used quite often in his letters to me at both Eton and Oxford, as if he expected me to submit to such behavior. It only showed how little he knew me.

Nothing in my conduct at either location had given Father reason to believe I would bring shame to the family name. In all reality, as the younger son of the Marquess of Granton, I was an obedient son, obedient to a fault.

Oftentimes, my mates prodded me to break a rule here and there... generally with little success. I could never do anything that might substantiate my father's poor estimation and, truthfully, I preferred being regarded as a man of good repute.

Even my three younger sisters might agree. Genevieve, the oldest at nineteen, with whom I shared most confidences, often told me how proud she was but lamented over my decision to fight. The night of our goodbye was filled with an inordinate number of tears. Although little was said on the matter, I knew much of her despair arose from her fear of what might occur in my absence. Her disagreements with our father and our older brother Justin, the heir, often centered on her encumbered future.

They both sought to find a suitable match for the oldest Walsh daughter, regardless of her input.

I had tried countless times to come to her assistance and attempted to influence their decision based on Genevieve's desires, but I was met with little success. She would be betrothed before I returned from war, I was sure of it; and if I wasn't mistaken, it would be to the dishonorable Lord Brant, Earl of Duxton, only esteemed for his wealth and standing... nothing else.

My fingers gripped the railing tightly at the memory of her tears. If only I had been born first and had the power to take care of my sisters on my own. I would never force any of them to marry, and especially not to a man they loathed.

Removing my helmet with its horsetail crest, I ran a hand through my shorter than normal bangs and sighed heavily, praying that I would even make it home to see their beautiful faces once more.

The fighting against Napoleon's troops had grown worse in the last year, which was why my friends and I were dispatched. As younger sons, we shared the duty of finding occupation in the most foreseeable ways… military, church, or law. None of us were truly cut for the cloth but found an equal desire to serve our country. Thus, commissions were acquired, and goodbyes were made.

Despite our desire to serve at an earlier age, as sons of titled men, we were required first to complete our education. The war had already been going on for nine long years, well, longer if you counted all the Anglo-French Wars throughout history.

Justin, at twenty-six, my eldest brother by three years and heir to the title, would have never been asked to risk his life in battle. But as the spare to the heir, I yearned for acceptance, for I certainly didn't feel it at home with the men of my family.

My thoughts shifted to my brothers-in-arms, the ones I had said goodbye to mere days ago. Jaxon, Zachary, and Hunter were my right *and* left arms… sometimes even more than that while away at school. Our goodbye at Brooks's had been a mixture of pride and soberness. They were men of honor; not one doubted the need to stand up against the enemy.

But what would we face upon return, *and would we all return?*

Chapter Two

Helena

11 April 1814

"Helena, I'd like to introduce you to Baron Foxton of Castleton." My father, the Earl of Tafney, pointed to the gentleman before us who wore a shocking, yellow-colored cravat and brown waistcoat. "Baron Foxton," Father continued with a great deal of veneration for a lesser peer. "I present to you my daughter, Lady Helena Webster."

I dipped into the appropriate curtsy for a man of his standing and smiled my most charming smile; the fabricated one I had perfected over the last year to hide my true feelings. "I am pleased to make your acquaintance, Lord Foxton."

The man's lips lifted in a sly smile. His eyes roamed the length of my pale pink silhouette dress while his tongue slid against his lips as he spoke. "It is entirely my pleasure, Lady Helena, I assure you."

I bit the inside of my cheek through my smile.

This was the fifth titled man my father had introduced me to in the course of three-quarters of an hour. Normally, I would expect a half dozen introductions the entirety of the night, the sort that carried a lighthearted sentiment culminating around the evening's amusements. Only recently, Father's urgency in such introductions brought forth undue pressure to dance or converse, and he had never asked me to entertain any particular man... until now.

Whipping my delicately painted fan open, I stole a glance at my father. A thin layer of sweat coated his abnormally pale forehead. While the Cavendish ballroom was a bit suffocating from the number of attendees, we stood close to a perfectly lovely Baroque-styled window left ajar. Papa should not be sweating or shaking. He avoided my stare—one of several oddities that had transpired recently.

Only yesterday, upon arriving home after visiting my modiste on Bond Street, I interrupted a spirited argument between him and his longtime solicitor, Mr. Branby, in the foyer. Of course, it ceased the moment I arrived, but I could not recall any time in my life that my father had raised a voice to anyone, much less a trusted friend.

The annual Cavendish Ball marked how swiftly the end of my second season approached. I had not only been fortunate that my father allowed me to enter society when I was ready, but he also had not compelled me to accept any courtship without ensuring a love match could be made. Therefore, at twenty years of age, I remained quite unattached.

Though I had been introduced to a multitude of potential suitors in the last year, I did not find any one man to be sincere enough to pursue. There was no end to the handsome, titled fops I danced with, but it did not take long for me to see what assets the men of London found essential... a lovely face, womanly figure, and a significant dowry. A woman's mind was not considered to be of great importance. That was always made clear the moment I spoke of politics or societal inequalities. Men went as far as to ask me why a beautiful woman would have need to read or to speak of such *masculine* topics. I would smile demurely as I silently crossed them off my list. My mind carried more value in my eyes than the fashionable gown I wore.

"Might I have the pleasure of the next set?" Lord Foxton rubbed his jaw. A gaudy sapphire ring graced his second finger.

"I believe it's a waltz, my lord, and I am not allowed." Though the intimate dance had grown in popularity amongst the *ton*, my family had always maintained a higher standard of modesty and this conviction had always brought a reprieve at the most opportune times.

Father cleared his throat and twisted his hands together nervously. "Oh, surely we can make an exception for Lord Foxton, my dear."

My eyes flashed to my father, though he quickly looked away. He had never risked my reputation before. When my eyes met the baron's once more, he swiftly drew them from the neckline of my dress to my face. Though I was properly covered, his examination of my figure made me feel as though I stood stark naked before him.

He held out his arm.

I glanced back at my father with one last plea, but he subtly motioned for me to take the man's arm.

I swallowed hard in an effort to quell my building tears. If Mother were here, she would have placed herself across the dance floor if only to stop me from being subjected to such a man. *Oh, how I missed her.* Placing my hand lightly over the gentleman's forearm, I walked beside him and toward the dance floor.

From the corner of my eye, I saw my dearest friend, Genevieve, standing below the soft glow of a candle sconce. She gasped, then quickly covered her mouth with her gloved hand. Hiding her emotions were never her strong suit. She moved beside a generous bouquet of pink dahlias and watched us. The lavender dress she wore balanced between her duty to grieve and obeying her brother's command to attend. The newest marquess insisted the exclusive Cavendish Ball should not be missed... even by a sister in mourning.

Once we reached the other dancers, the baron, who was undoubtedly twice my age, wasted no time in reaching around my waist and pulling me closer than socially appropriate.

I stiffened at his touch. "Please, my lord, I shouldn't be held in such a way, people will talk."

The scent of garlic and tobacco wafted freely as he leaned in. "I don't see any harm in such an act for a woman I am soon to court."

I took a step back, shocked at his boldness. "I have not consented to such a propensity, sir."

The man's fingers pressed into the fabric at my waist as he tightened his hold. "It is not your decision to make, now, is it?"

"It most certainly is." I withdrew another step and, regardless of what tongue wagging my action might generate, I marched off the dance floor and swiftly toward Genevieve. With her hand in mine, we fled out of the ballroom and down the hallway to the ladies retiring room.

"Can you believe that man?" I cried once inside and reached for the handkerchief tucked carefully inside my satin glove. "Such nerve! And before the eyes of all of London!" I dabbed the fabric against my flushed cheeks. "How could my father even allow such a man to take liberties with me when he has never done so before?"

Genevieve led me to a settee and took my hands in her own. "I cannot begin to tell you what I feared when I saw you walking out with Foxton. The man's reputation is atrocious." Her mouth pressed into a tight line. "Then when he touched you so intimately, I was near to rescuing you myself."

I wiped the perspiration off my nose and took an extra breath to calm my racing heartbeat. "Why would he do that?"

"Because he's a cad," Genevieve spouted.

"No," I whispered. "My father."

Genevieve placed one arm around me. "It is peculiar. Has he ever done that before?"

"No, never. Well, recently he has shown more urgency in his introductions and complacency in his choices." I thought back to the majority of men he had introduced me to tonight. Most were twice my age with wandering eyes and all reeked of regurgitated liquor.

"Calm yourself, Helena." Genevieve brushed the tear from my cheek. I had tried so hard to keep them from falling. "I believe you avoided a scandal, it's a crush out there and I'm certain very few guests saw you give the man the cut direct."

Genevieve was being kind, but we both knew in this society it only took one person to see something for the entire ballroom to be chatting about it by the end of the night.

"But what could your father be thinking?" She questioned as she re-twisted one of my dark curls that had fallen loose and secured it with a pin. "As women, our reputation is all we have."

"He clearly *wasn't* thinking."

"Lady Helena?" A voice called from the doorway. "Lady Helena Webster, are you present?"

My brows crinkled together as I looked at Genevieve then back toward the door. "Yes, I'm here."

"Pardon the intrusion, miss." A servant stepped inside. "Your father is asking for you."

I took a deep inhale. "Good. I would like a word with him." I did not intend on having a row with him here in public, but I couldn't stop the anger that blazed through my veins at this moment.

Genevieve's eyes widened. She had known me since our come out together last year and we became fast friends. She also knew me to have many liberties in my house, unlike her own where her father and eldest brother dictated everything. Her expression showed more worry than anything else.

14

"I'll be fine, Genevieve. My father knows where my heart lies. I will not agree to a courtship unless I know there is a possibility of a love match. He and my mother were in agreement of this, and he knows how important that is to me."

"Be careful, Helena." Genevieve kissed me on the cheek. "Your father does not seem to be himself lately and I don't want to see you suffer for it."

I smiled. "There is nothing to worry about. May I call on you tomorrow?"

"Of course."

Though I sounded confident with my sweet friend, my legs trembled beneath my dress. I had always had an open and comfortable relationship with my father, especially after the death of my mother four years ago. It had not been easy on either one of us, but through our grief we grew closer.

I stepped outside and saw my father's silhouette near a window in a darkened corner of the hallway. I tugged on my gloves and approached him with limited control over my voice. "How could you permit that man to—"

"Enough!" My father's hand rose outward and when he stepped into the moonlight, his face twisted in a madness I had never seen directed my way.

I gasped and came to a solid stop. My eyes followed his hand as it slammed down on the nearby Demilune, making a matching pair of porcelain vases wobble atop the French accent table. The thunderous noise bounced off the walls and echoed through the empty hall. I glanced behind me, praying that Genevieve remained in the ladies' room.

Father took one step forward and reached for my wrist. His hold tightened as he led me into a side room. The glow of a moonbeam shining through the window outlined a handful of instruments in what was presumed to be the music room. Thankfully, we were alone.

"How could you humiliate the baron in such a way with your childish behavior? And me in the process."

"P—pardon?" I stuttered. I wrenched my hand free though the pain he had incurred from his hold remained. "Humiliate you?" I took a step back, rubbing my wrist tenderly. *Who was this man before me?* "Do you even know where that strange man's hands and eyes were fixated, Father?"

His jaw tightened, but he ignored me. "He will not be a stranger for long."

I choked. My breath came out faster than any words. "What? What did you say?"

Father stood to his full height, which easily towered over me, and straightened his cravat though it was perfectly in place. "I intend to give Lord Foxton permission to court you."

"No!"

"You will do as I say, Helena!"

"Father! He is not a man I would choose."

"It is not your choice."

"Since when?" I tried to catch his eye, but he kept them away from me by looking at everything but me. "You and Mother have always promised me that privilege." He blanched slightly at the mention of his late wife. "Why have you taken that away from me?"

His eyes snapped back to me. "Since you have decided to prolong the event."

"I have not found the right man yet, but that does not mean he is not out there."

Father breathed heavily through his nose. "You have wasted enough time. You will be a spinster before long and we cannot wait."

"A spinster?" I pressed my gloved hand to the laced bodice of my dress. I suddenly felt nauseous. "I'm twenty and only in my second season."

"Precisely… with no prospects."

"I will not agree to this, Father."

He pointed a stiff finger in my direction. "You will obey, or you will be cut off." Then he fiercely turned around and slammed the door, leaving me alone in the room.

This time, I couldn't prevent the tears from falling as I slid dejectedly into the closest parlor chair. The strong scent of mossy wood assaulted me as if its last occupant had left his snuff box nearby, a smell I had grown accustomed to at night as a child when my father read bedtime stories to me.

My hands shook while I retrieved my handkerchief once more. *How could he do this to me?* If he wanted me out of his life so quickly, I could think of a dozen other men who did not have the rakish reputation Lord Foxton had. Though many of these men would bore me to death, they would not misuse me. Of that I was certain.

The door creaked open, and I launched to my feet, afraid Father had come back to inflict more pain.

Genevieve appeared.

I sighed and fell to the chair once more, my hands covering my face as I wept. My sweet friend rushed to my side and kneeled before me, trying to comfort me.

"I'm so sorry, Helena. I overheard your conversation." She paused. "In truth, I eavesdropped on purpose. Forgive me."

I shook my head, grateful I didn't need to repeat the dreadful exchange. Just having it spin inside my head was damaging enough. Genevieve placed her arms around me and pulled me in for a tight embrace. "We will figure something out, Helena. You cannot marry Lord Foxton, he's a horrible man."

I cried onto her shoulder. It seemed there was little else I could do.

Chapter Three

Lucas

20 April 1814

I stepped off the plank slowly and took several strides to the right to allow the other disembarking passengers to pass by. Taking a deep inhale to the fishy smells of the port, I never knew arriving back onto British soil would be as equally invigorating as repugnant. At least I was leaving the scent of tar, bilgewater, and rum behind with the ship.

That was not the only thing I was leaving. Well over one hundred discharged soldiers onboard were being brought out on stretchers, many with missing limbs, and some with missing minds, having been diagnosed with "nostalgia"—a debilitating cerebral ailment. The return across the channel had been a solemn one, reflecting on our abundant losses despite the veritable win.

I had remained in France an additional sennight upon Wellington's request and witnessed the famed Napoleon Bonaparte sign the Act of Abdication which was swiftly followed by The Treaty of Fontainebleau. The legendary general, who once ruled over many nations, was now reduced to an island princedom in the middle of the Mediterranean. The same man who was responsible for the deaths of tens of thousands of British soldiers and many thousands more who, although they might return home, would certainly not come home in the same manner in which they left.

I chose not to accompany the men who volunteered to escort the former leader on the frigate "Undaunted" along with a garrison of French soldiers to his newest accommodations, the isle of Elba. It had been over two years since I had set eyes on my home. It was time to return.

"I will see to arranging a hackney, my lord." Giles, the man who wore many hats—valet, batman, friend, and now footman—set my trunk down beside me.

I hesitated, hoping to savor the moment a bit longer but was instantly overcome by a flurry of female squeals as my sisters descended upon me. I had sent word only six weeks ago that I would be arriving near this date, though I had not indicated precisely what day or which ship I would be on. Apparently, it didn't matter.

I caught Giles' attention. "No need." I chuckled. "The cavalry is here."

"Lucas!" Sariah, my seventeen-year-old sister, cried as she threw her arms around my neck. I winced at the pressure. Though I had the good fortune of returning whole, my body felt the torment of war in every aching muscle.

Time spent in battle had yielded a harsh toll. I might never be the same. Deep bruises penetrated into the core of my chest, arms, and legs and a long scar from a saber marred my back thanks to a sous-lieutenant. Not to mention the layers of filth and blood that never seemed to disappear regardless of how many times you tried to wash it off.

"Oh, dear me." Sariah covered her mouth with her dainty glove. "Are you injured?"

I forced a brave face for them. "I am well enough." I never detailed such injuries in my letters home, it would have been for naught. The girls would have only worried, and father would have cared little.

Josie, at fourteen, wrapped her arm through mine and laid her head on my arm. "We've waited every day for six days. I cannot tell you how unsettled we've been." Tears filled her eyes. "We've missed you so."

I kissed the top of her golden curls. As siblings, our relation could never be mistaken, all of us with blond hair and though two of the girls sported blue eyes, Genevieve and I bore a unique blend of gray. "I've missed you all as well." Then I looked around. "Are you alone?"

Each of the girls' eyes went to the ground in an instant.

"Where is Father? Justin? Or at the very least, a chaperone?"

It wasn't until I took in the sight of the girls' dark dresses that I realized something terrible must've happened in my absence. I pulled Josie off my arm and faced them directly. "Why are you all dressed in mourning attire?"

The girls sniffled and looked down at their feet.

"Genevieve?"

"Papa passed," Josie blurted out.

"What?" Though my relationship with my father was less than civil, the news of his death was monumental. I could not believe my ears. "When? And why was I not informed?"

The girls all burst into similar cries. Guilt swept over me for being the cause. "Forgive me," I led them aside and out of the way of the other happy reunions. "Please, please tell me what happened."

Genevieve shook her head. "Justin sent word, but I presume from your reaction you never received it. Father passed two months ago."

I leaned against a stone wall and removed my cap. "How?" I ran my fingers through my matted hair. "Was he ill?"

Genevieve shook her head.

"Sariah?" I knew she, more than any of my sisters, would be the one to tell me the whole truth.

She tried to look away. "Sariah?"

"It is unknown." She sniffled.

"Pardon?" My cry alerted all within ear's reach. I held her hand and pleaded, "Unknown?"

Giles stood behind the girls. His expression of confusion mirrored my own.

"We know very little," Josie added.

I tamed the shock in my voice and spoke in a gentler tone. "Tell me what you do know."

Sariah chewed on her bottom lip. "He had informed us he would be at his club for the evening. It wasn't until the next morning that we learned he never returned home and was found far from Mayfair and Saturn was discovered near the bridge on the Thames."

Genevieve sniffled hard then added, "Father was found trampled to death."

My mind reeled. Not only was I coming home from war to news of my father's death, but under suspicious circumstances. "Where's Justin?" My jaw tightened at the absence of my older brother, now the new marquess. "He should be here with you."

"Miss Abagale is." Josie pointed to the older woman who waited a short distance away. I was relieved at the sight of her. At the very least, their reputations were secure. "He's too busy trying to make sense of Father's accounts. Something about the tenants."

Sariah spoke up now. "He left for Longbriar two weeks after the burial to meet with Mr. Blakely, Father's man of business."

"So, he's left you alone in London?"

"We're not alone," Josie said quickly as her eyebrows lifted. "We have Mrs. Parker, Miss Abagale, Davies, Max, Patsy…"

"All servants." I tried not to reveal my anger.

"They're more like family," Genevieve justified. "You know this, and he knew you were coming home, so he felt his time was better utilized in the country with Father's interests."

I mumbled with irritation, "*You* should be his primary interests." Then I swiftly forced my hard feelings from my mind. I didn't want this reunion to be any more sullied than it already was. Though the news of my father's death was shocking, I hated to admit that I wasn't entirely grief-stricken over it.

"I wish it was you, Lucas," Josie grumbled.

"Me, what?"

"I wish you were the heir."

"How can you say that, Jos?" I held her hand and rubbed the fingers of her gloved hand. I knew that Father was not the most compassionate man when it came to his children, but he wasn't inhumane either, and Justin was much like him when it came to business. He would make sure their dowries were intact and all would be well. "Justin will do right for the title. He has been trained up for it since he was a child."

"He's changed, Lucas," Sariah whispered.

"On what grounds?"

"He's always been serious, but now he's short with us, impatient."

"I'm certain it will pass; he has a lot to measure up to now."

Genevieve sighed. "He has already told me he will find me a husband by the end of the season." Her eyes resembled the frightened look of a fox during a hunt. "Lucas, that's in less than two months."

I looked over to my closest sister. Her bonnet shielded her eyes, but from my view, I saw her hands shaking. I didn't want to admit it at the moment, but I was relieved she hadn't already been given away. "Surely not while you're in mourning."

22

She finally looked up at me. "I said such a thing to him. He said it would be of no matter to my betrothed…" Then she grumbled, "Whoever he may be." She frowned. "Last week he demanded that I re-engage in social events. The elderly Harper sisters chaperoned me for the Cavendish Ball."

My eyebrows pinched. My brother and I hadn't been the closest growing up, but we had always been able to resolve our differences logically. This didn't sound like him at all. Granted, I hadn't had communication with him in the two years I'd been gone, other than a random letter or two, but that was expected.

"Do not fret, Genevieve, we will sort this out. When does he return?"

"He said in his letter this morning that he hoped to return in a month."

"Well, this will give us time to work up a plan, if necessary." I kissed my sweet sister on the cheek. "All will work out, dear one." Then my lips curved into a devilish smile. "Now, shall we go home and you can catch me up on the latest *on dit?*"

All three girls giggled at that. They knew how much I detested gossip but, to appease them on more than one occasion I offered a listening ear for their merriment and, secretly, I was truly desperate for any semblance of normality.

Chapter Four

Helena

"Helena, do not keep Lord Foxton waiting."

Father stood at the bottom of the grand staircase as I descended slowly. My walking boots felt more like blocks of lead than the fine leather they were made of. I had no desire to rush to see the detestable man who had called on me twice already since the Cavendish Ball.

Once, Father had left me alone with him in the drawing room which I hoped was not on purpose, but now I questioned even that.

Did he want me to be compromised? Scandalized?

If it weren't for my dear lady's maid, Eliza, who instantly recognized the impropriety and entered, thwarting any advances from His Lordship, I might be married within days. Lord Foxton might already have the special license from the Archbishop of Canterbury for such a purpose.

Eliza, who had been with my mother her last two years until her death and then with me for the last four years, had recently heard whisperings below stairs. Speculation I didn't want to believe—hints tying Father's finances to his state of urgency in securing a match. Despite Lord Foxton's inferior placement on the peer hierarchy, the man had deep pockets. This was a surety amongst the *ton*, but other things about the not so seemly baron were also a surety... such as the mistresses he kept, his connection to *gaming hells*, and his overall vulgarity.

I had no desire or intention to become associated with any of this and only appeased my father's demands until I could reason with him or come up with a plan. Whichever came first.

"Lord Foxton has requested permission to take you riding along Rotten Row today, Helena."

I stiffened. The more I was seen with him in public, especially during the fashionable hours, the more people would speculate an understanding. I had agreed to nothing. "Father, I do not wish to go today."

A sharp pain pierced my elbow, causing me to shriek with surprise. Father's grip held tightly as he moved me to the side of the stairs and away from the parlor where the baron awaited my arrival.

"You *will* go!" Father hissed. The proximity of his face near mine showed there was no question in his displeasure. Wrinkles I had not seen before deepened around his mouth and eyes and a red, almost purple, color flamed his cheeks. "And you will enjoy his company. Do you understand me, young lady?"

I lost my voice and nearly my breath as I watched the man I had adored my whole life turn into a man I now feared. "F—father..." I stuttered. "Wh—what has happened to y—you?"

He shook my arm and the sharp pain resurfaced. "I have granted you too much independence your entire life. You're my daughter, and you must obey. Do so and do it now, or you will face dire consequences."

I fought the desire to dissolve into a fit of tears. It was a new emotion for me. Since my mother's death I had found a way to rise above my sorrow and had mastered the skill of indifference. Only now, this man who stood before me was more of a stranger than ever before, and the very thought cut me to the bone. He flashed me another irritated look. My heart pounded feverishly beneath my dress and my hands trembled at my side. *What might he do next?*

Father turned to Eliza who waited obediently for me at the bottom of the stairs. "Retrieve my daughter's pelisse, she is going for a ride, and you will be accompanying her." Then he stormed off. Thank goodness he had the decency to permit Eliza's accompaniment, allowing me a smidgeon of dignity by having a chaperone. I can only imagine what would happen if Lord Foxton and I were alone.

While waiting for Eliza to return, I walked over to the forward-facing alcove with the window set that faced Grosvenor Square. The sun shone past the cerulean blue drapes, but the sheer tulle prevented the heat from reaching my face. On any other day I would have delighted in the sights before me—Mrs. Spire leading her charges down the walk, the elderly Captain Jones sitting on a bench holding his wife's hand, and Sir Humphrey trotting by on his black shire horse. But this was not any other day. I felt as though I had entered an unknown terrain and was paralyzed by it.

"Who was that man?" I whispered to myself. Certainly not the kind and loving man who had raised me. What had happened to him in a few short weeks? Could he really be facing such dreadful circumstances that he would be forced to pawn his only daughter off to the highest bidder? If this was the case, I was certain we could come to a solution together. I didn't need my enormous dowry. If I was to marry for love, money would not be a factor and five thousand pounds could surely rectify any number of financial debts.

I took a deep breath and wiped my eyes. I could not let Lord Foxton think he'd found a vulnerable miss. He had to know I would never submit to his requisites willingly.

When Eliza arrived with my navy-colored velvet coat, she quickly guided my arms through the sleeves as my father stood and watched from the mezzanine above. Though she and I had spoken of my recent concerns, I willed her to stay silent at this moment. We could only speak in the quiet confidence of my bedchamber. If my father or anyone else knew that we shared more of a friendship than that of a maid, she could be swiftly dismissed, and I needed her now more than ever.

"Good afternoon, Lord Foxton," I said without enthusiasm as I entered the parlor with a shallow curtsy.

The man, wearing a gawdy red greatcoat and gripping a conical black hat, allowed his eyes to linger the length of my figure from my toes to my chin and I had not been more grateful for the comfort of my layers at any other time. It seemed as though this might be his customary greeting and I wanted to bathe from the way it made me feel.

"Lady Helena, you look..." he licked his lips as if he was about to take a bite. "Most heavenly."

I clenched my teeth and nodded with a tight smile. "Shall we go?"

"By all means." He lifted a hand and waved for me to lead the way out the door.

When he held his hand out to help me into his barouche, I released it as quickly as possible and, though he shared my bench he scooted closer than was socially appropriate. I kept my gloved hands tightly wound together on my lap, hoping he would not try to reach for them during the ride.

Eliza took the footman's hand and sat facing me. We knew each other well enough for me to know she was strategizing Foxton's murder step by step in her mind.

27

The baron faced me. "What a lovely day to ride, wouldn't you say?"

I nodded. "It is indeed, thank you for the invitation." Though I wanted to be rude, my upbringing forbade it, so I kept my responses appropriately short.

"That is a pleasing bonnet you're wearing." He tapped an umbrella on the forward bench and signaled for the driver to go. "It matches the blue in your eyes."

If he had taken the time to look at my eyes instead of my figure, he would have seen that they were green, not blue. "Thank you," I mumbled.

"Will you be attending the Charleston Soiree tomorrow night?" Lord Foxton adjusted his cravat and glanced around, looking more at the passing carriages than me.

"I am unaware if my father has issued a reply."

"I am certain he will once he is aware of my own attendance."

I cringed. I had always enjoyed the events in Town, the musicales, dinners, balls, and soirees, but now I wanted nothing more than to hide in my quarters if Lord Foxton was to be present.

Silence weighed heavily between us for several seconds.

"You are quiet this morning. Are you ill?"

"I fear I am a bit under the weather." I lied, hoping this might shorten the ride.

"Maybe I should return you home."

My heart leaped at the thought. I sighed for exaggeration.

He tapped his umbrella on the forward bench once more. "Turn around, Martin." Then he leaned in my direction as if to whisper. "It is imperative that you are well rested for the Higgins Ball."

I swallowed hard. *Why is he saying this?* "The Higgins Ball?" I leaned sideways covertly. "In a sennight?"

"Yes." Lord Foxton reached for my hand. My fingers stiffened beneath his touch. I had never been so grateful for a piece of fabric as

I was for my glove in that moment. "Has your father not informed you that he plans to announce our betrothal at the ball?"

My lips parted and a small gasp escaped.

His mouth curved into a sly smile as he stared at my lips. "You tease me, milady."

My brows furrowed.

"Your lips are inviting me to take part, but as you know we are not alone." He glanced over at Eliza who had placed her hands in her lap, though I saw her clenching them tightly. If looks could kill, the man would be dead by now. He droned on. "But I'm certain I can find a way for us to be alone in the coming days. Do not fret, my sweet. Your needs will be satisfied."

Heat flooded my cheeks, but not from humiliation. My temper flared. "Do not mistake me, sir," I growled. "Being alone with you is the least of my desires."

Just then, Mr. and Mrs. Dutton approached in their phaeton and waved to us.

A dark chuckle emerged at my side. "I do so love a spirited woman."

I turned stiffly away from Lord Foxton and waved at the Duttons as they passed. "Please return me to my home. I am unwell."

He chuckled again. "As you wish. I do so want you in the peak of health for our upcoming societal demands." He brushed a hand over my knee and I jumped.

"And keep your hands where they belong, sir."

He winked. "I assure you, Lady Helena, they will be right where they belong in due time."

I scooted farther from him on the bench and, the moment we arrived in front of our townhouse, I didn't wait for him to help me down, I practically launched for the cobbles. Lord Foxton was still chuckling as I kept my back toward him and waited for Eliza to descend. It was the most unladylike way to exit the carriage, but I didn't care, I needed to get away from him as soon as humanly possible.

I waited at the door only briefly until the sound of his carriage and horses had disappeared down the road and grabbed my maid's hand to walk in the opposite direction. Across the road and through a path of trees, I found the secluded bench I had sought comfort at more than once.

"What a 'orrid man, miss." Eliza moved to my side once she knew there was no one to witness our exchange. We were alone in the solitude of the trees. Between the newly formed blossoms, budding leaves, and nearby hedges, we remained well-hidden.

"He's..." I could barely speak. My anger had tipped over and come full circle. Perspiration drenched the back of my neck, and none of it stemmed from the temperature. "He's..." In truth, I couldn't even think of a word wicked enough to describe the man.

"What're you gonna do?" The woman who was only five years my senior laid her hands over mine like a mother.

I stood and paced between the hedges. "I cannot marry him, Eliza. I would kill him first."

Her mouth tightened like an overripe raisin. "Well, miss, we can't have you goin' to prison, or get hung... I s'pose I should do it."

I glanced over to her and stopped walking. "I'm just speaking my mind, Eliza. I won't kill anyone..." I wanted to smile at her unfailing loyalty. "Nor will you." I untied my bonnet and pushed the limp curls hanging forward behind my ears. "Maybe..." I chuckled darkly though there was nothing humorous about our conversation. My mind spun in a blur of activity. "I can leave. Where do you suppose I can go that is out of that man's reach for the next year? I'm only one year from my majority."

"I've a cousin who works the docks at Billingsgate, maybe 'e can get you on a ship to the continent or perhaps employment 'lsewhere. What about yer mama's kin? She chatted so fondly of 'er sister."

I shook my head. We had lost touch with my only known relative, my mother's twin sister, and I wasn't quite sure why. I lifted my chin in defiance. Any living, even poverty would be better than what I believed a life with Lord Foxton would be like. Of course, that was easy for me to think having never suffered privation. My father's title and wealth had always provided a comfortable life. But if the rumors below stairs were true and my father's finances were in trouble, the poorhouse was where I was headed, regardless.

"Maybe Mr. Coventry?" Eliza's voice lifted with enthusiasm.

I bit my lip. I had refused his offer last season. He was an amiable man but overly shy and I could not see myself with someone who could not converse more than two or three words at a time. Though *anyone* looked better than my present option.

"Or that Sir Jackson? You told me 'e was quite 'andsome an' tolerable to talk to."

Sir Jackson had probably come the closest to my approval. He was handsome and witty, rich, and charming, but he wanted to establish his home in the West Indies to be closer to his investments. I had no desire to leave England because of my father, yet now... leaving England didn't seem so dreadful. I hadn't seen Sir Jackson this season so he may have already married and left the country.

"I don't know, Eliza." My body wilted in despair. "I feel utterly helpless."

"Well, it seems to me, miss, we 'ave to think of somethin' fast."

31

Chapter Five

Lucas

"Hyah!" I shook the reins of our phaeton carriage and urged our matching bays forward. Then realized my word choice and chuckled. I had spent too much time on the continent and become a heathen of sorts around horses. Coming back to my senses, I clucked my tongue. Nutmeg moved first, Cinnamon followed but moved reluctantly, showing a hint of rebellion, but both moved to a decent trot within seconds. I had never been a fan of riding during the fashionable hour, but my sisters loved it, and I loved them so, of course, I was more than willing to do anything they asked… *within reason.*

Rotten Row was packed, as usual, lined with barouches, single riders, cabriolets, landaus, and lines of casual strollers. Why the girls enjoyed this so much was beyond my comprehension. It took everything in me to maneuver in such a way to avoid a collision.

I sat alone up front with all three girls in the back pressed together like tightly packed tarts. This was the first opportunity we had to leave the house in two days. Rain had cancelled our plans to ride, play blind man's bluff, and visit the opera at Covent Gardens. The girls had to settle for hours of indoor games like charades, whist, and pinochle instead.

"Look over there!" Genevieve pointed to an overly plump man on a rather small horse. "That's Sir Reynolds. Justin introduced us last season."

The man was far from anyone I would let near my sister.

"Please tell me he also introduced you to gentlemen closer to your age."

"He actually spent most of his time playing cards with Father, but occasionally they would venture out to make some dandy happy with my hand for a set."

I wrinkled my nose. Mother would have never allowed such a feat.

"And that woman over there." Genevieve pointed to an attractive woman on a grey mare as a gentleman trotted beside her. "She is known as the Ice Princess."

"That sounds cruel."

Genie laughed. "I'm only telling you what Mrs. Quaker told me, but I believe she's betrothed to someone you know."

I glanced over at the woman who sat stately in a finely cut riding habit. Though her presentation was lovely, Genevieve was right, you could almost feel the chill from here. "Who is she betrothed to?"

"Lord Matthews."

"Hunter?" I nearly choked. I had yet to see my friends since I returned but I was certain a betrothal would warrant his contact.

"No, silly. His brother, Josiah, er, Lord Devon, the marquess."

"Oh." I took a breath. In this instance I was happy for my friend that his twin brother had earned the family title simply by being born first. To be forced to wed, regardless of how incomparable a woman might appear, would be a dreary lot indeed.

"Helena!" Genevieve called out to a barouche that approached us from the opposite direction.

The woman she called to waved back. What I could see behind her well-placed bonnet, I did not recognize.

"It's my friend, Helena," Genie leaned forward and whispered, then nearly growled, "with that awful man."

She was unable to elaborate before the man's buggy was beside us. I slowed my team to a stop and shifted my body sideways. Though it was not customary for a gentleman to drive his own carriage, it was the only way all of us would be able to ride together without taking the formal coach.

"It is so wonderful to see you, my friend." Genevieve held out a hand to keep them from proceeding. The man in the carriage seemed annoyed with the interference.

The woman Genevieve referred to as Helena carried herself with grace, she was a woman of standing, though it did not take much to see that her smile curved unnaturally. Genevieve motioned in my direction. "Lucas, this is my friend, Lady Helena Webster." Then, pointing toward the brunette, she said, "Helena, this is my brother, Lord Lucas Walsh and my sisters, Lady Sariah and Lady Josephine."

"It's a pleasure to meet you all." The woman's smile warmed. When she turned in my direction, her bonnet shielded her eyes, but her velvety voice resonated. "I have heard a great deal about you." Then her tone steeled as she turned to the man at her side. "Baron Foxton, may I present Lord Lucas Walsh, Lady Genevieve Walsh, Ladies' Sariah and Josephine."

"Pleased to meet you, sir." I dipped my head acknowledging the older man. There were no kind pleasantries and the exchange ended almost as quickly as it started with Lord Foxton tapping his umbrella against the back of his driver. "Onward, man," he called out and they departed abruptly.

34

"Well, that was… odd." I turned to snap our horses to a trot once more.

Genevieve sat back against her seat with a heavy sigh. "Odd and terribly wrong."

"How so?" This piqued my curiosity.

"Helena, Lady Helena, is being forced to allow Lord Foxton to court her."

I scoffed, "The man must be twice her age or more."

"Precisely," Genevieve cried.

"Of course, it's not unheard of." I shrugged my shoulders. "Many marriages are arranged for convenience along with any number of reasons."

"But her father has always been kind, allowed her to believe she could choose her suitors and even search for a love match."

I shook my head. "She certainly did not look as though she chose *him*."

"Not in the least," Genevieve grumbled. "In fact, she detests him. He is a deplorable man."

I managed a sideways glance back at the carriage and at Lady Helena who inched her way as far as her body could manage in the opposite direction of Lord Foxton.

"Then why would her father all of a sudden change his mind?"

"We don't know."

"We?"

"She's my friend, Lucas. I'm trying to help her."

I brought the phaeton to a halt and circled around to face my sister. With a stern expression, I warned, "You have no business getting entangled in another's domestic situation, Genie. It is a conflict you are unequipped to contend with." I tilted my head for emphasis, knowing full well her ability to get ensnared into situations she knew little about. It was that compassionate heart of hers. "We have our own issues to deal with… especially once Justin returns."

35

"If Justin returns," she countered.

I gave her a wry look. "Of course, he will. He can't stay away from the London life for long, he loves the excitement too much."

"What if he forces me to marry someone like Lord Foxton?" Genevieve whispered.

Though I didn't know the man, I knew enough from the looks of him and where his wandering eyes focused to know I would never let my sister anywhere near a man like that and I would fight Justin to the end over it.

I let go of one of the reins and reached for my sister's hand. "That would never happen, I promise you."

She closed her eyes and when she opened them a layer of moisture remained. "I refuse to let it happen to Helena either. She's the kindest person I know."

"Genevieve Marie Walsh…" I only used her full name when I readied for a scold. "We must not get involved."

"I only ask of one thing, Lucas."

"No, Genie."

"Please?" She batted her eyelashes in such a way I could not continue to refuse.

"Stop that."

"Is it working?"

"You know it is," I retorted with a playful roll of my eyes.

Sofia and Josie giggled in the background.

"Please, my sweet brother who missed out on two of my critical impressionable growing years."

"Fighting Napoleon for King and Country mind you, getting shot at and pummeled at each and every turn."

She inched forward and wound her arms around me, squeezing tight. I winced at the pressure on my back but said nothing about the pain. "I know, dear brother, and I'm so grateful you have returned. I missed you so very much."

36

I kissed the top of her head. "And I you."

As she leaned back once more, she smiled.

"Fine, what is it?" I shook my head. Heaven help the man who marries her. "What is it that you so desperately need to ask of me?"

She kissed my cheek. "All I ask is that you carefully inquire around your club as to why her father has suddenly hit dire straits."

"I cannot inquire into another man's finances!"

"Isn't there a way to do it without being obvious? Maybe there are rumors about his finances being unstable. Why would he suddenly turn to Lord Foxton? Why would he give this rake of a man permission to court Helena?"

"Ahhh, Genevieve," I growled, rubbing the back of my neck. "You are asking too much."

"Please? Aren't you meeting Lord Zachary there this afternoon?"

"Yes, but we haven't seen each other in two years, I hardly want to spend my time inquiring of another man's private affairs when I have a chance to see to my friend's welfare post war."

"You didn't see him at all on the continent?"

"Just once, in the beginning."

"Very well, Lucas. Just promise me you will look into it sometime soon. If we can't find some way to help her, she will be affianced shortly to a man who is known to mistreat women."

I sighed in defeat. "I promise, Genie, I will inquire discreetly. But not today."

It was the first time in two years I had surrendered to the opposition.

Chapter Six

Helena

"Thank you for joining me on the ride, dearest Helena."

I cringed. Father had forced me to ride with Lord Foxton a mere two days following the first disaster and, even though I tried to tell him of the way the baron spoke so indecently toward me, it fell upon deaf ears.

The only bright spot of the entire day was seeing Genevieve Walsh and meeting her family, albeit cut short by Lord Foxton and his grumblings about pretentious gentry. Yet, what I knew about Genevieve was far from pretentious. As the daughter and sister of a marquess, she had a right to airs, though she never demonstrated a condescending trait in her character.

"I believe we are too early in our acquaintance, sir, for that kind of familiarity." I fought to keep derision out of my tone. "By no means should you refer to me by my Christian name." I scooted to the far end of the bench and prepared to step out of the carriage on my own once more.

He reached out to touch my cheek though I turned aside. "Oh, I do believe familiarity is quite near, my sweet."

My limbs braced at the liberties this man continued to take.

Lord Foxton exited the barouche before me and remained at the door before I could step out on my own unassisted. He held his hand up for mine and, though I loathed to touch it, I knew my father was most likely watching from a window, and with his growing temper, I could not chance another confrontation. His outburst over something as simple as lamb for dinner last night remained fresh on my mind.

I quickly tried to release the baron's grip once I reached the ground, but Foxton's fingers curled tightly around mine. Leaning in, he caught me off guard as his lips grazed my cheek on the way to my ear. I leaned back but his clutch tightened. "I don't know why you fight me so, *Helena*." He smirked when he said my name. "The contract is being drawn up two days hence."

I jerked away and pulled my hand back against my middle. The nauseousness I felt as of late had surfaced once more. Forcing a quick curtsy, I hustled toward the front door with Eliza on my heels.

Once inside, I removed my pelisse then untied my bonnet and handed it to Eliza, whispering, "I wish to be alone. Please make sure I'm not disturbed. If my father inquires, tell him I am resting." Not that she had any ability to keep my father at bay, I merely hoped that he would respect that one simple wish.

I rushed toward the stairs but not fast enough.

Father appeared at my side. Shuddering at the sight of him, I wondered what ill-mannered behavior he might engage in. All of our recent interactions had hovered between aloof and disagreeable. I preferred aloof over the latter.

"How was your afternoon, Helena?"

I weighed the consequences of speaking the truth, though it had always been encouraged in childhood. I lifted my chin and took a deep breath. "Do you really care to know?" I knew my response was dangerously insubordinate.

His jaw tightened. "Well, I trust you will be more..." Father seemed to be searching for the right word. "...*accommodating* when he comes to call on you tomorrow."

"Tomorrow? Why?" I couldn't stop the rise in my tone.

Father's face turned a deep red and when he stepped forward, he raised a hand as if to strike, though quickly lowered it.

My arm flew over my head in swift reaction to his raised one. *Did he really intend to hit me?* It wasn't until I heard his footsteps retreat that I lowered my own defenses. *What is happening?* What had turned my kind father into a crazed man?

I quickly ran up the stairs to my room and pulled the bell rope, hoping Eliza would ignore my last request and come. I rushed over to the corner desk and retrieved a quarter sheet of foolscap and uncorked my ink bottle. Within minutes, my maid entered. "Please Eliza, I must get this note to Lady Genevieve Walsh on Arlington Street... immediately."

"Are you okay, miss?"

I wiped the growing perspiration off my brow and shook my head. "I don't know. I honestly don't know."

Chapter Seven

Lucas

As I passed the doorman and entered the ambiance of Brooks's, one of the choicest and most reputable clubs in Town, I called to my oldest friend who was already seated at a corner table, "Zach!"

Truly we should have met at home, but I didn't want my friend to be sweetly assaulted by my sisters, especially not knowing what effects the war had on Zachary. If it was anything like me, it might take more than a couple of months to adjust.

"Luke." Our nicknames for each other were whispered with accompanying hugs. There was a soberness that hadn't been present in Zach before today, but I refused to jump to conclusions with this being our first visit.

I knew war could easily change a man... it had changed me after all.

I waved the waiter over. "Port, please, and two glasses."

"Thank you, Luke." Zach resumed his seat and the preoccupation of tapping his pen knife on the table.

"Are you well?" I eyed my friend curiously. It was a foolish question to ask any man who returned from the ravages of war but a question that needed to be asked, nonetheless.

"Well enough, I suppose." Zachary deepened a crack in the table with the blade. This drew my attention.

"Where did you serve, Zach?"

"The Iberian... Badajos."

"Badajos?" I blew out a long puff of air. There wasn't a man around who didn't know the horrors rumored to have taken place there, especially the madness that consumed the men from their losses. "Was it as they say? Our troops with their drunkenness and pillaging?"

Zachary's jaw clenched. "I am unaware of what you heard but the behavior was far below that of any gentleman. One other man and I escorted the French governor and his two daughters out of town... my sword was drawn for hours in an effort to keep the ruffians from having their way with the young girls. It was a shameful response to a brutal battle."

Once our drinks arrived, Zachary placed his knife down and reached for the glass I had just poured. I eyed him carefully. Much had changed, indeed. I noted that he kept his left hand under the table and out of sight.

"What about you, Luke? Where did you serve?"

"Salamanca, Burgos, and Vitoria."

"Under Wellington?"

"Yes."

"I heard he was a beast of a man with his defensive strategies. Some are even saying he might have a chance at Prime Minister."

"Beast, no." I recalled many interactions I had with the legendary commander. "But a tyrant when it came to his daily tea."

42

A laugh surfaced that sounded more like the old Zachary and it relieved me.

"What are your plans, my friend?" I took another sip of my drink.

"I plan to resume my duties as a rake and dine and delight myself into oblivion." He smiled, though it didn't reach his eyes. War had taken a part of him much like it did me, but I had much to return to. Much to keep me more than occupied—my sisters being the greatest occupancy of mind. Although Greenbriar, the small estate my father left me, would eventually need my attention.

Zach had only his townhouse, his inheritance, and a long reputation of broken hearts to live with.

"Are you and your brother still out of sorts?"

Zach gave me a shrewd look. "I think 'out of sorts' is putting it mildly. He behaves as though I don't even exist."

"He's here for the season, isn't he?"

He nodded and took a long swig of his drink. "And I'm certain if we passed in the street, he would not even acknowledge me."

"But you're his brother, his family. A hero."

His eyes darkened. "I am no hero." He emptied his glass and waved the staff down for another bottle.

"Take your indulgence slowly, man," I suggested. "Ease into a routine but don't rush to return to such a reputation. You might find you want to settle down."

He scoffed, "Hardly."

That's when I saw it… the two missing fingers on Zach's left hand. He pulled it away nearly as fast as he produced it as if he had forgotten and let it slip. Zach's eyes met mine as if he dared me to say something, even though we had been the longest of friends.

I felt this was one area I needed to leave be… for now. "How is your father, Zach?" An easier subject to delve into.

"He is well." This time his smile came naturally. "He is resting easy at Havenscrest as we speak. I hope to visit at the end of the

43

season." His eyes softened. "I heard of your father's death, Luke. I am truly sorry."

I absent mindedly touched the black band on my sleeve. It had been over two weeks now since I had returned and learned the news, and while I had moments of sadness, my father and I had grown apart long ago, and I did not mourn his loss like the others.

I had yet to see Justin, but he sent word on his detainment and his trust that I could handle things in his absence. "Thank you. It was unexpected."

Zach looked at me with narrowed eyes. "But not a terrible thing."

I glanced up, shocked at his candid comment, though he spoke the truth. He had definitely become graver in his demeanor. "It grieves me to the soul for my sisters. They only have Justin and me now."

He chuckled. "Just you." Zach knew the intimate details of my life more than I wanted to admit.

I took a long sip of my drink and an even longer time to swallow.

"Has a perpetrator been apprehended for your father's death?"

I shook my head. "I know remarkably little, and Bow Street knows negligibly more. I might not be crushed over his absence, Zach, but to die so insignificantly... it's an injustice of the vilest kind."

"It seems rather odd for a gentleman to be traversing in Southwark at so late an hour, especially alone."

The tightness in my chest returned. While it would not have been unusual for father to seek companionship with a woman since Mother's death, a brothel seemed uncharacteristic of him.

"So, Justin has inherited?"

"It seems so." I appreciated the shift in our conversation. "I have yet to see him. Family business has taken him to Longbriar."

Zach lifted his glass upon refilling it. "To His Lordship and all that may entail. May he be a better man than the previous."

My lips pulled tight. I didn't want to speak ill of the dead, so I remained silent.

"How are your sisters? Genevieve?" Zach smiled his rakish grin. He had always teased about Genevieve's fair features, but it had always been in jest. He knew I would never let him set his cap in her direction and I was certain that's why he paid her particular attention, if only to get under my skin.

"They are all older... more beautiful, and their needs are much more involved." I chuckled. "Thank goodness for Miss Abagale. Her skills in attentiveness are positively formidable. Genevieve outshines many young misses in both talent and beauty."

Zach's eyebrows furrowed. "She is out in society? While in mourning?"

"Justin feels she has adequately mourned our father. He now hints at the hunt for Genevieve's husband."

Zach rubbed his jaw, frustration clouding his eyes. Though I never asked it of them, my friends shared the burden of protecting my sisters.

"What of Eveline?" I spoke of our mutual childhood friend. Her estate bordered both of ours and we spent many summers together. "Have you seen her upon your return?"

His eyes darkened even more than I thought possible, and his body stiffened.

This was not the response I had expected. I knew that Zach kept his affection for Eveline a secret from others, but not from me. Though we had both seen her grow from girl to woman, it was Zach who loved her, I had no doubt. "What happened?"

He shifted uncomfortably in his seat, then exhaled long and hard before he spoke. "She has married."

"Married?" I nearly spit my sip of wine out on the table. "I had not heard."

"Eight months ago, it would seem."

"To whom?"

Zach shook his head. "I must be off." He stood up and quickly erased the grimace from his face. "Give my regards to your sisters." Winking dramatically, he swiftly slipped his hand into his jacket pocket, his right hand leading into a low bow.

I stood and reached out for a brotherly embrace which, at first, was stiffly met, most likely from our recent topic. Finally, Zach relaxed. Something had happened to the man, but at least not all was lost. I leaned in. "It really is good to see you, Zach."

"You, as well, Luke."

Chapter Eight

Helena

"Quickly, miss, yer father is deep in 'is cups." Eliza rushed into my bedchamber and pulled my small, prepacked trunk from the connecting room. It had been readied hours ago for this very moment. "If yer to leave it must be now."

The reality of running away washed over me, forcing me to freeze in my stance. Glancing over the room I've had since I left the nursery, every part of it reminded me of the happy childhood I had. My four-poster mahogany bed with brass curtain rails and satin trim, the small desk in the corner where I would write letters to my parents and slip them under their door. The window seat where I read for hours was now marred by recent memory.

Eliza glanced between me and the door. "We must leave 'fore he wakes. 'e's in the library."

I pressed a cold hand to my cheek. The bruised mark from our most recent confrontation yesterday grew in size and discomfort. The sting radiated as painfully now as it did then and, though Eliza applied arnica to the wound last night, it remained a beastly sight.

"Quickly, miss." Eliza opened my jewelry box and handed me a diamond pendant along with my ruby earrings and brooch. "Put 'em in yer reticule. You cannot leave the lovelies yer mama gave you."

"Yes." My hand gripped them tightly before I put them inside with what pin money I had saved. "I may need to sell them."

Eliza's lips pulled into a frown, but I was grateful she said nothing. I could not bear the guilt on top of everything else I was feeling. Reaching for my pelisse, she held it out while I reflected on what caused my father to react so violently.

The entire scene played back through my mind like spokes on a spinning wheel.

I had defied him.

Despite Father's insistence, I adamantly refused to dress or attend the Higgins Ball—the very ball Lord Foxton continued to threaten my future over. When Father came to check on my progress and instead found me still in my morning dress, propped in the window seat reading, he flew into a rage. Seizing the book from my hands, he struck me across the cheek with it. The spine left a welt the size of my palm from my cheekbone to my mouth. When I tried to run from the room, he grabbed my dress, tearing the sleeve and pulled me backward. Stumbling, I fell to the floor as he loomed over me shouting words I'm sure I would've understood at any other time, but at the moment, I could only comprehend one thing.

My father hit me.

The very notion ached nearly as much as the wound itself.

I was grateful no one had witnessed the event. Eliza might've tried to help me and found herself in a similar state or without employment. However, once she discovered me and realized my injury was at the hands of the earl, I had to beg her to keep it confidential.

She left early this morning and went to the Walsh residence on her own. My dear friend Genevieve arranged to send her coach to me later this evening and Henry, a trusted stable hand, notified us of its arrival. Now everything was in motion.

Each step from this moment on determined my future. What little reputation remained after Lord Foxton's public affection, and my father's financial state, would now be in tatters. I knew that once I walked out this door there would be no undoing my past. I would have to disappear or face the injustice of my peers.

With my pelisse now secure, Eliza led me down the servants' stairs with Henry close behind carrying my trunk. They had made sure that no one else would be witness to our subterfuge and face a similar consequence from my father.

The moment we stepped outside, a light breeze wafted over us. If I hadn't been trembling, I might have seen it as a sign of comfort, guiding me forward, giving me the confidence to continue.

With a full moon, no additional lanterns were necessary as we stepped into the alleyway and past the mews where the Walsh driver and one footman met us at the carriage. Neither one said a word as they secured the trunk and opened the door for both Eliza and I to enter.

"Don't yous fret, Lady Helena." Henry tipped his cap. "I won't say nothin' to no one." He sealed his promise with a nod. I believed him. Though he was paid by my father, it was my mother who insisted we hire him ten years ago when he was but thirteen. He was as loyal to me as Eliza.

As the coach pulled away, I leaned out the window and watched the silhouette of my home disappear, and my chest tightened, wondering if I would ever step foot inside it again.

While the drive to the Walsh residence was not far, the lateness of the hour would force Genevieve to stay up past a reasonable hour to receive us. I frowned with the burden of shame that already crept through my limbs and weighed down my soul. I was asking people to take great risks on my behalf.

I knew of the recent death of the marquess and also knew that his successor was absent. Genevieve had told me that her oldest brother, Justin, was seeing to the family affairs at their country estate. However, it was not Justin I met while riding with Lord Foxton at Hyde Park, it was her brother, Lucas, recently returned from war on the continent. My only consolation to this terrifying plan was that despite Lord Lucas Walsh's presence in the house, Genevieve assured me he would know nothing of our design.

I only needed this plan to work temporarily. At least until I found my aunt, my mother's sister, in Northampton, or found a means to live by.

Chapter Nine

Lucas

I rolled over in bed.

The sound of wheels clattering along came to a stop outside, but I had gone to bed quite late and had only just fallen asleep, or so it seemed, so surely I had to be dreaming.

I hadn't quite grown accustomed to the sounds of the city yet. Much of my time on the continent had been spent in less than copious means with only a tent and a bedroll for comfort. One would think with the luxurious lifestyle now at my fingertips I would sleep like an infant in a mother's arms.

A door creaked, then footsteps padded up the stairs and down a hallway.

What in the world?

I rose wearily. I moved slower now, especially since I slept on my side avoiding the scarred flesh of the saber wound. The injury itself had occurred over seven months ago and received the best care a field hospital could offer, but the slash had damaged muscle and flesh that may never fully recover. I peered down at my attire, having fallen asleep in my shirtsleeves and breeches again. Nights were especially unkind to me and, while it would have been easy to drown my memories in an endless bottle of whiskey or laudanum, I knew too many soldiers who struggled to return from such methods. I couldn't do that to my sisters. They needed me.

Though I had not planned to leave my bedchamber at such an hour, being partially dressed made the task infinitely easier. I ran my hands through my longer than normal strands. Since my return, I deviated from the short military haircuts required of a uniformed officer and, while I always dressed to perfection each time I appeared in public, I quite enjoyed a less stringent appearance at home.

The sound of doors opening and closing filled the otherwise silent corridor. My sisters were no strangers to midnight snacks, secret conversations, and visits to one another's bedchambers. I was sure this was just another one of those nights but, as the sole man of the house, it was my duty to see to their safety. I lit my candle and reluctantly opened the door.

Of course, there would be no sound now.

I shuffled to the far end of the family wing and knocked on Genevieve's door.

No answer.

"Genie?"

I waited, leaning against the door frame, then knocked again. Genevieve was naturally a light sleeper, I was certain she must hear me. Twisting the knob, I cracked the door open just as a voice rose from behind me in the hallway.

"Lucas?"

I circled around to see my sister in her nightclothes with her dressing robe tied tightly at her waist. Her eyebrows were raised in a way that made me feel as if I was the one in question.

"I knew it," I groaned and ran a hand down my face, then rubbed my tired eyes. "Playing night games again?"

Her cheeks turned a bright red under the flame of both our candles. She looked away. I stared harder, she could never look me in the eye when she was fibbing. "Uh, Josie had a fright. She needed comfort."

I eyed her suspiciously. It was true Josie had nightmares occasionally, especially since our mother passed. She was only seven at the time, but there was something more to this. "Should I go check on her?"

"No." Genevieve grabbed my sleeve. "She is asleep again. Resting comfortably. I sang her Mama's song and she fell back to sleep."

"Alright." I reached for the hand that gripped my fabric and clasped it gently. Genevieve had become a mother to her sisters, not intentionally, of course, but it had happened, nonetheless. Pulling her in for a hug I kissed the top of her head. "Get some sleep. We have a dinner party to attend tomorrow."

"We do?"

"Have you already forgotten that Justin sent a list of events you are to attend?"

She rolled her eyes. "Only because he has resumed Father's crusade to see me married."

I tilted my head, forcing her to see me. "Actually, Genie, I was quite relieved you hadn't wed in my absence."

"Thank heavens I was not."

I lifted one brow curiously and scanned over her fair features. She offered all the correct checkmarks for a woman of marriageable age— she was a lovely, well-bred woman with a titled family and a substantial dowry. "But." I could not prevent my next question from surfacing. "Why were you not?" When she sent daggers my way, I swiftly threw my hands up defensively. "I'm only asking. Don't misunderstand, I am grateful you are not."

She smiled wickedly for one brief moment and the younger, wilder version of Genie appeared. "I may have sabotaged a courtship or two."

I laughed out loud then quickly covered my mouth to not wake the others. "How?"

"Miss Abagale helped, but do not judge her harshly. It was I who required it of her."

"What did she do?" I braced for bad news.

Genevieve shifted in her stance and bit her bottom lip before she spoke. "She sent word below stairs that I might be unable to bear a child."

My face went still. "Genie…" I needed to craft my sentence carefully as to not sound like Father or Justin. "That is nothing to jest about. It could have damaged *all* of your future prospects."

"Then fine!" She fisted her hands on her hips defensively. "I would be delighted to remain unshackled my entire life if it means I can avoid the likes of men such as Lord Brandt or Lord Foxton."

I had to agree with her. I had feared to return and find her bound to such a man.

"Well, you mustn't concern yourself now. Get some rest. We will be attending the soiree if only out of respect for Father's close connection to the Drake's."

"I'm not sure if I should go."

I eyed her warily. Now I knew something was up. She *never* turned down a social event with close friends. Was she this terrified that Justin would force her into an abysmal match? "I will be there, Genie," I assured. "I would never leave you to the clutches of a blackguard."

She coughed into her hand. "It is not that… I believe I'm catching a cold. I would hate to risk infecting the guests."

Did she really believe I was that daft?

"Love you, brother." She swiftly kissed me on the cheek and slipped past and through to her bedchamber, closing the door before me. I stood in the dark corridor stewing for several more minutes. Something strange was happening right under my nose and I couldn't put my finger on it.

Once settled back in my quarters, I blew out my candle and smiled. Since coming back from the war, my senses were heightened. In battle, I had learned how to vet out the enemy and had become one of the best scouts Wellington employed.

Allowing my sisters time to believe they have their brother fooled would not only be an amusing adventure but, in the end, the lightheartedness might remove the dark shadow that had reigned here for far too long.

Chapter Ten

Helena

I stretched out comfortably beneath the feather coverlet and sighed. The luxurious bed I slept in was not unlike my own, but it was just that... *not my own*. Only here, the moment I stepped foot onto the property, there was an undeniable sense of safety that I had not felt in weeks.

I only had to be discreet.

Last night when Genevieve met me and Eliza at the coach and led us through the servant's entrance to the top floor, she reminded me that, if we were careful, Lucas would remain completely ignorant to my presence.

She had initially presumed he might go to his own inherited country estate soon, but then she admitted with the new marquess absent, Lucas wouldn't leave his sisters alone. He felt too much of a responsibility for them.

The way she spoke of Lucas, I couldn't help but adopt the name in my mind. Lord Lucas Walsh felt so formal, cold, and stiff. And when she described his desire to protect her, something much more congenial took root... then jealousy inadvertently crept over me. If only I had such a brother or such a protector, my circumstances could be entirely different.

I had previously believed it was Father who filled that occupation. My hand once again went to the injury on my face and, while it was quite tender to the touch, my sorrow was more about the act itself than the result. I would have never believed my father could resort to such conduct and it pained me deeply to dwell on it.

With Lucas here, it presented a complicated situation for me. If he discovered me, he would most likely consider it an obligation to return me to my home regardless of the reason I left or the danger I felt living there. Men of the *ton* did not question other men on how they managed their households or their families.

A soft knock at the door brought Genevieve inside, holding a delightful tray of breakfast foods.

"Oh, my dear friend." She quickly placed the tray down on a nearby table and ran to the side of my bed. "Oh, please tell me that did not occur at the hand of your father."

My hand went instinctively to the bruise. I knew it was unsightly and was ashamed by it. I had forgotten that upon my arrival in the dark, the hood of my pelisse would have shrouded the horrors from her last night.

Genevieve reached out to me and embraced me lovingly. "You are safe here. I promise."

"But for how long?" I whispered. "I cannot hide here forever."

"Until we figure out a plan. We will think of something."

I adored her cheerfulness. She was possibly the only person I could think of who had such a pure heart.

"Until then, stay in here," she cautioned. "You are in a guest chamber that is quite overlooked. I know the condition is less than you are accustomed to, but you would be discovered in the nicer bedchambers." She handed me a cup of warm chocolate. "And the good news is that it's only my family here, we have no guests due to arrive any time soon."

"And what if your brother learns of me?"

"He won't." She patted my hand. "Lucas will have no need to venture in this direction, and very few know you are here outside of your maid who is staying right there through that door." She pointed to a connecting door that opened at that very moment and Eliza stuck her head through as Genevieve continued. "Also Mrs. Parker, our housekeeper, and Henrietta, my maid will make sure you have all your meals here and no one will be the wiser."

"Thank you, Genevieve." I kissed her cheek.

Eliza picked up the tray and brought it to me. I took a nice, long sip of the chocolate drink, allowing it to warm me from the inside out.

Stepping over to one of the windows, Genevieve pulled the drapes open. The sun brought light to all the delicious foods before me. Bacon, sausage, fried tomatoes, baked beans, and toasted bread. "Eat," she commanded. "Eliza is considered a new hire here so she is free to roam the halls as necessary and retrieve whatever you may need." Genevieve moved toward the door. "We have a proper library, though it is not as large as the one in the country." She smiled. "I will bring you a new book every afternoon. I might have to leave on occasion in the evenings now that I am out of mourning."

"Out of mourning?" I gasped. "Entirely?"

"It is Justin's request. I'm sure his objective is prompted by husband hunting."

I made a face. The very thought of husbands made my stomach roll, but it brought comfort knowing that Genevieve shared my plight.

"Fear not, my friend." She smiled and winked. "Lord Foxton's hand cannot reach you here."

I returned her smile with a sincere one of my own… something I had not felt in a very long time.

Chapter Eleven

Lucas

"Lord Lucas Walsh, welcome home."

I stepped up to the receiving party and bowed. "Thank you, Lord Drake," I said, then turned to his lovely wife and bowed over her hand. Though this evening's soiree was not as elegant as a ball, they spared no expense on their Greco-style décor. The sight was a refreshing change from the field officer's *mess* I had grown accustomed to overseas.

Instead of exotic bouquets gracing expertly carved columns, we had a wooden table and a half dozen chairs. Instead of marble likenesses of Poseidon, Apollo, and Athena, we had a couple of chickens and a goat. Instead of the lovely Grecian garland adorning the ballroom entrances, we had a few mismatched plates, bowls, and cutlery. And instead of a row of colossal Hellenic vases, we had a row of half-filled bottles of rum.

Despite Justin's recent missive demanding that Genevieve abandon the mourning attire and attend every social event possible, I could not deny the comfort it brought to immerse ourselves in humanity once more and restore old friendships. The Drakes were one of the oldest relationships our family had. Theirs, and our neighbors from the country, the Collins and Browns—Zachary's and Eveline's families, respectively.

"I'm deeply sorry for your family's loss." Lady Drake lovingly smiled.

"Thank you, that is kind of you to say."

The pleasant mother with two daughters of her own then turned to Genevieve. "Dear girl, you are a vision. If you are not snatched up before the season ends, I will be most astonished."

Genevieve flashed a panicked look my way before she curtsied then smiled a tight grin to the hostess. "You are too generous, ma'am."

Although our families had spent considerable time together, our fathers shared the deepest connection. Unfortunately, the Drake daughters were painfully shy and spent most of their social appearances circumventing any conversation by cowering behind the largest pillar they could find. Genevieve eventually stopped seeking amiable familiarity with the girls years ago.

"Please enjoy the evening, despite your heavy hearts," Lord Drake added as I bowed our goodbye.

Genevieve wrapped her arm through mine and leaned in tightly. "What did Justin say after you mentioned that there was no need to rush my betrothal?" I had not told her the entirety of the contents of his letter. It angered me too much.

"He is overwhelmed with the tenants." I had never lied to her, but this was not the time to tell her the complete truth that Justin mentioned in the latter part of the missive he was considering offers of her courtship through correspondence. "He has much on his mind. Do not worry, you are of little concern at the moment."

I smiled and nodded as we passed the handsome Mr. and Mrs. Gregor who were engaged in a conversation with the Howards. I leaned closer to Genevieve and whispered, "It will be easier if Justin and I speak in person. But don't fret, please, I will make sure nothing happens."

She frowned at my side. "I don't recognize anyone, Lucas. Why did we have to come tonight?"

I stopped in place and eyed her carefully. She usually enjoyed societal affairs. Was she really that frightened of marriage? "You know why. Father and Lord Drake were childhood friends. It is a duty. Didn't you come last year?"

She shook her head. "I was unwell. Father and Justin came without me."

I glanced over the assembly. Pockets of noble men and women huddled in each corner, many much older than Genevieve, whispering most assuredly over the latest *on dit*.

"Were you aware Eveline Brown wed?" I had remembered the news Zachary had shared with me, though he didn't elaborate.

She nodded and lowered her voice. "We believe their change in circumstances required her to marry so swiftly."

"What change in circumstances?"

Genevieve's eyebrows pinched. "Lord Ashton died shortly after your departure. I wrote you and told you the dreadful news."

I could not recall receiving such an account and I was stunned to learn of it now. Both Lord Ashton and our father, neighbors for decades, passed away within two years of one another? How odd. Poor Eveline, her mother Joanna, and younger sister, April. Though Zachary and I were two years Eveline's senior, we spent many summer days amusing ourselves at the pond which signified the cross section of all our estates.

I handed Genevieve a glass of orange-colored punch. She took a sip before continuing. "With her father's passing, his troubled financial state was exposed. The wedding came as a shock to us all. A small affair last September, shortly after the banns were read. Speculation suggests she married to save her mother and sister."

My heart pounded in my chest. If only Zachary had known, there was no doubt in my mind he would have rescued them. Eveline may have refused out of pride, but Zachary loved her. I was sure of it. No wonder he responded tersely to my inquiry.

Now it was too late.

"Did Lord Ashton not have his affairs in order? An addendum to provide for the women of his family?"

"Apparently not. A distant cousin, the closest heir, now resides there. A man by the name of Curtis is the new Lord Ashton. Justin might be familiar with him, but I am not. I refused to be acquainted with a man who callously turned the women out shortly after the wedding breakfast."

"He did what?" I had never heard such a thing.

"It is rumored that he was the one who introduced Evie to her husband then obliged her to wed posthaste so as to not take on the added burden himself."

"Who is the man she married?"

"Sir Colin Turner."

"What do you know of him?"

"He is much older than her. Fifteen years her senior."

"Fifteen!" I lowered my voice as eyes curiously flashed in our direction.

"He is a businessman of sorts. They have rented rooms here in London."

"Have you seen her?"

"No."

"Whyever not?"

"Justin forbade me to."

The muscles in my jaw clenched to her confession. Justin must've seen her fall from grace as a reason to sever ties. "For heaven's sake Genie, she's our friend and former neighbor."

"I know," she said as she shook her head. "I have so few as it is and the ones I do have are facing severe hardships."

"Such as?"

"Good evening, Lady Genevieve." A tall, shapely older woman wearing a gaudy, feathered headdress interrupted us. "Don't you look dazzling, my dear."

Genevieve's lips lifted in her false smile. I fought to keep my chuckle buried as I looked over to receive the strange woman.

"Who is this dashing young man beside you? A new suitor?"

"Suitor?" she choked out, then quickly resumed a polite façade. "Forgive me, I presumed everyone who was acquainted with my family knew my brother. Mrs. Louisa Cunningham, I present to you, Lord Lucas Walsh."

The woman's eyes brightened at the word "brother". Then with little tact, she perused the length of my form from the tip of my head to the toes of my boots. I must've passed her approval because she ended her scrutiny with a sly smile and held out her hand for me to bow over. "Pleased to make your acquaintance, my lord."

"The pleasure is mine."

Genevieve gracefully lifted a hand in the air. "Mrs. Cunningham is visiting London from Bath." She pointed to the elderly gentleman at the refreshment table. "Her husband, Mr. Frederick Cunningham, is a recent member of the House of Commons."

"Very impressive, my dear. What a memory." With one last pointed look in my direction, Mrs. Cunningham walked away with an extra sway to her hips. I turned to Genevieve for an explanation. She shook her head. "I don't have the patience to elaborate tonight. I only warn you, do not say a solitary thing in her presence that you don't want spread across Town by morning."

I chuckled.

"The woman always makes me feel like I'm an exhibition."

"You do look beautiful, Genevieve. She wasn't wrong."

Just then my sweet sister looked up at me with her bright eyes that appeared more hazel in the light of her shimmering gown. "Dear brother, it will not be long before you are taken with someone." She tugged on my white cravat as if to straighten it, although I knew Giles would not have let me leave the room had it been less than perfect. She smiled. "And you would be quite the catch."

I grimaced. "I am not in haste. My dear sisters must be cared for first."

"That is Justin's responsibility now," she said with a frown.

"And where is he?" My teeth clenched, then I resumed a pleasant face for my peers. "I'm sorry, that was uncalled for."

Genevieve gazed up at me for a long while and chewed on her bottom lip. "There is something I must speak with you about, but not here."

"It sounds serious."

"It is."

"If it isn't the infamous Lord Lucas." A deep voice surfaced from behind me.

"Matthews!" I circled around to find the intimidating figure of one of my closest friends. I gripped his hand in a robust shake. Typically, in a public setting, I would bow, but this was not any man... and it was the first I'd seen Hunter since our parting drinks at Brooks's over two years ago. "It is so good to see you, mate."

"Any news from the others?" he asked.

"Yes," I nodded. "I saw Zachary recently, but he had not heard of your whereabouts. When did you arrive?"

"Last night."

I didn't mask my surprise. "And already out socializing?"

"Of course. I couldn't miss the Drakes." He chuckled. It had been a long-standing joke that we had all been forced to endure. In our youth, we entered a bet to attend one specific event each season. If we were in Town and did not attend said event, the negligent sod bought a night's round of drinks at Brooks's. The Drake soiree became that time-honored occasion.

"Any word on Jaxon?" I inquired.

Matthews shook his head sternly then tipped his head inward. "We need to speak privately."

I glanced over to Genevieve. "Lord Hunter, you remember my sister, Lady Genevieve Walsh."

Hunter smiled warmly in her direction. Despite his height and broad shoulders, he could charm anyone with his smile. "How could I forget one of the most beautiful women in the room?"

Genevieve blushed and curtsied. "My lord."

He lifted one eyebrow. "I do believe close friends can forgo that ridiculous title," he whispered only within our earshot. She giggled and I rolled my eyes. Most of the time we said it to each other just to get on each other's nerves.

"Come Genevieve." I reached for my sister's hand and tucked it into my arm. "I need to speak with Matthews, might I leave you to Mrs. Harding's care?"

The elderly matron, more like a grandmother, always looked out for Genevieve at every turn during our months of residence in Town.

"Lucas," Genevieve whispered. "Please don't abandon me all night."

"I won't, I promise."

Following Matthews, we stepped out to the veranda for some privacy. "I understand congratulations are in order for your brother's betrothal." I leaned against the balustrade with both of my arms

66

folded over my chest. "I caught a glimpse of the woman at Hyde Park. She sports a fine seat."

"And a cache of icicles at her fingertips," he countered.

I chuckled. "So, the title stands."

He shrugged. "The Ice Princess is not my concern. Josiah must tolerate her, but I will say…" He rubbed the back of his neck. "If he doesn't tame his wild ways, she might plunge one of those icicles in his chest while he sleeps."

I shook my head, knowing full well the trouble Hunter's twin brother caused the family. Though he was the heir by mere minutes, his reckless behavior had caused the family their fair share of grief. I wondered why their father had not yet circumvented some law to cut the eldest out of his inheritance.

"What did you wish to speak to me about?" I studied his face for a hint. "Is your brother the reason for that grimace?"

"Not this time. I didn't want to answer your earlier inquiry in front of your sister." He sighed heavily. "Jaxon has been reported as missing."

"What?" I choked. I had not expected this though I knew the possibility of losing a friend in war was vastly real. "What do you know?"

"We were together on the peninsula."

"Zachary and I were there as well."

"Yes, I was aware of that," Matthews continued. "I worked for the War Secretary and I was able to keep tabs on all of you. Your company's whereabouts, transfers, moves, and so on. Jaxon worked as a topographical spy. His final mission took him reasonably close to Bonaparte's center of operations."

"A perilous mission indeed," I added.

He nodded. "He met often with a group of Spanish guerillas who intercepted dispatch from an unnamed French officer under Marshal Soult and then forwarded the collected confidential information. I got word this morning that he missed issuing his final report mere days before Napoleon surrendered."

"Jaxon's missing?" I repeated, unable to fathom the idea of one of our own out there alone.

"Listed as missing could very well mean prisoner. They have not accounted for all of our interned men."

"What do you suggest?"

"I am petitioning to return to the peninsula. I will meet with the Foreign Office within the week."

I folded my arms over my chest. "I want to be included."

He exhaled loudly and looked out over the Drake's well-tended gardens. Despite the variety of exotic foliage they displayed, it was the fresh scent of mint that filled the air. "I will keep you informed, Walsh. As you know, things were tenuous in the end. Despite Bonaparte's exile, there are many French sympathizers who believe the war is not yet over."

"But it's Jaxon Gray, a significant part of the secret intelligence for these two years. For heaven's sake, his father worked under Sir Evan Nepean and his surveillance system in London for many seasons. They wouldn't refuse your request and leave him on his own… would they?"

"There are still many unknowns. Negotiations with the French have been slow and *Verdun* is rumored to house thousands of detained Brits. We can only hope that Jaxon is alive and not have gone unaccounted for in a mass grave somewhere."

I frowned deeply at the very thought. I wanted more than anything to assist but feared my own domestic state might prevent it. I could not leave Genevieve to Justin's rash decisions and, if he continued to stay at the country estate, I could not leave my sisters alone here in London.

"Thank you for telling me."

"Anything for a brother." Matthews slapped me affectionately on the back and I winced.

His eyes narrowed. "That was not a hard slap my friend, what are you hiding?"

I shook my head. "Nothing that most of our men haven't faced in battle. I'm fine."

He nodded and bowed, but his eyes said a silent mouthful before he departed. I knew he, more than anyone, would understand. He would be just the man I could confide in when divulging details of my inner demons.

I remained on the veranda alone, unable to stop thinking about our friend. I met Jaxon in our second year at Eton. As the son of a duke, he could have befriended any number of gentry offspring, but he chose *me* to be the bowler of his cricket team. You would think the son of a marquess would have confidence aplenty, but I kept to myself and had only two friends—Zachary and Eveline.

With my decent bowling arm and a bevy of new friends, my societal demands improved and, by our fifth year, not only were we undefeated but also the pinnacle of rank at the notable college. Lord Jaxon saved me from social rejection. Although that was seemingly small compared to what he now faced, I owed him. I knew what pitiable circumstances a military man faced in a foreign country, but a detained soldier most certainly encountered ten times that.

My mind flooded with memories of the carnage, chaos, and death that occurred during battle. And the smell... there was nothing more dreadful than the metallic scent of blood and rotting flesh. Notably, not every man lost was killed by the enemy. As Dragoons, we had an elevated perspective over the Foot Guards or Rifles on the frontline with their muskets and bayonets. I had seen many men succumb... *could Gray have been with them or killed for espionage?*

It wasn't until Genevieve had located me outside that I realized I had missed the entire event. I had neglected my sister's pleas and been an abysmal escort, but despite this recognition, I couldn't bring myself to focus on anything but my friend.

Chapter Twelve

Helena

It had been two days since I left my father's house.

Did he miss me? Or only the financial windfall I provided with a marriage of convenience?

Frustration plagued my mind. What could Lord Foxton possibly want with *me*? He didn't need my dowry. He was filthy rich... emphasis on filthy. His reputation with women, more particularly with mistresses involved in the theater, made it so he didn't lack female companionship. He could veritably ask any woman to be the lady of his house.

Why me?

The mystery needed vetting. If my father chanced upon dire straits, Lord Foxton's connection would be beneficial to my father, but what did the man have to gain from my betrothal other than a wife of higher standing? Was his intent to improve his aristocratic status through marriage that significant?

I turned in my bed and tossed the coverlet aside. Though the hearth now only offered an amber glow in place of a once roaring fire, a fervor heated my body. The sun had descended hours ago and yet I could not get my mind to settle long enough to fall asleep. I even read for several hours from the book Genevieve brought me and, most of the time, reading had lulled me enough to a peaceful rest.

Not tonight.

I stood up and drew one side of the rose-colored drapes aside. Genevieve said this room was not one of the finest guest chambers, but the impeccable décor surpassed with preeminence. A woman's touch most certainly influenced the silk damask wall hangings and the vibrancy of the matching ornamentation.

I glanced out the window. The full moon provided a lovely view of the rear garden. Oh, how I wished I could walk through the latticed arbor draped with wisteria or the neatly trimmed evergreen hedges leading to the marble birdbath. Instead, I was hidden away like a secret prisoner inside my bedchamber.

It was certainly not Genevieve's fault I felt so confined. If anything, she had saved me and I would be eternally grateful to her, but to be so constricted—well that was torture in itself.

Retrieving my dressing gown, I covered my shift. I needed to breathe air that did not circulate in this small space. Walking over to the door, I cracked it open. With the late hour and everyone asleep, I hoped to wander the halls without being discovered. It might provide a tiny semblance of freedom… and maybe allow me a chance to locate another Chelsea bun similar to the one Genie brought for me with tea this afternoon.

My stomach growled. The answer was clear; I needed to satisfy it.

I returned to the mantle, lit my sole candle, and stepped out into the corridor cautiously. I knew my bedchamber did not coincide with the family floor, but I wasn't fully aware of how the house was designed, aside from my familiarity of the traditional townhouses of Mayfair and their narrow build.

I tiptoed down the hall and descended the stairs. The glossy marble made the task easy for my slippers to be silent. Reaching the next floor, I wandered through an overlong hall. In the glow of my small flame, gilded frames protruded from each side. A portrait gallery.

Being a London townhouse and not a country estate, the portraits appeared to only go back a century ending with 1813. The late marquess to be sure. I lifted my candle to examine him more closely. Although the man with light-colored hair and an angled chin proved handsome for his age, his stern brow and unrelenting glower presented a clear insight to the man Genevieve had spoken so little about.

I returned to the stairs and quietly made my way to the next floor. A handsome portrait of a striking woman graced the entire wall in the small alcove of the mezzanine. Her blond curls tucked up into a fashionable style, her gown a vision of cobalt silk and pearl lace, ending with a kind, enchanting smile. I lifted the candlestick closer to see bright blue eyes peering back at me. Genevieve's mother, no doubt. The similarities were too substantial. Sadly, she had lost her mother at the tender age of thirteen—right in the beginning of transitioning from a girl to a woman—another reason she and I became close, having both lost our mothers.

I brushed a finger across the stunning sapphire necklace that circled her throat and the matching dewdrop earrings. How would it be to be the lady of such a grand and reputable house, respected and revered?

A loud bang sounded from the opposite end of the hallway, shuddering me back to reality. My insignificant flame did nothing to penetrate the darkness and I failed to identify the impending danger. Spinning around in the small alcove, I searched for a place to hide, but only a pair of chairs and a bookcase could be found. Noting a modest gap between the bookcase and the corner wall, I squeezed inside and blew my candle out.

My heart pounded in my throat as I peered around the edge. Though darkness filled the corridor, moonlight from the expansive window nearby cast enough of a beam to show the silhouette of someone walking forward.

I bit my lip and prayed it was a woman, but from the heavy footfalls against the tiled floor and the breadth of the shoulders, it was confirmed... the approaching figure was most certainly a man.

I had only seen Genevieve's brother Lucas once in a carriage, but I believed with certainty it was he who headed in my direction.

I braced for discovery when he stopped at the forward-facing window and flung the drapes aside. Though it was too difficult for me to see his facial expression, his movements were sharp and filled with frustration. Clutching the sill with both hands, he tilted forward, breathing heavily.

From my dark refuge in the alcove, I watched him with curious eyes. Reaching for the window latch, he cracked the glass open and invited a chill inside. I shuddered as he began to pace. In an instant, he wrenched his shirt over his head and crumpled it in his hands before he tossed it to the floor, leaving a light-colored pair of breeches as his only attire.

Despite the profound wickedness of the act, my eyes molded to every angle before me, slowly trailing the contours of his well-shaped chest and arms. His skin appeared moist in the moonlight. I had never seen a man without, at the very least, his shirtsleeves.

Do they all look that defined and I daresay... attractive?

My cheeks heated at the immorality of my thoughts. I glanced down at my fingers gripping my nightclothes and I suddenly felt confined and claustrophobic. If I were to be discovered spying on this man in his precarious state of undress, not only would I face

74

humiliation, but I would risk what remained of my fragile reputation. Though it briefly crossed my mind that a marriage to Genevieve's brother would likely be better than the alternative, I would never oblige another to lose their freedom for my own selfish purposes.

Lucas ran his hands through his hair and groaned.

Something troubled him deeply.

"Bloody nightmares," he grumbled, exhaling loudly before he leaned out the window allowing the cold night air to cool him.

As he turned his back in my direction, I nearly choked at the sight of a long, jagged scar that ran from his shoulder blade crosswise to his waist. It was a decent half meter long; clearly the man had survived a dreadful wound.

Though I believed my palm had prevented my gasp from escaping, he circled around in the dark and held still as if he sensed that he wasn't alone.

"Genevieve?" he questioned. "Sariah?"

I pressed my hand tighter against my mouth and willed my legs to stop shaking. Holding painfully still, I watched and prayed he would not seek an answer to his query between the bookcase and the wall. He might not react properly to my spying on him, despite the innocence of it.

He leaned against the windowsill once more. Shadows flashed across his face and, though I couldn't see his expression clearly, his movements suggested great vexation. He suffered from night terrors. Genevieve had confided in me often about her brother who had gone off to war and how she feared for his life and his return. The way she spoke of him revealed a true fondness. I knew she loved him very much.

Within seconds, the man latched the window closed and retreated the same way he had come. Once I was sure Lucas had gone downstairs, I took full advantage of his disappearance to flee back to my quarters, abandoning my desire to seek out the sweet pastry that lured me from my bedchamber to begin with. Moving as fast as my feet allowed, I rushed carelessly, fearing he might see me.

Once back in bed and under the security of my covers, I no longer attributed my restlessness to my father or Lord Foxton. The mystery of the man who lived below stole my complete attention and contemplations.

And yet… he knew nothing of my existence.

Chapter Thirteen

Lucas

I hardly slept.

Though I had initially fallen asleep with ease after a night of games with my sisters, I awoke only hours later to fresh images of death as if I relived my walk through a pasture of dead bodies. Smoke swirled hazily overhead, and the crack of cannon fire assaulted my ears. After Burgos and Vitoria, I wasn't sure the bloody scenes would ever leave my head. The men from both sides of the battle had been slaughtered like sheep—and I was a part of that.

I had to take lives in order to preserve my own. Twice, I had looked my opponent square in the eye before my sword ran him through. Eyes that once beheld the virtue in others, now silenced at my hand.

Sitting on the edge of my bed, I peered over to see the early light of sunrise peeking back. I never fully closed my drapes for fear of confinement, but after I awakened several hours ago from the images of the battlefield, I had to get out of the room. Thank goodness I hadn't awakened my sisters with my restless wanderings.

Last night proved to be insufferable. I recalled dashing out of my bedchamber, drenched in sweat. When I reached the end of the corridor, I felt stifled and overwhelmed. Unlatching the window brought minimal relief. If my mother lived, she would have scolded me for allowing the crisp night air to penetrate the warmth of the house, but I was alone... *or so I believed.*

When I turned to inhale the cool air from outside, I was sure I heard something from within the alcove, though I didn't see anyone, and no one answered my call. It could very well have been my grievous mind dispensing additional cruelties, but in the end, I was eternally grateful that neither Genevieve, Sariah, nor Josie stepped forward.

With my bare skin exposed, I shivered, then remembered the state of my shirt... crumpled on the floor somewhere. I ran both hands down my face and exhaled. If my sisters had seen my wound, I would have never forgiven myself. I had no intention of distressing them any further.

I tugged on the bell pull and Giles arrived.

One look and he knew.

"How can I help, my lord?"

My fist lightly tapped my forehead. "I doubt there is anyone that can help." Though my sisters and the season had offered some distraction, the relief remained short lived.

"If you permit me, sir," Giles said calmly as he prepared for my shave. "I have learned of restorative efforts underway at Greenwich Hospital for the men who have returned... less than whole."

I removed my hand from my forehead and peered over at him.

"They have a pressing need for additional benefactors. Might I suggest that your involvement in such a cause may ease your mind?"

I steeled my jaw. *Was peace to my soul even obtainable?*

I moved to the chair as Giles wrapped a linen around my neck and proceeded to dip the blade in a scuttle, scrape, and dip again. Silence magnified between us, but it was a comfortable quiet, never cumbersome. "Once you are finished will you have Max prepare Ace? I'm in need of a bruising ride."

"Anything you ask, my lord."

Twenty minutes later, I entered the breakfast room to find Sariah already present. I began to fill a plate from the ample display of breakfast foods that adorned the sideboard. "Sariah?" My sister glanced up at me as she swallowed a sip of her juice, though she said nothing and only watched me curiously.

"Would you like to ride with me today?"

Of all my sisters, only Sariah rose early enough to ride. With the crush of the city during the season, the best time to go was before nine in the morning when most members of the *ton* were still abed, sleeping off the corollaries of the previous night's entertainment.

"Oh, yes, Lucas! I would love to." She shoved the rest of her scone in her mouth in a most unladylike manner and stood up.

I chuckled. "No need to hasten, I'm here to break my fast."

"It's alright, I'm finished," she mumbled while she chewed. "I'll dress and meet you in the foyer."

I loved that she enjoyed the pastime as much as I did and, at this rate, she will exceed Genevieve in her skills on a horse.

As we walked to the mews behind the house, I felt it necessary to rule her out of my late-night suspicion. "Did you sleep well?"

She tilted her head sideways. "If you are asking if I had an inkling for more of Betty's shorties, the answer is yes; but no, I did not leave my warm bed for a midnight snack, Lucas."

I chuckled. I knew my sisters often snuck down to the pantry for nightly treats.

"And Josie wasn't up with a nightmare?"

She eyed me curiously. "Not that I know of, but you know it is Genie that gets up with her, I sleep through everything." She spoke the truth.

Max retrieved Sariah's side saddle and readied Nutmeg while I looked over my mount. Within minutes, I led Sariah out past the strains of the city, trotting across the Thames and into open spaces. Though the gaps were far from what we had at the country estate, I had managed to discover several hallowed treasures.

As we slowed and trotted side by side, Sariah appeared troubled.

"What's rummaging around in that sweet little head, Sariah?"

She frowned. Though she had the kindness of her older sister Genevieve, she had a fiery streak that tended to surface at all the wrong times. And despite the trouble it caused, it was one of the traits I loved about her. That and the true nature of her sincerity.

"If Justin forces Genevieve into marriage, what hope do I have?"

This surprised me. She delayed her come out this year due to father's death, but I never knew her to be as interested in society as her older sister. "First off, I will fight Justin in a duel if he forces *anyone* to marry against their wishes." I teased, of course, but said it to bring a smile back to her forlorn face. "Second of all, you have plenty of time to find your intended. There's no hurry, you're only seventeen."

She wrinkled her nose. "Are you certain I will have a say in the matter?"

My brows furrowed. "What are you not telling me?"

She looked away, then slid off her horse on her own.

I joined her and grabbed both sets of reins as we walked through a wooded arch of linden trees and deeper into Epping Forest. She took a seat on a large boulder and clasped her hands in her lap.

"Sariah," I reached for one of her hands. "You and I have always been open and honest with each other. What is troubling you?"

When she looked back up at me, there were tears in her eyes. "I met someone."

"What?" I slid beside her. "Without a proper introduction? Who is this man?"

She shook her head. "Don't be angry. We were at the bookshop. Genevieve, Josie, Miss Abagale, and I. He bumped into me." She looked at me. "It was innocent, I assure you."

"What transpired next?"

"He apologized and then offered to help me find a book."

"Who is *he*?"

She wrung her hands together. "He is the bookshop owner's son. Mr. Osborne."

Blowing a subtle breath, I knew I had to tread lightly. "So, he is the son of a tradesman?"

She nodded. We both knew Justin would never concede. I might be able to sway his direction toward honorable gentlemen, but a man without substantial means and influence would be impossible.

"How many times have you seen him?"

"Three times at the shop."

I did not miss her play with words. "And where else?"

She groaned and stood up.

"Sariah? Tell me the truth."

She fisted her hands on her hips. "Why must I?" Her eyebrows furrowed. "You have secrets."

"This is not about me."

"Why have you not spoken of your days on the continent? Why must I be forthcoming if you are not?"

I rubbed my jaw and stood to join her. Taking her by the hand, I led her back to the boulder to sit upon. "You are correct." I gently squeezed her fingers. "However, war does not make for pleasant conversation at tea. It is a brutal narrative, one that I would like to spare you from if I could."

81

She kissed my cheek. "I only want you to know that I'm a good listener, Luke."

I smiled in return. "That, I already know. But back to the issue at hand."

She closed her eyes and braced for the continued questioning.

"Where else have you seen Mr. Osborne, the younger?"

She opened her eyes slowly. "At church…"

"And…" *I knew my sisters too well.*

"Oh, bother, Lucas," she grumbled. "In our garden."

"Our garden?"

"Yes."

"Alone?"

"No, I would not risk such behavior. Emily was with me."

"Your lady's maid."

"She's an excellent chaperone," she countered.

"That is not the point. The man dares to enter the garden of a woman he has not been given permission to seek out."

"I thought you of all people would understand."

"Why me?"

"Because you care for us… unlike Father did. Or Justin. You care about our sentiments, our fears, and our futures." She began to cry.

I retrieved a handkerchief from my pocket and dabbed her cheeks. "Dear Sariah, if it were up to me, I would let you choose the man you cared for regardless of his circumstance. I'd only be concerned for his ability to provide for you and, regrettably, the son of a bookshop owner cannot give you the lifestyle you are accustomed to."

"I don't need it. I don't even want it!" She shook her head. "I don't fancy the finery, the jewelry, or the attention. I only want to be loved."

My heart sank for her. How could I want anything else for her? I squeezed her hand. "You must tell Mr. Osborne he may no longer come by the house. If Justin learned of this, he would see that the man faced a far worse penance than simple humiliation."

She nodded. "I know. I just can't bring myself to do so."

"Why don't you let me speak with the chap?"

Her eyes grew wide. "Oh, Lucas, no. He would be horrified I shared our secret."

"A secret a young woman from a respectable household should not have." I said this in the gentlest manner possible and wrapped my arms around her, drawing her to my chest.

She sniffled against my coat. "Have you ever loved anyone, Lucas?"

My mind reflected on past years. While I may have flirted, danced, and even charmed a number of ladies... I could not say with any smidgeon of truth that I had fallen in love.

"No, Sariah, but when I do, you'll be the first to know."

Chapter Fourteen

Helena

Once the sun's rays pierced the window in my bedchamber, the glass reflected the warm light alongside my face. It should have felt comforting, but the overnight battle between fatigue and restlessness wore footpaths upon my body and mind.

Eliza left early this morning to meet Sally, my father's maid of all work, in hopes that she might be encouraged to help us discover my aunt's whereabouts. In order to write her a letter, I required more information.

My Aunt Patricia lived in Northampton, but I also understood that to be a sizeable place. The plan was to have Sally discreetly search for any old correspondence while she cleaned my father's study. I prayed she would acquiesce, but she faced a significant risk, and bringing more people into this subterfuge did not sit well with me. Their lives were as fragile as my own.

I left my bed and paced anxiously between the window and the armoire. The weight of my future hung precariously before me. It felt as palpable as dense fog after a summer rain. Then, as if I didn't have enough to occupy my thoughts… that deuced man from last night had settled into my mind for an unsolicited visit.

Images of Lucas standing there in only his breeches kept a constant heat in my cheeks. If I ever made it back to church, I would need ample time to repent. The man was flawless. Yes, he had wounds that marred his body, but even with their intent to ruin, they failed.

This aggravated me to no end.

Had I never seen such a thing, I would have never known a body such as his to exist. But now… now I knew, and I was certain such a sight would remain engrained indefinitely.

"Helena." I gave a start as Genevieve entered the room. "Whatever is wrong? You look utterly vexed."

I quickly drew the palm of my hand from my forehead. I could never tell her what I saw, but I wondered if she knew of it. *Did she know her brother had been wounded in such a violent way?* "I am well enough, just restless I suppose," I said, although I continued to wear a path in her floor.

"I have brought you breakfast. Also, news."

I stopped pacing.

"I believe Lucas plans to be gone for the day."

I peered over to her with wide eyes. Did she know that he had settled into a tiny corner of my mind? Well, to be honest the corner wasn't as tiny as I wished. I swallowed hard, though she didn't seem to notice. "Then I can take you to the library to select your own book."

"Oh." I smiled with relief. "Yes, I would love that."

She brought the tray to the table and pointed to the edge of the bed. "Come sit down with me."

I picked up an orange and brought it to my nose. The rich, tangy scent tickled my toes.

"We need to devise a plan if you are unable to find your aunt."

"Yes, yes that has been on my mind."

"I have been scouring the advertisements for positions. You know, as a governess or companion. Mostly hoping for something in the country, away from your father."

"Thank you, Genevieve." I hugged her, immensely grateful for all she continued to do for me. "It has been three days, have you heard any chatter involving me or my father?"

"No." She shook her head. "Nothing. But I have only ventured out once since you arrived, so I haven't been privy to additional hearsay. I truly hope he has waylaid his diabolical plot."

I frowned, recalling the darkness in his eyes the day he struck me. "I doubt it," I whispered. "If his debts were as substantial as believed, he would not leave it be."

"I wonder how long it will be before he will be arrested and taken to debtors' prison?"

My throat tightened. I had not considered this. Of course, he would face consequences if he could not settle. *What had I done?* "I'm utterly selfish," I whispered.

Genevieve wrapped her arm around me and pulled me close. "He is in the wrong for forcing such a wretched man upon his daughter. It is his duty to protect you." I looked over at her. She, herself, faced similar machinations from the new marquess.

"Now that your oldest brother has ended your mourning, has he chosen a suitor for you as well?"

Genevieve sighed. "Not that I am aware of, but the longer he stays away, the better. Lucas has assured me he will see that the man is worthy of me."

Lucas again.

Instantly my cheeks heated.

"Are you well, Helena?" Genevieve stood up and opened the window just a crack. The breeze that slipped through brought a slight reprieve to my flushed cheeks. I prayed a time would come when his name failed to bring forth such an ardent reaction from my body.

"Yes, I'm fine, thank you."

"I must go, now, but I will return for you when it's safe. I'm sure a little time outside of this cage will do your constitution a world of good."

I smiled tightly, thankful she didn't know about my wanderings last night.

When Genevieve left the room, I sat down at the lovely pedestal desk in the corner and retrieved the ink, quill, and foolscap. I needed to formulate my thoughts on paper, including how and when I would sell my jewelry, how long I could await word from my aunt once I've sent a letter, and the latest I could remain hidden on the Walshes upper floor before I must leave.

And leave I must!

Chapter Fifteen

Lucas

Tipping the glass back, I swallowed the last of the brandy while I watched the glowing embers darken in the hearth. My stare intensified parallel to the recollection of the day's events. I spent most of the day and into the night searching out military connections of those who might've known something of Jaxon or his whereabouts. I proceeded with caution. With Napoleon's defeat so fresh, there were rampant concerns of loyalty and mistrust—and a fair number of French who still resided in London.

I only paid one social call. Thankfully, His Grace, the Duke of Camberley, accepted my unexpected visit. I had met Jaxon's parents on several occasions over the years, including several balls in that very townhouse. Their reaction to my visit did not reveal anything but a joyful reunion, furthermore, I quickly learned that they had not been apprised of the latest news—the suspicions that Hunter had shared with me the night of Lord Drake's soiree. He, and the duchess, still anxiously awaited their son's return.

Was he dead? A prisoner of war? Was it even possible to bring him home?

So many questions surfaced... with an equal number of unknowns.

Glancing at my right hand that held the glass, I remembered my thumb bent in an unnatural way due to a break sustained while on the continent. So little compared to the other wounds I bore, but one so apparent that I saw it every time I lifted a glass to my lips. I knew my circumstances were fortuitous—a survivor who, despite the horrors of battle, might one day overcome the nightmares, the pain, and the past. But there were so many who didn't... and wouldn't.

On my return home tonight, I rode past the white colonnade of Greenwich Hospital, though I couldn't bring myself to stop. *Not yet.*

Standing and stretching, I reached for my cravat that I had untied hours ago. That, and the coat I shed, were draped over the back of one of the matching wingback chairs. Night after night, the seclusion of Father's study had become a place of refuge for me.

Glancing at the ormolu clock on the mantle, I noted the minute hand pointed half past one. I groaned. I had promised to go riding again with Sariah early in the morning. I had allowed my deep contemplations to overshadow my good judgement. Lighting my sole candle with the few remaining embers, I placed it in a chamberstick and stepped out of the room.

When the darkness of the hall enveloped me, I took comfort in the quiet. The sounds differed vastly in the daylight, and it was these moments of solitude I cherished... at least until I fell asleep.

A dull thump sounded from across the hall and drew my attention.

Someone was in the library.

Setting my coat and cravat on a table in the hallway, I approached the door in question with my chamberstick still gripped in my palm and pressed my ear against the wood. Minute shuffling sounds emerged.

What are those girls up to now? Genie had better not be up reading again.

I cracked the door in near silence and watched a small flame dance across the books from the hand of a girl whose back faced me. Her dark plaited hair confirmed that she was *not* one of my sisters. Would a maid have breached such boundaries?

As I widened the gap in the door and moved closer, I realized it was not the form of a girl after all, it was a woman… in her night dress… stretching on her tiptoes as she reached for a book.

Stunned at the sight of this strange figure before me, I walked directly into a table, slamming my knee against the corner. "Blimey!" I cringed in pain at the same moment the woman squealed and dropped her book.

When I looked over, she not only dropped the book but her candle as well. Though the wick had doused shortly after impact, it was not before the flame caught fire to the thin threads of my mother's favorite Ghiordes rug. The fragile strands were like pitch shavings and, within seconds, the fire sprinted along the edge like a detonation cord leading to dynamite.

"What the devil?" I cried and stamped the rug with my Hessians, putting a stop to the aggressive flame. Reaching for my own candle, I lifted it up and glanced back toward the shelf. The woman had disappeared. My indecent language surely didn't help.

With the candle still in my grip, I crossed my arms over my chest and huffed. I had more than my share of complications, I didn't need to add to that list. "Show yourself," I demanded.

Part of a head peeked out from behind a bookcase.

When the woman inched forward, she kept her head lowered.

"Who are you?" I grumbled, aware of only one recent hire… one with a vastly different stature. But as my eyes took in the quality of the embroidered design on the front of this woman's dressing robe and the fine lace at the cuffs of her sleeves, it became instantly apparent... she was most certainly *not* hired help.

"Forgive me." The woman found her voice.

I set my candle down on the nearest table and waved my hand. "You have nothing to fear, come and explain yourself."

When the woman stepped into the glow of the candle, I had to temper my breath. Her dark, rich hair hung down in a loose plait on one side of her chest. The angles of her nose, chin, and cheekbones suggested poise and grace and a clean and pale complexion, despite her flushed cheeks, evidenced nobility. When our eyes met, I steadied myself. I had never seen that shade of green before.

"Forgive me, sir," she repeated. "Did I wake you?"

"I was already awake." One of my eyebrows lifted. "But the greater question is who are you and what are you doing in my house?"

The woman's eyes flashed to the door, and I sensed she was going to try and make a run for it. The moment she did, I slid in front of her forcing her to a solid stop. When she bumped into my chest, she squeaked again, then peered up at me with an angry expression. I held both her arms lightly as I scanned her face in this new proximity. The color that I had assumed was blush was actually an unsightly bruise along her cheekbone.

"Release me," she demanded.

"Not until you answer my questions." My tone softened a smidge.

She tightened her mouth into a perfect little bow. "Fine." Stepping back, she crossed her arms over her waist. "I am Miss Helena Croft. I am a guest of Genevieve Walsh. I could not sleep and sought to read a book."

My body relaxed. She was a guest I had not been informed of, but a guest, nonetheless. "Well, that wasn't too difficult, was it?" My lips lifted in a playful smile as she wrinkled her pert little nose at me, and I noted a charming dimple that appeared at the lower side of her mouth.

"Permit me to leave now, sir, I am hardly dressed appropriately to be in a gentleman's presence."

My eyes betrayed me as I snuck a glance down at her nightclothes once more, then quickly stepped away. "Forgive me for delaying you, I had not been informed that we had any guests. When did you arrive?"

"I—uh, I arrived r—recently."

It wasn't a complicated question, why did she stutter?

I dipped into a low bow. "I bid you goodnight, Miss Croft," I said, then I opened the door wide to permit the lady leave, but my eyes remained fastened upon her until she disappeared up the staircase.

Blast that Genie! Irritation pulsed through my veins. Why hadn't she mentioned anything of this to me? I might not be the marquess, but I am currently the man of this house, and she had no right to keep this from me.

I had intended on waiting until a reasonable hour in the morning to confront my sister, but I lay awake, tormented with all manner of questions. I had never heard of a family by the name of Croft or a Miss Helena Croft, but from what I saw, regardless of her informal appearance, she would have cause for men to notice her. *I* would have noticed her. But then, something about her nagged at the familiar, and I couldn't put my finger on it. Was it possible I had seen her at a dance? I wasn't the greatest judge of age but assumed her to be between nineteen and twenty-one. If we had met at a social event prior to my departure for the continent, she would have been a young partner, and I generally circumvented the fresh misses with energetic mothers.

I rolled to my side then slid into a seated position. If I wasn't going to get any sleep, then neither was Genevieve.

She did not feel the same.

"Wake up, we need to speak." I patted her shoulder three times before she pulled the blanket off her eyes.

Cracking one eye open, she groaned and turned her back to me. "Good heavens, Luke, the sun has not even risen. Go away. You know I don't rise this early."

I tapped her again. A little harder and on top of her head this time. "Fine. I will just see that your *guest* is kindly shown out."

This got her full attention and she rose abruptly. I headed for the door to make my bluff as realistic as possible and Genevieve leaped from the bed, falling short with the blankets tangled around her legs. I clasped my hands behind my back and stared down at her, fighting to keep my smile hidden. She looked ridiculous as she struggled to get free from the fabric.

"No, please, Lucas, don't!"

"Who is Miss Helena Croft?"

"Croft?" She looked down at her hands. "I do not know who you are referring to."

"Tall, shapely, brunette, green eyes, small scar on the bridge of her nose, oh, and a large bruise on her jaw." I pursed my lips. "And apparently a guest in this house who I was not informed of or have seen except in the very late hours. And in her nightclothes, mind you."

"Her nightclothes? You saw her in her night rail?" Genevieve's eyes rounded in shock.

"Yes, *her*, who apparently you do not know."

"Uh, um…" she stuttered. "Um, yes that Miss…"

"Croft," I interjected. "Or is that a falsehood as well?"

She looked away and I blew out a breath. "Genevieve! Who is this woman you have brought into our home under such deceitful means?"

She lifted her chin as she took a seat on the edge of the bed. "Miss Croft is my friend. She's staying here for a bit while her parents are touring the continent. She's uh… shy."

One of my eyebrows arched. "She is not shy; I can assure you of that."

She grimaced.

"Why must I find out you have a guest by discovering her in the dead of night, fumbling around in our library?"

"She what?" She rubbed her eyes clear. "You what?"

"I met Miss Helena Croft in the most ungentlemanly way possible. Why did you not ask me… or at the very least inform me, for mercy's sake?"

Genie stood up and brought me back to the edge of her bed, forcing me to sit down. "This is what I tried to talk to you about the other night at the Drake Soiree when you disappeared with Lord Matthews. I didn't see you again until we left." She frowned persuasively.

"You could have told me in the carriage."

"You left me alone, Lucas; besides, you didn't speak to me at all on the ride home."

I rubbed my cheek. The new growth scratched beneath my palm. I hadn't realized how neglectful I'd been to her. Jaxon's disappearance troubled me immensely.

"I tried again yesterday, but you were gone all day."

I sighed. "I'm sorry Genie. Can you forgive me?"

She laid her head on my shoulder and whispered, "I'm sorry I deceived you. I hadn't planned on that, but she had to come quickly, and I didn't have time to ask."

"How long has she been here?"

"Four days."

My mouth gaped open. "Four days?"

Genevieve threw her head down into her hands. "She is facing a complicated situation."

"So, her parents *aren't* touring the continent."

She shook her head.

"Tell me the truth. No bouncer."

She bit her lip. "Her mother has passed away and something dreadful has happened with her father. Trust me, Lucas, she needed to come here."

I inhaled deeply then blew the air out of my cheeks slowly. "But do you know what the servants will say about a woman—a woman who looks like that, here in our home sneaking around with an eligible gentleman here?"

"A woman who looks like what?"

"Uh, um…" I coughed to clear my throat.

She stared at me.

"Um, someone who is of marriageable years. It could be assumed she is my lover."

Genevieve burst out laughing. "Lucas!"

I didn't crack a smile.

"You are the most proper man I know, and everyone knows you would not keep a lover."

"The gossipmongers don't care much for the truth," I mumbled. "Just the sordid deviation."

Genevieve sobered and wrapped her arm through mine. "I'm sorry. I didn't realize what kind of conundrum this might create. She's my friend and in need of my help. Can she please, please stay here a while longer?"

I studied her for several seconds. She looked more and more like our mother and, while I celebrated her advancement into womanhood, a sharp pain gripped my chest at the loss we all felt. "It's fine, Genevieve, we just need to be courteous hosts. No sneaking around and no more late nights. It does not look proper for a genteel young woman like Miss Croft to be here without my knowledge or Justin's."

Genevieve smiled wide and kissed my cheek. "Thank you so much, brother. Thank you!"

"And Genevieve..."

"Yes?"

"How did she get that ghastly bruise?"

She looked down at her hands. *Deuce!* She was about to lie to me again. "She uh, fell off her horse."

I waited until she looked back up at me and sighed. I would not push for the truth at this moment. "Do we need to send for Dr. Sawyer?"

"Oh, no. A surgeon has already attended her. He said she will not suffer any prolonged consequences."

"Please invite her to join our meals, but I must make arrangements to stay in a rented apartment while she's here."

"Is that necessary? Won't that raise suspicion if you leave us here alone?"

My brows furrowed. Of course, she was right. "Genie, you do realize that even my reputation can taint yours."

"Forgive me, I had not thought this through," she replied, lowering her head.

"No, you didn't."

"We are waiting to learn of her aunt's location to write her and I am seeking other... well, other alternatives."

"We can discuss the details later."

"Thank you, brother," she said, planting a light kiss on my cheek.

I mussed her hair. "Go back to sleep. You can give Miss Croft the news at a later hour."

Chapter Sixteen

Helena

My heart pounded wildly the entire way up the four flights of stairs, down the long corridor, and continued for several minutes after my bedchamber door was closed. I had been so careful the first few days. Well, except for the previous night when I saw Lord Lucas in his breeches. The memory brought a warmth to the back of my neck. I needed to cease these intrusive thoughts!

I crossed over to my pitcher and poured water into the basin. Taking a cloth, I dipped it into the cool water and wet my skin, wiping my forehead, cheeks, and neck. I felt ablaze, and not only from the run. Good gracious, I had been caught in my night rail, but somehow, even in my urgency to leave, I could not draw my eyes from him and the small square of skin below his neck. Miniscule compared to what I glimpsed the night before but daunting just the same. The way this man's striking handsome face stared back at me... was... well, I couldn't quite identify how it made me feel, but it wasn't anything I was familiar with. Thank goodness he had his shirtsleeves on this time.

I paced beside my bed. *How could I be so foolish?*

Fortunately, I kept my wits about me, despite the warm timbre of his voice, and ingeniously provided a false family name. Had I given my real one, he might've known my family or my father… especially if they had crossed in business or at the gentlemen's clubs.

I slid into bed, hoping to have an ounce of sleep after that very unsettling encounter, but I knew better. Our ruse was exposed because of me, and I feared Genevieve's disappointment.

I rolled over to my side and pulled the coverlet to my chin. *Maybe our secret might remain intact.* I had only met her brother once before when I was riding with Lord Foxton, and the meeting was ever so brief. I could not judge this man's character or devotion on such a fleeting encounter, I would have to rely on what I knew of Genevieve, and she was the very best of everything.

Several more minutes of trying to rid my mind of the confrontation, I surrendered my bed and fumbled my way through the dark to light my candle with the tinderbox on top of the mantle. Once lit, I set it down on the desk and retrieved the writing tools.

Somehow my pragmatism still managed to surface as I pondered my next step. If I could have a completed letter ready to send to my aunt the moment I learned of her whereabouts, I might not have to wait as long for a reply.

Uncorking the ink, I reflected on my mother's funeral. Portions of it I still couldn't recall, but I often wondered why Aunt Patricia chose to stay out of my life after that day. It couldn't entirely be due to my appearance. Although Mother and I shared the same figure, hair color, and dimple, there were more differences than similarities. I dipped the quill into the ink.

Dear Aunt Patricia,

It is I, Helena, your niece.

I tapped the tip of the vane against my chin, attempting to formulate my next words. What does one say to someone they had not seen in four years? *My father is forcing me to marry a detestable man, may I please come live with you?*

I'd be a laughingstock. I'd even endeavor to say most marriages are not at the will of the woman. By law, my father had the right to force me to do anything, at least until my majority or my marriage and, even then, my husband would be the one giving the orders.

What woman finds that appealing?

It was only last year that I had entered society with the hopes of finding that one special man. The one who would love me, edify me, and appreciate all that I had to offer as a woman, including an intelligent mind. Then as the balls and the events commenced, night after night, my aspirations began to crack and finally break. These men didn't want a companion, they wanted a pleasing woman who charmed their fellow peers and brought healthy male heirs into the world.

I looked down at the paper and realized I had made a hole in the parchment from pressing too hard. *How had I turned so cynical in such a short time?* Did I really believe all men were a similar version of Lord Foxton? I set my quill down and then laid my head across my arms.

Maybe I could be my aunt's companion, or a teacher at a nearby school, or even a governess. Though I had not heard of many noble daughters turning to this, I had the mind to do very well if only I was given the chance.

I stood up and gazed in the mirror. Running my hand across my cheek, I examined the injury. My bruise had become only a slight discoloration now. It was healing properly on the outside though I wasn't sure I would ever heal on the inside.

What must my father think now? Is he concerned for my welfare? Is he angry?

I needed to proceed carefully. If Genevieve's brother believed I could bring dishonor to his family, he might not hesitate to deliver me home.

I went back to the desk and started over.

Dear Aunt Patricia,
It is I, Helena, your niece.
I am sorry for our separation these last few years and am not entirely sure why there was one, but please accept my apology for any part I may have played in you distancing yourself.

I am writing to ask a favor. My father and I have recently had a disagreement. I can elaborate in person if you would permit me to visit. I am currently staying at the house of a friend, Miss Genevieve Walsh of Mayfair. I have not participated in anything dishonorable or disreputable, if that might be your concern. I can pay my way by public coach, but desire to know if this might be agreeable to you.

Yours sincerely,
Helena
If you reply, please, for safety's sake, I ask that you use the name Helena Croft.

Chapter Seventeen

Lucas

Once I left Genevieve's bedchamber, the fact that I would not be getting any sleep became a forgone conclusion. Without wasting another minute, I sent for Giles and, despite the unreasonable hour, he fulfilled his duty and helped me dress.

Refusing my morning shave, I scratched a simple note to Sariah apologizing for my need to postpone our ride until tomorrow. I could not be in the house today. Everything about last night unnerved me, and I longed for air and distance. Though the rides that Sariah and I most often engaged in led us far outside of the city's frenzied bustle and densely polluted air, at this precise moment, it was imperative that I proceed alone.

Images of Miss Helena Croft lurked in all the turnings of my mind—from the state of her dress to the flash of stubbornness in her eyes, to the faintest hint of something sweet, possibly jasmine or amber. Then those eyes... those emerald eyes that glimmered even in the dimness of the room. I could not face those eyes right now in the light of day despite my request that she join the family.

And that bruise.

How could a woman of her standing sport such a dreadful mark from the hand of another? *A pugilist maybe?* I chuckled darkly to myself then sobered. No, she was running from someone. A husband perhaps… and despite the evils of laying a hand on a woman, the law sides with the man. He can correct her however he deems necessary. The "rule of thumb" authorized a man to beat his wife as long as the *rod* was smaller than his thumb. A new heat coursed through my veins. I would kill any man who laid a hand on my sisters.

With my coat and hat clenched in my fists, I descended the stairs nearly two at a time. I did not need another run in with anyone.

Stepping outside, I allowed myself a deep inhale. Any unpleasant smells of the mews were weakened straightaway by the soothing sounds of the horses. Upon my arrival, Nutmeg's soft neigh contradicted Cinnamon's snort and clop, but it was Ace who stood absolutely still. He knew I had come for him. I had been present at his birth five years ago and rarely rode another steed except while at war. While I would have taken him to the continent with me, travel for a horse across the channel was abysmal at best and if I had lost him in battle, I would have grieved fiercely.

Brushing my hand across his rich, chocolate hide, I marveled at the genetic Chapman muscular build that prepared him for not only the rigors of the countryside, but the harsh cobblestones of the city. He nudged me gently as I inspected his bit and halter, then with a single fluid motion, I settled comfortably on top.

"Onward, Ace." I prodded him forward and waited until we were outside of Mayfair before I led him into a trot, then to a gallop.

With a full day ahead of me, I intended on doing some more digging regarding Jaxon but my aimless wandering around the city brought me across Tower Bridge and the Thames. When I finally became attentive, I realized our jaunt had traversed toward Southwark. Slowing my mount as I approached Boss from Tooley, I hesitated. This was the precise location that my father had taken his last breath.

The few details I knew provided some context to where he was found. Ace trotted in place for several minutes while I imagined Father's final moments. Though we did not have affection for one another, I was not heartless. I would have never wished for such a fate to fall upon any man, cold-blooded or not.

I descended my mount and strapped the reins to a nearby post as I paced between the intersecting roads. Glancing down the street both ways, I calculated how off-course my father must've been if he had, in fact, been at White's. Perplexed, I rubbed my chin thoughtfully. This particular neighborhood was nowhere near the gentlemen's club, nor did it pass parallel to it, being on opposite sides of the river. *What was my father engaged in?*

Days after my return from war, I had chosen to leave the mystery of his death buried. Bow Street had not found a culprit with the presumed runaway phaeton and my father had been laid to rest beside our mother at Longbriar. I had not yet ventured the distance to pay my respects properly, fully aware a trip to the family estate would force Justin and I to speak of things we did not agree on. And in his newly inherited role, he would always be right… even if he wasn't.

So why was I standing here, trying to calculate the model, speed, and impact?

I shook my head. In this part of town, it could very well be a drunken patron of a nearby gambling establishment who, to this day, might not even know he killed a man.

I studied the businesses along the road—brothels, gaming hells, and all manner of ill repute. *What was the marquess doing here?*

Crouching down, I used the popper on the end of my riding crop to push some rubbish aside along the gutter. It had now been over three months since his death, and I was certain the waste had only tripled in size and depth. What was I looking for anyway?

I stood up disappointed. Even if some sort of clue as to what happened was found, I wasn't entirely sure what to do with it. My father had never been kind to me. He, most certainly, never thought of me or my welfare on the continent in battle and I should reciprocate that disregard now that he was gone.

Only, the truth of the matter stirred within. I was *not* my father and never would be.

Chapter Eighteen

Helena

Scratches on my door shook me out of my stupor.

Since finishing the letter to my aunt, I had done little else than think of what occurred in the library mere hours ago. Even now, a thin layer of perspiration coated my skin at the memory of the encounter.

Though I failed to respond, I received Genevieve warmly as she entered my room and rushed to my bedside. "What were you thinking, Helena? Leaving the bedchamber last night?"

I winced. "He told you?"

She nodded and clasped my hands.

"Forgive me, I thought everyone was asleep."

"Thank goodness you gave him another name." She exhaled rather loudly. "He cannot know your family name. Lucas is an honorable man, but it's too dangerous to reveal your actual identity.

Who knows what your father would do if he found out you were hiding here."

I grew weary of the scheme. "But I can't stay here forever, Genie. I can't bring such strife to your family."

"Was Eliza successful? Did she learn of your aunt's location?"

I shook my head. "Not yet, but she is meeting with Sally again tonight. I pray for better news this time."

Genevieve settled in on the edge of the bed. "Didn't you say that your aunt is your mother's twin sister?"

"Yes. I have fond memories of visiting her before my mother became ill."

"Do you recall anything about her home? Did she live in the city or on a country estate?"

"Country estate. She was a widow and…" I pressed my fingers to my forehead. "It was called Wood… or Forest… or… oh, I don't know!" I couldn't hide the frustration in my voice. "Maybe it was nothing like that. I had only been there a few times and the last time was when I was nine."

"What about the colors or the style of the home? Was there a stable?"

"Yes, a lovely stable. I rode a horse called Clementine and there was this man, the groom, Mr. George, I believe. Oh, it's all so vague, I doubt we could find anything with so little."

She patted my hand. "I wonder why your family became estranged from her?"

I chewed on my bottom lip, trying to recall the details I had elicited overnight. "She came to the funeral. Like my mother, she was tall and willowy with a pleasant disposition. After we departed the churchyard, I saw my father speaking with her privately then she departed in her coach. I never heard from her again. Once, shortly after the funeral, I asked my father if I could write to her. He told me that she had asked to be left alone, that her sister's loss was too painful. They were identical, you know." I buried my head in my hands. "Oh, what if it is still too painful and she wants nothing to do with me?"

Genevieve wrapped her arms around me. "Please do not despair. There is always hope."

Hope seemed so far away, like the tiny light that appears on the horizon, but the closer you get the farther it is. "Thank you, Genevieve. Thank you for all you have done for me."

"I would do anything you ask, my dear friend." She stood to leave. "Oh, and Lucas insists you join the family for meals. Now that he knows you are a guest he will not agree to you remaining in your quarters."

"Is he cross that I'm here?" I questioned timidly.

"No. I mean he was at first because I kept it a secret, but Lucas forgives easily. He always has. It's Justin who is unpredictable. We just need to hope that he stays away until you have departed."

Genevieve laughed, but I didn't find any humor in her words. It could take weeks to receive correspondence from my aunt and that would not even happen until we located her precise whereabouts.

"I'll notify Eliza to help you dress and join us for breakfast."

I acquiesced to her command as she knocked on Eliza's door and updated her on the latest news. Though I was relieved at the thought of leaving my bedchamber, I couldn't help but fear seeing Lucas in the light of day.

Brushing my hands across the skirt of my pale-yellow morning dress, I entered the dining room less than thirty minutes later. Eliza had styled my hair in a simple chignon and, though I felt ready to join the others, my chest swelled with apprehension—apprehension over who I might see.

The aromatic smells of freshly baked bread, black pudding bangers, and malt vinegar kippers competed for my attention against the room's opulent features and instantly calmed my beating heart.

That, and the reality that only the sisters were present. I suppressed my relief that we were alone but kept a watchful eye out for Lucas. He could appear at any moment.

Throughout the day, I couldn't deny the lightness that settled in with being out of the bedchamber and free to roam the townhouse. Engaging in all manner of pleasantries with the Walsh sisters, my body ached from laughing so often. They were a delight to be around.

Between cribbage and literary charades, an improvised puppet show written and performed by Josephine, who insisted I call her Josie, and an enlightening contest of Questions and Commands, the day passed rather quickly and, before I realized it, preparations for dinner had come upon us.

As I walked to my quarters to dress, the tightness that seized my body earlier returned uninhibited. The notion that Lucas might possibly be present for the evening meal surfaced in each shallow breath I took. *How could I face him after the past two nights?*

Strangely enough, however, both dinner and a lively game of Whist passed uneventfully without any sign of the man. Even more peculiar was the curiosity that accompanied his absence. I tried to convince myself it was only to catch a glimpse of him in something other than his casual attire. After the humiliation of being discovered in my nightclothes, it couldn't possibly be anything else.

Nothing. At. All.

Chapter Nineteen

Lucas

"Well, if it isn't our elusive guest, Miss Croft." I stood to my feet when Genevieve and her friend entered the breakfast room the morning after my disappearing act. I had needed that time to clear my head for many reasons, but she was most certainly one of them. Even now, seeing her here with her hair styled and in proper dress, my eyes could not find a solitary thing more tempting to gaze upon.

She stopped in the doorway and her brief surprise was replaced with aloofness.

I continued, "You look so refreshed in the morning hours. It's nice to make your *official* acquaintance."

Genevieve waved her hand in the air. "Ignore him, Helena, he's probably just grumpy because you saw him without his cravat properly in place."

"Truthfully it was more than that," I grumbled and resumed my seat.

The woman flashed me a frustrated look. "I was the one dressed indecently, sir."

Sariah and Josie's eyes widened, flashing between us. I smiled when her face turned bright red the moment she realized what she had said and who had heard it. "Drat it all," she mumbled. "Never mind."

"That I will, Miss Croft," I said, chuckling to myself. Though I knew in all likelihood that task was impossible. I doubted I would ever be able to get the image of her in her night dress out of my mind. She looked altogether too... I stopped that thought before finishing it.

Stabbing the kipper on my plate with my fork, I pointed it in Miss Croft's direction before I took a bite. "I'm sorry about your injury." I watched carefully as her face went from red to pale white. She glanced at Genevieve with a look of sheer panic.

Just what I thought... *another lie.*

Genevieve stuttered, "I—I told Lucas about your a—accident... you know when you fell off your horse."

I didn't miss the subtle wink.

Genie then added for emphasis. "I trust you don't mind."

"Oh." Miss Croft blew a slight breath out of her lips and color returned to her face. "Yes, I fell off my horse." Her hand rubbed the bruise tenderly. From the healing discoloration I could only imagine the state of the injury the day it happened and, for some reason my blood pumped faster at the notion. I had received similar bruises in combat, but this woman hadn't been to war.

I continued to watch the two women as they tried to cover up and did a wretched job of it. They were hiding something, and the determined part of my nature was bound to vet it out. Especially if this woman was to be a guest in our home, I needed to know if she brought scandal with her. My sisters' sakes depended on it.

"Do you ride poorly or did your horse get spooked?"

She jutted out her chin. "I would have you know, my lord, I am a fine horsewoman."

The corners of my mouth twitched as I wrestled with a smile. I didn't realize when we first met how vastly entertaining it would be to irritate her. "I'm not so sure of that. Horses are rarely spooked in the city. They are accustomed to the noise."

"Are you suggesting I am being dishonest about my skills?"

I shrugged. "There is only one way to ascertain."

She looked at me, her eyes narrowed. When they flitted over my attire then over to my sisters, who also wore their riding habits, she shifted awkwardly in her seat. "I could not impose."

"Could not, or unable to prove otherwise?"

She glared at me. "Seeing I did not pack my own riding habit I would not feel comfortable trespassing on your family's already generous hospitality. Thank you very much." She slid from the table, dipped into a shallow curtsy and marched out.

Genevieve stood and faced me with a grimace. "What in the world has gotten into you, Luke? You never behave this way in front of a lady."

"You are misrepresenting her." I lathered a large dollop of honey across my scone. "Mark my word, Genevieve, you can either confess or I will discover it on my own."

She stiffened.

Then I swiftly added before she departed. "And I will tell you why Wellington chose me as a trusted scout detecting the enemy... I am quite good at it. Do not underestimate my abilities."

Genevieve snorted and stomped out of the room after her friend. I chuckled, though it might not be as amusing as I first believed. If this woman brought dishonor to our home, it was up to me to put a stop to it, immediately.

After taking a few more bites of my bread, I smiled broadly at my silent sisters as if nothing irregular had occurred. "Ready to ride?"

Sariah and Josie's wide eyes finally blinked as they both nodded with enthusiasm.

I waved my hand toward the doorway and marched out, determined not to dwell one additional moment on the exasperating woman.

Chapter Twenty

Helena

There was nothing I could do but feign a megrim for weeks on end if I was to avoid Genevieve's bully of a brother. Although he wasn't as terrible as I built him up to be, he did have a way of saying all the right things to drive me mad.

Though I was fortunate to have missed him upon his return from riding with his sisters, I somehow found myself face to face with him in the corridor on my way to the parlor for tea.

As much as he vexed me, seeing him now in his proper dress was a sight to behold. It wasn't a look I was unaccustomed to seeing on other gentlemen, but somehow the insufferable man improved the view. His ocean-blue cravat drew an unusual streak of blue from his gray eyes and his cream-colored waistcoat matched the beige in his tailcoat. He cut a striking figure... though I already knew that... a little too well.

"How long will you be in residence, Miss Croft?" Lord Lucas inquired as I attempted to pass by with only a light curtsy.

Unable to be rude to my host, I stopped and faced him. It was a perilous act. "Genevieve has been so kind as to extend the invitation indefinitely." She hadn't really, but I had no doubt she would if it came to it. I only said this to see his reaction.

"Indefinitely?" Caught by surprise, he coughed, then quickly cleared his expression. I tried not to appear so pleased by it.

Despite the dimmed hallway, I discerned a mischievous gleam in his eye as he continued, "Well, I say the timing is most providential."

"How so?" One of my eyebrows arched.

That blasted smile emerged. "I have a stack of invitations on my desk that are awaiting our acceptance. I look forward to adding your name to our party."

Though Lucas kept a straight face when he spoke, his objective was most certainly to taunt. A man, not of my relation, and not courting would never risk the damage a little chinwag can do.

Regardless, my heartbeat sped up at the suggestion of being exposed. "Oh, I could not impose, my lord." I tried to keep fear from easing into my tone. "I only brought one evening gown and it is not quite up to fashion, I'm afraid." I glanced away and toward the door of the parlor. *What might he think if I ran for it?* "I wouldn't want to humiliate your family."

The casual way he stepped in front of me appeared natural, but he seemed to sense my plan to flee much like the night we met in the library. I peered up to see his lips curved partway in our new proximity. A subtle, rustic aroma swept over me.

Incorrigible man.

He crossed his arms over his chest and tilted his head. "I imagine Genevieve would extend her generosity beyond her invitation to stay to include her wardrobe. She has plenty to share."

I narrowed my eyes in a challenge. I could never trust him with the truth. "Unlike some," I paused for emphasis, "I value propriety and do not take pleasure in pestering others."

He laughed out loud, and I gritted my teeth. Even his laugh was attractive. *Drat it all!*

"Helena, there you are." Genevieve appeared in the hallway. "We have been waiting for you." Her eyes shifted to her brother. "Are you joining us for tea, Lucas?"

He moved aside and waved his hand forward and once I had the exasperating, enticing scent of the man outside of my immediacy, I could finally breathe.

"Oh, no dear sister. I wouldn't dream of interfering with your female agenda."

Genevieve linked her arm through mine and guided me away. His deep chuckle continued to reverberate in my ears until we disappeared into the drawing room.

Though I should have had a pleasant visit with the Walsh sisters that afternoon, my mind flitted back to the meeting in the corridor and the way that Lucas teased me. He knew more than he was letting on by the way my presence had become sport to him.

Now, there was no question that weeks-long megrim looked better by the minute.

Chapter Twenty-one

Lucas

Leaving earlier than anticipated the next morning, I rode directly to Greenwich Hospital before I lost the courage. Truthfully, it was not about courage, but facing the realism of how my life was spared compared to so many others. I wasn't quite ready to be reminded just how thin those threads of circumstance were.

Entrusting Ace into the hands of a stable master, I began my slow walk past the grand colonnade. Each pillar I passed along the lengthy causeway weighed heavily upon my heart equal to each step I took. *What might I see or feel once I reached the end and entered the building?* Though I had physically departed from the battlefields on the peninsula, a haunting unease lingered as if the torment followed me home, destined to remain forever.

Month after month witnessing the gruesome acts of men killing each other changes you and at night when the fighting ceased, and only the smells remained, it was enough to drive one to lunacy. There was truth to what was written in the London papers like The Times. Prior to my departure for the war, I had read periodicals recounting battles against Napoleon and contemplated its accuracy. While much of the detailed carnage was suppressed for propriety's sake, the romantic notions of war were devoured by the public.

I no longer partook in that particular diversion.

Stepping through the main doors, I approached a man in a surgeon's cloak.

"Pardon me sir. I am looking fo—"

I did not even finish my sentence when he ushered me through a nearby set of double doors.

"See that nurse over there, she is the one you need to speak with." He pointed to a slightly plump woman in a white uniform. Her cap barely fit over her brown, tightly knotted hair. "Speak to Nurse Watkins."

I waited until she was finished directing other nurses in their duties then stepped forward. "Pardon me, ma'am?"

Her eyes took in my attire. I should not have tried so hard in my dress, but since my return, I enjoyed the respite from the uniform and the return to gentlemen's clothing.

"How can I 'elp you, sir?" Her eyes narrowed. "Or is it m'lord?"

I smiled. "I understand you're looking for benefactors... for the hospital."

"That's not 'ere." She pointed to a row of men lying in beds suffering through various degrees of injuries. "This uh, 'ere is a recovery ward. Take your quid to the central agency fer that."

"Recovery ward?" I swallowed hard, my gaze darting toward the men. The sight summoned unwelcome memories—not of pristine hospital rooms, but of the harrowing chaos of field hospitals and blood-soaked battlefields. While their surroundings were much improved, the familiar emptiness in their eyes remained unchanged.

I turned back to the nurse, sensing her scrutiny. Her eyebrows lifted in a silent question before understanding washed over her features, softening her. "You fought yonder, din't ya?"

I took a deep breath and nodded.

She wiped her forehead with her sleeve. "Y'all 'ave the same look."

"What look?"

"Like yer lost."

I thought about that. She was right, I *did* feel lost.

"Why don't ya dally 'round 'ere, 'fore ya git. Ya might 'appen to find…" She hesitated as her own eyes flitted over the men. "One ta natter with."

The muscles in my jaw tensed. "About what, precisely?"

Her mouth pursed into a thin line. "The like," she affirmed, gesturing toward the row of beds. "These fellas have yet ta see a single caller and the lot of 'hem have fits of the blue devils. A chat with a fellow bloke'd be 'ppreciated. 'Specially from one who gits it."

I followed her gaze, uncertainty gnawing at me. *Where would I even start? What would I say?*

Offering a silent nod of gratitude, I stepped aside and watched as the doctors and nurses shifted from one patient to another. Some men bore the scars of lost limbs; others were swathed in bandages, and a few lingered on the precipice of death. It was the unmistakable scent of mortality that stirred the most vivid memories in me.

The nurse patted my arm. "Take yer time, but if ye can spare 'n hour, start with 'im. 'e was cupped tis mornin'." She pointed to a man the third bed down. His entire head was bandaged above his mouth along with both of his arms from the recent bloodletting—her reference to him being cupped.

I gripped my hat in my hand. I was certainly overdressed for such a place, but I would not be ashamed of my lineage. My prosperity has placed me in a position to make a difference and I was determined to do just that.

Retrieving a stool from a corner, I stepped over to the man's bedside then sat down.

"Nurse, is 'at you?" The man's voice creaked under strain. Most likely from the excessive length of silence.

I cleared my throat. "No, I'm not a nurse."

He moved his head toward the sound of my voice but could not see me. A tender mercy at this very moment.

"Please mister, im a tad befogged, git me a sip of somethin'?"

There was a glass filled a third of the way on the small table beside his bed. I reached for it and casually sniffed it, curious of its contents. Diluted sherry, I surmised, and lifted it to his mouth. He struggled to drink, even with my help, but in the end received enough to wet his throat.

When he leaned back against his pillow, he winced in pain, then mumbled, "'re ya ta preacher?"

"No," I chuckled lightly. Though it might have been a more docile choice of occupation over military, I wasn't sure it would have been for me. "I'm just visiting. My name is Lucas."

"Much 'bliged, Lucas."

In this proximity, I saw that there were additional bandages on his torso and legs. I was no stranger to seeing the damage a cannon can do. He must've been far enough away to not be killed but close enough to receive the shrapnel and the burns.

"What's your name?" I asked when he had finally settled back to a somewhat comfortable position.

"Pete."

"Nice to meet you, Pete. Where's home?"

"Woolwich. My pa runs ta ferry."

I smiled. "I've been on that a time or two. Lord Roseberry was a friend of my father's."

"A chum?"

I cringed. I didn't want to reveal anything about my status just yet. "Yes. I remember when he and my father spoke of the ferry. Even back then, Lord Roseberry mentioned how he intended for it to be free for all to access."

"'e's a right fella."

Yes, my father's friends *were* good men which surprised me that their character and conduct didn't rub off on him more.

I spent the next two hours speaking with Pete about what I recalled of Woolwich—the local farmer's market, the Royal Arsenal plant, and even the foot tunnel under the Thames that led to Newham.

And as the day passed, I recognized that Nurse Watkins was right. Only three other visitors arrived during that time—a woman with two young children in tow. When she settled next to a man's bed, presumably her husband, she nearly swooned. The man was missing his right leg.

After Pete fell asleep, the man in the bed beside him introduced himself as Grant. I didn't have to ask too many questions; it was quite apparent these men were anxious to talk... just talk.

By the time I left the hospital, I had visited with five men. Only one was due to leave soon with his body mostly intact and, though the guilt I bore earlier hadn't vanished, a renewed spirit of purpose swept over me. I couldn't heal their physical ailments, but I could erase the memory even for a moment.

Retrieving Ace, I checked the time on my pocket watch. It confirmed I would certainly miss the dinner hour at home, so I stopped at the nearest pub for a steak and ale pie. I could have gone to my club, but for some odd reason, after the day I had I felt more at ease around men who didn't speak of prized horses, parliament, or tenant disputes.

When I reached the townhouse, it was well past 9 o'clock in the evening. Was it too much to hope that the women had gone to bed early, and I was entering a quiet house?

Apparently so.

One step through the door assured me that the complete opposite was afoot. Davies took my hat and coat. Glancing up the stairs, I acknowledged my desire to slip past the parlor and directly into my quarters. The day had exhausted me but, in the end, the lively sounds that surfaced from the drawing room lured me in.

I leaned against the wall just outside the doors and listened as my sisters engaged in a spirited game of Whist. They all proved to have sharp minds and I was proud of their ability to calculate, assess challenges, and strategize against an opponent.

"You have won again, Sariah and Helena," Genie cried. "That makes it 5 to 2."

My ears perked up. *So, the trespasser has an equal spark of intelligence.* I weighed my temptations. The first… in the direction of my study and a bottle of brandy, and the second… to see this woman in action.

I ran a hand through my hair, straightened my jacket and cravat, and then stepped through the door.

Chapter Twenty-two

Helena

I had gone the entire day without a minute of harassment, but I knew that had come to an end the moment Lucas stepped inside the drawing room during our evening pleasantries. I hid my frown behind a pasted smile. I refused to let this man see how he affected me—an effect not limited to his teasing.

After greeting his sisters amiably, he turned to me once again with a glint in his eye. Nonetheless, after my streak of good luck tonight, my confidence soared.

Let the games begin.

As Lucas approached the table, I shuffled the cards, trying hard to keep my concentration on the task at hand. When he stood before us, I turned to Genevieve. "Even though we won, you can be the elder hand this time." I smiled and pretended not to notice Lucas reaching for Sariah's hand. In my peripheral vision, he kissed her knuckles. The man exuded charm. "Sariah, my dear, I so desperately want to hear you play *Robin Adair* on the pianoforte." He helped her to her feet. "Would you please do us the honor?"

I no longer averted my eyes and watched the exchange curiously, then my mouth parted with realization. If he took Sariah, *my partner* away, that only meant one thing. He and I would be playing the card game as a team.

I pressed my lips together tightly as Sariah sweetly smiled at her older brother and dutifully made her way to the instrument in the corner. When I glanced at the other two pairs of eyes looking my way, there was nothing but cheerfulness displayed. Was I the only one wise to his machination? Did Genevieve not remember how much he dislikes me? Why isn't she volunteering to be my partner and Josie his?

I peered over at Lucas dressed in the peak of fashion with his white cravat and burgundy waistcoat as he nestled into her seat casually and when he caught my eye, he winked.

Winked!

I glanced down at my fidgeting hands then realized this only made me appear weak. Lifting my chin with poise, I hesitated a brief second before I smirked subtly in his direction. If I didn't enjoy winning so much, I would lose on purpose just to humble the man.

"What is the trump suit?"

"Hearts."

Several times over the course of the game, Lucas tried to catch my eye.

"No hints, Luke!" Genie cried during one of those very times.

He lifted his hands in feigned humility. "I assure you I am a paragon of innocence."

I scoffed.

He narrowed his eyes playfully. "You doubt me?"

Our eyes locked and instantly a warmth bled into my cheeks. I glanced away.

123

"We have two honors, one more and that's two additional points," Genie announced.

I played the ace of hearts. "Ten tricks."

"Lud, Helena. You have the highest Trump again." Josie scowled. "I do believe you have won more tricks than anyone I know."

Lucas cleared his throat. "I *do believe* she has a partner, Jos."

"Yes, but she was winning even before you arrived."

Lucas watched me curiously. "You have a sharp mind, Miss Croft." He *sounded* sincere.

I looked over at Genevieve. She had the makings of a smile but lowered her head as if to hide it.

I peered back at Lucas with a clear intent to provoke him. "Is that a hindrance, my lord?"

"No," he said with a chuckle. "Why would it be?"

I stared at him trying to decipher his honesty. "I have difficulty believing that."

He tilted his head curiously as he leaned forward, and I got a whiff of the masculine scent from yesterday—the hint of something woodsy and raw breeched my carefully constructed barriers. I stifled my breath, determined not to succumb to its allure. Then his voice cascaded over me, ensnaring me with charm similar to what he used on Sariah. "In case it has escaped your notice, Miss Croft..." He grinned. "I've three sisters. Their brilliance and keen intellect have always been encouraged."

I folded my arms and leaned back in my chair trying desperately to smell more of the fumes from the hearth than from this man. "And what if the man that intends to marry them does not appreciate such brilliance and keen intellects?"

Genevieve looked up now and arched an eyebrow. She knew I baited him, but something else flashed across her countenance. Something I didn't recognize, like she knew what was about to happen.

Lucas' stare held me captive once again, his piercing eyes sought to read my thoughts. I averted my gaze as he delivered his next words with unwavering conviction. "Then the man is not worthy of her."

My eyes flashed disobediently back his way after he said this. *Was this true?* Did he really feel this way about a woman's mind? I glanced over to Genevieve again and she giggled. "I believe, dear Helena, you have met your match."

"My wh—what?" I stumbled over my response until I realized she had not meant for him to be my match literally, just in our rows apparently.

Lucas stood to his feet and bowed low in my direction. I dipped my chin as he said goodnight, then went to each of his sisters and kissed their foreheads before he departed from the room.

I turned to Genevieve. "Was he in earnest?"

She nodded, then frowned. "But he is not the one to have the final say. Justin is."

"He must have some say."

"There is no doubt Lucas is a defender, a protector in everything he does and says, especially regarding us. He insists he would not let anything untoward happen to us. I have to believe that."

My eyes flitted to the empty doorway and, though Lucas had long departed, I unwittingly missed his presence. "I wish I had such a brother," I mumbled. My longing was pointless for I had no brother, and I no longer had a father who sought to protect me, either.

"Come, walk with me to my room, Helena," Genevieve said after Sariah and Josie said goodnight and left the parlor to retreat to their respective quarters.

Arm in arm we walked up the stairs and to the family wing.

"Have you written to your aunt?" she asked innocently.

"Yes, though I have yet to be successful in terms of her whereabouts."

She squeezed me close. "I have great hope it will be discovered soon."

I shared her sentiments. "I will also need to beg for it to be posted. The pin money I have will need to be used for my transportation."

"Oh, that is little to ask, of course we can post your letter. Then hopefully her response will be swift. I do not mind however long you must stay, Helena. Frankly, I wouldn't mind you staying forever, but I fear you would never be able to go out or enjoy the city's amusements ever again."

"I am indebted to you," I whispered. "I owe you everything."

Genevieve wrapped her arms around me. "You don't owe me anything. It was the right thing to do."

After our goodnights, I took several steps upward toward my bed chamber then decided to go back to the library once more. This time without having to sneak or creep through the hallways.

Only when I opened the door, the smell that had assaulted me at the games lingered in the very room I entered and Lucas Walsh lounged in a wingback chair only with his shirtsleeves and waistcoat on, his tailcoat and cravat missing once again.

I froze.

Then I tried to back out when he spoke up. "Do not let me prevent you from getting that book you are so desperately in need of." He chuckled and looked over at me. I straightened my form and lifted my chin, determined to do that very thing and not look at him while I did it.

"At least we are properly dressed this time…" I suggested and peeked in his direction. "Well, at least I am." I walked toward the front shelf that he had frightened me from three nights before and held my candle up high, tracing my finger along the spines, though thoroughly distracted from reading them clearly.

"So, what do you like to read, *Miss Croft*?" He said my name with another tease in the tone. It caused me to spin around, but I had not expected to lock eyes. He knew that name was not real, but I would not be the one to tell him otherwise… too much was at stake.

I took a subtle breath. "Byron and Keats."

His eyebrows raised in the dancing light of the three-tiered flame resting on the table beside him. "Poetry?"

I faced the bookshelves once more. "Yes."

The creak of his chair surrendering his weight sent a shiver up my spine. Each measured step resonated in the silence, drawing him closer. Awareness prickled my skin leaving a trail of gooseflesh beneath my dress. My breathing slowed and nearly stopped as his arm brushed past my shoulder, bringing his body precariously close.

I watched as he retrieved a book. Taking a step back, he lifted my hand, our bare skin brushing as neither one of us donned gloves. I feared the rapid beat of my heart could be heard in the quiet stillness of the room.

Then he smiled.

The movement was so heartfelt and genuine that it stole the very air from my lungs. "Then you'll want to read this." His touch lingered far longer than necessary. I didn't dare move, held captive by his proximity and that dratted, intoxicating scent.

It wasn't until he had left the room that I realized I still hadn't moved, mesmerized by the entire ordeal. Tilting the book, I read the title on the brown leather spine. "*The Corsair.* A tale by Lord Byron." I gasped. This had only been printed recently, and nearly every copy had been purchased within days. How did they manage to secure a version of this most coveted work of art?

I held the book to my chest and claimed the very spot Lucas had evicted. Curling up next to the light of the three-tiered candlestick, I delightfully indulged in the newest words of Byron.

It was several hours before I convinced myself of the need for sleep. I could have probably read all night, though it would not have been proper for me to sleep all day tomorrow. I might be a guest, but I needed to somehow be of use and not just a recipient of the kindness from this family.

I arrived in my bedchamber shortly after midnight and, though I refused to retrieve Eliza, I had not forgotten how difficult it was to unfasten a gown on my own. The time spent removing my dress and stays was lengthened, which only allowed more time for my thoughts to revert to the library and that curious man… Lucas Walsh.

Thankfully, he did not pursue a line of interrogation again, though it was certain he did not trust me. Genevieve said little about his role in the war. The few men I had known who returned were greatly changed… even angry and broken. Then my thoughts shifted to the scar on his back—the dreadful injury I saw several nights ago. One that would have taken many months to recover from, even now it didn't appear fully healed. I had to tamp down a rising desire to touch it, to soothe his pain.

Everything I had come to believe of men of the ton had come into question the moment I met Lucas Walsh. *Was it truly possible there were men who revered character more than money and status?*

I envied the way he doted on his sisters and, as I laid in bed, I found myself suddenly filled with hope. If there were men like Lucas Walsh in the world, it's possible I might meet one; one that could change my own future and my fate.

If only I could be so lucky.

Chapter Twenty-three

Lucas

"Matthews! Collins!" I waved my hand in their direction as I handed my hat and great coat off to the doorman at Brooks's. This would be the first time that the three of us would be together since our return.

The men had already ordered, waiting for my late arrival.

"What kept you, Luke?" Zach asked, once again with his left hand hidden beneath the table. I wondered if Hunter had seen it yet.

"My sisters, of course." I chuckled. "What other pleasantries could possibly fill my days than their need to be entertained."

The men laughed alongside me though neither one had sisters to truly relate to my situation. Only Jaxon shared my fate with two of his own.

"If Genevieve is a handful, Luke—" Zach started to say.

I cut him off. "—She is not, and you need not concern yourself any further."

Zach smirked. He knew precisely how to get my blood pulsing.

"By the way," I pointed in his direction. "This round is on you for missing the Drake soiree."

"Yes." Zach grinned. "I wasn't in the mood. I will pay my penance."

I turned to Hunter. "Have you any news since the soiree?"

The table grew somber waiting for Matthews to expound.

"I have little else to go on. He is not being listed as a prisoner of war and his body has not been identified from the records of remains on the peninsula. Granted, there are still many thousands of papers to sort through."

I took a sip of my sherry and swallowed slowly. "I visited His Grace."

Both pairs of eyes went to mine with anticipation.

"They are unaware of anything and faithfully await his arrival. They did, however, share with me his last letter."

I reached into my pocket and unfolded a piece of paper. "Shortly after I departed, I went to my solicitor's office and borrowed supplies to write down all that I recalled by memory." Laying it flat, the others leaned in as we read the list.

"The letter was dated 28 October 1813," I offered clarification.

"Well done, Walsh. At the very least this gives us a timeline."

Zachary pointed to the next couple of lines. "He is speaking of Leipzig. I am certain of it. I had a comrade who spent a great deal of time there."

"Germany?" I questioned.

"I had suspected that with Napoleon's whereabouts in Germany, Jaxon would not be far behind. Now that we possibly have his last known location and date, we have a very good place to start," Hunter added.

"Have any of his effects surfaced?" Zach inquired. He clearly meant the family ring and the gold pocket watch he carried against his chest without fail.

Hunter shook his head. "Nothing has appeared in the files, and I have three men scouring everything new that is documented."

"Such items could surely have been stolen and found to be anywhere on the continent."

"Yes, I've considered that. I've spoken with two comrades who knew him and are convinced he's still alive. That is the mystery."

"When are you leaving?" I looked at Hunter.

"Within days."

Zach took a sip of his brandy. "I'm going with you."

"Are you certain?" The way Matthews looked pointedly at his hidden hand, I realized more had been shared between the two of them and, for a brief moment, a sliver of jealousy emerged. I had always been Zach's closest mate.

"I am certain."

Matthews glanced in my direction, and a grimace shrouded my face. I wanted nothing more than to go with him. Everything inside me wished for the freedom to make such a journey.

"Has Justin returned?" He knew my plight.

I shook my head. "No, and it might be another month before he does so." The absence of my older brother brought conflicting feelings. I could not leave my sisters, but if Justin were in London, he might take advantage of my absence and force an unwanted betrothal on Genevieve, possibly even Sariah.

"You cannot leave them." Zach spoke aloud what we were all thinking.

Heat rose on the back of my neck. "I should be with you."

Matthews nodded. "Yes, but you have obligations here."

"Keep me well informed, will you?"

131

"Assuredly." Hunter agreed then ordered another round of drinks.

Once the business at hand was passed over, I recalled the name Genevieve had asked me to make an inquiry of after our ride on Rotten Row. Both Hunter and Zachary had spent considerably more time in London than I and could very well be familiar with the family.

"Are either one of you acquainted with a family here by the name of Webster?"

"Lord Webster?" Matthews tilted his head curiously. "Earl of Tafney?"

"Yes. I believe that is him."

Matthews leaned back and rubbed his chin. "Why?"

I knew whatever I said in the presence of these men would always be confidential. I had no reason to be furtive. "Genevieve has formed a friendship with his daughter."

"Lady Helena Webster?"

"Pardon?" My mind spun.

"That is her name, Walsh."

My jaw tensed. The woman in my house and the friend Genevieve had concerns about were one and the same. *Lady Helena Webster.* I knew she wasn't Croft. I smirked at my good fortune. I had met her that day in Hyde Park. She was with the man twice her age. Lord Foxton. I couldn't wait to inform her of my newfound knowledge.

"I am unsure whether I should inquire of the volley of expressions that just passed over your face right then." Hunter chuckled.

I returned to a stoic look. "Yes, Lady Helena Webster."

Zach now grinned like a scheming cat. "She's an incomparable. Are you sure it's Genevieve who has taken an interest in her?"

I wanted to laugh. "I assure you I have no designs on the woman." At least I tried to convince myself of that.

Matthews eyed me warily in disbelief.

132

"Don't look at me that way." I poured another drink. "There seems to be some concerns..."

"With Lord Foxton?"

"You're familiar with the gentleman?"

"*Gentleman* is hardly the term I would use," Hunter said with a scowl.

"What do you know of him?"

"He's a lowly baron but has top tier wealth with no boundaries. If he wants something he takes it, regardless of who might be harmed."

"He's a bottom dweller," Zach scoffed. "He owns several gaming hells on Tooley in Southwark." The name of the street piqued my interest. It was there where my father had met his untimely death. *Was this a coincidence?*

"Have you heard anything relating to Lord Webster, Earl of Tafney's finances? Or why he might encourage a courtship between this man and his daughter?"

Zach shrugged. "He's a gambler but not an excessive one that I've seen. I do believe he has been ill-advised in speculation. Business with the war."

Hunter added to Zach's list. "His solicitor is an honest man, but I believe the earl does not always heed his advice."

The puzzle was starting to come together. If Tafney had debts, offering his daughter to a man with unlimited means would be most beneficial. And the social climber, Foxton, would gain status from marrying an earl's daughter. I rubbed my chin, taking all this recent knowledge to mind. "Is the Earl of Tafney known to be a violent man?"

Both men stared at me with blank faces.

"Why is this of such great import to you?" Zach questioned.

"It's of concern to Genevieve, and anything my sisters are concerned with is of interest to me."

Zach studied me. He might've noticed the change to my demeanor. I could not keep my frustration from splaying across my features. "For someone without a personal interest, your expression shows otherwise," he commented.

"Genevieve claimed that the earl has displayed moments of anger." Now that I said this out loud, it all made sense. Her father's mood swings, her need to escape, the bruise on her cheek. *He struck her!* A fury surged through my veins giving rise to a fiercely protective trait.

Both men waited for me to elaborate.

"I have only been introduced to her as of late but..." I lowered my voice. "She had a bruise on her cheekbone, as if someone planted a facer on her."

"She'd been struck?" Zach's lips parted.

"I believe so."

Matthews' jaw tightened.

I whispered, "We must keep this between us until we know more."

"I will seek out a friend of mine," Hunter assured me. "Someone who is well-versed in the underbelly of London. If Tafney is in trouble, Mack would know. I'll send word before we leave."

Zach added. "And if you need us before then, just send Giles."

I nodded and shook their hands. They were the best of men. Now if only we could be this successful in the mystery surrounding Jaxon.

Arriving home late, I reflected on all that occurred since I had met Miss Helena Croft who was really Lady Helena Webster.

The pieces of the puzzle came together easily. Genevieve's concern over her friend being betrothed to a scoundrel, the woman's cloak-and-dagger appearance at my home, the bruise on her cheek, and her need to give me a false name. Regardless of all that had transpired in the short amount of time, there was one thing that went without question—this woman needed to feel safe, not threatened, and especially not tormented by me.

I arose early again the next morning. My conduct was far from the idle behavior expected of a man of my rank, yet I continuously marginalized myself from such habits frequently.

Determined to address the issue with the women at a later hour, I departed for a prearranged consultation. While our family physician most regularly visited our home in times of ailment, per our fee per annum, he kept an office off High Street in Cheapside, and it was essential I met him there under the circumstances.

"Lord Lucas Walsh, welcome home." Dr. Sawyer shook my hand and invited me inside. "I cannot tell you how relieved I was to get your message and hear of your return." He frowned as he led me into a small separate room and to an examination table. "I fear too many have not."

I took a deep inhale. A daily reminder.

"How may I be of service?"

"First off, call me Lucas like you have since I was in leading strings." I then glanced at the young man at his side; a student of medicine to be sure by the way he watched our moves with curiosity. The chap could be no older than eighteen with his slight stature and pockmarked skin.

"Oh, forgive me, Lucas. This is Daniel Stone. He is a student from St. Bart's sent to observe my work twice a week."

I nodded in his direction but had no intention of allowing him to remain. "Please understand, Mr. Stone, I don't ask you to leave under pretenses that I'm a highbrow. My visit to Dr. Sawyer is of a highly sensitive nature and I would prefer privacy."

He looked at Dr. Sawyer who waved him out of the examination room. When the doctor closed the door behind him, he brushed the request aside. "Daniel receives more than enough education each time

135

we visit the rookery." He chuckled to himself. "Now what brings you here?"

I removed my coat and began untying my cravat. "I believe this might be as healed as it ever will be, but if you have any further advice, maybe a tonic or balm, I would appreciate it."

Dr. Sawyer replaced his spectacles and stepped closer as I unbuttoned my waistcoat and pulled my shirtsleeves up toward my head, exposing my back.

"Oh my," he mumbled. "Lucas, this is…" he didn't finish his sentence and I only nodded.

As he took the next few minutes examining the saber wound, silence filled the room. Occasionally I felt his fingertips brushing tender areas of the scar.

"Well, I do say the sutures did a marvelous job at keeping the skin together, but some of these edges still appear raw and tender. How do you sleep?"

"Terribly," I grumbled, then added. "But not only because of this wound. I have…"

"Nightmares." He cut me off and moved to my side where I could see him better. Removing his spectacles, he wiped his face with a handkerchief. "Yes, one might think the war is over, but it is still being fought on our home front—in our houses and in our beds."

I eyed the older gentleman curiously. "You fought?"

He pursed his lips and nodded. "Revolutionary War." Then he leaned over and pointed to the lower half of his breeches. "Nearly lost my leg."

"How did you…" I thought hard on how to carefully word my question. "How did you get through the guilt of returning when so many men did not?"

"That is the question of the ages, my lord." He sighed. "But I don't let one day pass without thanking God for his decision to spare me. I refuse to let that gift be squandered."

That seemed too simple.

"And I never hesitate to help a soldier… regardless of their station or bankroll. If he needs me, I will be there."

I mulled his words around.

He continued, "The more time I am focused on the needs of others, the less time I am consumed with my own insatiable needs. It has been my saving grace."

For as long as I had known Dr. Sawyer, I had known him to be a man of great character. He lived by those standards. There was no divergence between his words and his actions. I thought about the men at Greenwich Hospital and vowed at that moment I would do more, visit more, and help where needed.

As I dressed, not in the precise manner Giles would have done so, Dr. Sawyer retrieved two small bottles from his cabinet. "Have someone rub this on your back each night."

I arched one of my eyebrows pointedly. "You do know I am unwed."

He chuckled. "I have a remedy for that, too."

I laughed out loud.

Lifting up the first bottle, he pointed to the label. "White lead numbs the skin leaving it paralyzed. Though the result may be unsightly, it will lessen your pain." Then he motioned toward the second bottle. "This one is Gowlands lotion, a corrosive sublimate ground with spiritus vini, employed most commonly by fashionable ladies for eruptions of the skin. However, we have found it beneficial in soothing blade wounds."

He handed me both bottles. "I am glad you have returned, Lucas, but I am most sorrowful for your family and the loss of the marquess."

"Thank you, Dr. Sawyer." I placed the bottles in the pockets of my trousers, each capped well with cork. "His death came as quite a shock."

"I imagine so." He opened the door that led back out of the examination room. "Now take good care of those sisters of yours."

I smiled and shook his hand. "Always."

Chapter Twenty-four

Helena

"Oh, that one is simply lovely, Helena," Josie chirped at my side as she admired the blush-colored rose I held in my hands. The Walsh sisters and I stood amidst their garden's vibrant tapestry, carefully curating blooms for a dinner bouquet. Though their housekeeper generally shouldered this task, Mrs. Parker had kindly granted us the honor.

It was a needed distraction. One I yearned for to put my restless mind at ease and keep my eager hands busy.

"What about these white ones?" Genevieve pointed to several long-stemmed plants set against the black iron fence.

"Lilies," I declared as my lips curved into a smile from a happy memory. "Their elegance offers a perfect contrast. Cut six stems." The principles of floral arrangement were etched into my being, a legacy my mother patiently imparted during my early years. She enhanced flower arranging with her grace and passionate heart, and lilies had been her favorite.

Though I would have loved to see their beautiful gardens in full bloom during the summer, they had a lovely spring beginning, and I was thrilled beyond words to be in the midst of them, this being the first time I had ventured outside since I arrived a sennight ago.

After only a few minutes, Eliza entered from the rear gate and waved to me. My heart leaped at her expression. She was smiling. Today would mark the fourth day that she had met secretly with Sally in the hopes we would locate the name of my aunt's estate.

"Would you excuse me a moment," I said to the girls and wiped my hands on the apron I was given.

"Oh, miss." Eliza's eyes lit up. "I couldn't wait ta show ya. We got it."

Eliza handed me an envelope and in one corner written in perfectly lovely loops was the name *Mrs. Patricia Carver, Woodhouse Grove*. "Oh, yes." I tapped my head. "Woodhouse. I remember now." Then my eyes went to the name the letter addressed and I choked.

Lady Helena Webster.

Tears bubbled on my bottom lashes. "This was written to me," I whispered. I had no recollection of ever receiving correspondence from the woman. Eliza glanced over at the others as they watched us but kept themselves busy. My ever-devoted lady's maid has hugged me before but only in the privacy of my bedchamber. She dared not do so in such a public setting, despite my wish.

Placing her hand over mine to stop the trembling, she lowered her voice. "She wrote ya, milady, 'n look, the date be *after* yer mama was laid ta rest."

I wiped my eyes. "Thank you, Eliza." My smile shared my gratitude. "I will be inside shortly." Tucking the missive into my pocket, I turned to rejoin the Walsh sisters once more, resigned to read the letter as soon as I found a moment of privacy.

Spending an hour with the sisters in the garden was a dream come true. Without sisters, I had never experienced so much laughter and gaiety, and these daily delights were envied. What a pleasure it would be to have a sister to turn to, to share with, and to lean on.

Twice, I fingered the paper in my pocket. The seal had been broken and I was quite certain I knew by whom. The thought troubled me. Each day that passed, the more I wondered if I had ever really known my father at all.

As we moved to carry the blooms inside the townhouse, Lucas trotted up on a striking brown stallion. *Another envy.* His ability to ride anytime, anywhere. I once had that same privilege and missed my mare, Cleo, more than anything.

When our eyes met, something unusual passed in that solitary look. The suspicion that had rooted there for days was gone. Instantly, my skin tingled. What could have changed in so little time? When he dismounted, he handed the reins over to a groom who led the beautiful beast to the mews. Lucas strode over to meet us in a dark blue waistcoat and pale-yellow cravat. Once again, he cut a dashing figure. I bit my tongue. Those thoughts had no right to passage.

He reached us with open arms. "Here, allow me to help." He retrieved the flowers, scooping them from all of our hands, then followed us toward the rear doors.

Once inside, he handed the blooms off to two maids who arrived to meet us and removed his coat and hat for Davies.

I lifted a hand to stop the two girls. "We're going to arrange them for tonight." I didn't want to lose the opportunity to prepare them ourselves. Then glanced back at Lucas. "I'm teaching your sisters how to create an arrangement."

He raised a brow thoughtfully. "Very well." He faced the maids. "Place them in the parlor, but leave them be." When he circled back to us, his eyes revealed a seriousness I hadn't seen before. "But first, we must talk."

I felt the blood drain from my face. I knew something had changed. He must've tired of my secrets and would now demand my departure.

Genevieve looked between us both with confusion. Josie and Sariah waited patiently for elaboration as well.

"Josie, Sariah, please excuse Genevieve, Miss Croft, and I. We have something to discuss in the study." He pointed the way down the hallway. I took an extra breath and followed Genevieve. Lord Lucas' heavy steps echoed against the marble floor behind me and, with every second, I wondered what would happen next.

My hands slipped into my pocket while my fingers pinched the parchment tucked safely within—the very one that might provide my needed rescue. If only he would let me post my letter first... before he sent me away.

After Lucas closed the door, he moved around to the other side of his desk, or his father's desk, I presumed. The room appeared quite opposite of the man who stood before me. The stiff resilience of walnut carved furniture and a set of solemn bronze statues resembling Socrates and Aristotle fashioned a cold atmosphere. I pictured Lucas a warm, mahogany type.

The pounding of my heart matched the pulsing in my veins as I waited for him to speak.

"Please have a seat, Lady Helena."

Genevieve gasped and my mouth separated at his use of my real name.

Though the moment was not a humorous one, Lucas's mouth lifted into a slight grin. "The presumption that you were never Miss Croft should not come as a surprise, though I am disappointed in myself that I didn't make the connection sooner between you and Genevieve."

I slowly took a seat in one of the two wingback chairs that faced him. Apparently, I was exceedingly foolish, for I thought we had mastered our subterfuge well.

"I was introduced to you mere days before your arrival at our home, though it was brief." He looked pointedly at me. "Did our introduction not merit a recollection?"

If only he knew what crossed my mind that first day, he would not be saying this. I hoped between being hidden by my bonnet and the swiftness of our departure, he would not have remembered, but he most certainly made a lasting impression on me.

Lucas' smile faded. "And your face was absent of the bruise at the time."

I stole a quick breath before I spoke. "I fell off my horse the next—"

"Don't." He held a hand up. "Genevieve knows I value honesty and integrity above all."

I lowered my eyes. Both traits I held close to my heart as well.

"It wasn't her fault," Genevieve spoke up in my defense, but he must've willed her to silence.

"Forgive me," I whispered.

There was a long pause and when I finally lifted my head, Lucas had moved around from the opposite side of the desk and stood before us. He leaned against the furniture in a casual stance. His countenance only exuded compassion.

A knock at the door interrupted us.

"Come in," he said.

The butler entered with apologies and handed Lucas a message. "The messenger said that his master, Lord Matthews, insisted you receive his missive immediately, sir."

"Thank you, Davies."

He unfolded it and quickly read over its contents, then his eyes slowly lifted to me. The frown on his face confirmed the note contained something related to me. *Oh, please not about my father.* I hoped he still remained unaware of my whereabouts.

Lucas folded up the letter and placed it inside his waistcoat pocket. "I'm aware of your father, Lady Helena." He exhaled slowly. "I understand there was a significant change in his circumstances that has led him to desperation."

The icy touch of fear gripped my heart and paralyzed me. I had not cried in days but once the shock wore off, I could not keep the tears from breaking free.

Did he also know the depth of my father's deeds?

It was then that I realized I had made a dreadful mistake by seeking refuge at the Walsh residence. I erroneously entangled them in my family's plight. My head fell to my hands with a wave of humiliation, sorrow, and bitterness.

A gentle warmth seeped through the delicate fabric of my dress as a hand touched my arm. I raised my tear-streaked cheeks to meet Lucas' reassuring gaze. He had crouched down before me and the intensity that blazed from his eyes was filled with unyielding conviction. "Please know, Lady Helena, that my word is sincere," his whisper, a fervent oath. "You are safe here."

Genevieve moved to my side and wrapped her arms around me. Leaning her head against mine, she soothed. "All will be well, Helena, you'll see." Then she handed me her handkerchief.

Lucas stood up and paced the room as I disciplined my sentiments. I rarely showed emotion in front of others, yet quite recently it had become a daily event.

Lucas ran a hand down his face. "Now, despite the innocence of your residing here, we cannot harbor you forever." He paused. "Do you have any family to turn to?"

Genevieve spoke before I could. "She's waiting to get her aunt's—"

I cut her off and lifted the missive from my pocket. "I only received it a moment ago from Eliza."

Genevieve squeezed me harder. "Oh, Helena, that is spectacular news and since you have already written a letter, we can send it posthaste." She looked up at her brother. "Can we, Lucas?"

"Yes, of course. Where does she live?"

"Northampton."

"And she has the means to take you in?"

I bit my lip. "She has the means, but I am unaware if there is a desire. I have not had a relationship with her for years."

"Hmmm." Lucas clasped his hands behind his back while he contemplated. "Well, we will carry on until we receive word." Then he peered down at me. The truth reflected from his eyes stopped my breath. "I will not send you home."

Genevieve kissed my cheek and I smiled warily. The fact that I no longer needed to hide behind a secret felt so liberating. "Thank you, Lord Lucas."

"Lucas, call me Lucas."

Lucas. I smiled in his direction. He had always been Lucas to me. lord was a name that fit the older, fiercer version of the marquess.

He continued, "It only seems natural, in light of the circumstances, that we become friends. However," he paused. "I fear you must remain inside. I need to investigate your father's state of mind and, since he has turned to violence against you, I worry over what he may do if he learned of your location. For your safety, *and that of my sisters*, please stay inside the house."

I nodded. It was true. I had never seen my father behave the way he did before I left. *What would he be capable of if he discovered me?*

When Lucas moved past me, I reached up and clasped his hand. This was brazen behavior for a lady, but I could not let the moment pass. Wanting him to understand the significance of his decision, I gently squeezed. "Thank you, Lucas." He looked down at me. The way his gray eyes pierced through me they unraveled my soul. "Thank you," I reiterated.

He nodded and I released my touch.

Once I was alone with Genevieve more unbridled tears fell. All the emotion that had been built up over the last several weeks crashed down as if the fragile walls of my resilience shattered under the strain.

"Oh, Helena." Genevieve kneeled beside me and took my hands in hers. "There is nothing to fear. I promised you that Lucas would protect you. He's had years of practice already." She chuckled.

I shook my head. "*That* is what I fear." I sniffled. "I have only become an added burden to a man who already bears the greater responsibility of his three sisters."

She kissed me on the cheek. "You are hardly a burden." She wiped my cheeks and pulled me to my feet. "Now, come and show me how to arrange those lovely flowers we picked."

Chapter Twenty-five

Lucas

I emerged from the study with my fist clenched. When Helena's hand lingered on mine it left a phantom sensation. Part of me wanted to rub it raw to erase its memory, the other part, a selfish part, longed to savor it and preserve it within my grasp.

When I first confessed to what I knew of her identity, I couldn't help but smile at the knowledge that she had been caught, but I didn't expect her reaction. The strength I admired dissolved, and I saw a terrified woman. When I read Hunter's missive, my whole being froze. His words only confirmed what I suspected about her father, his financial woes… and behavior.

Then an instant sensation overcame me. A desire to keep her safe… I *wanted* to protect her.

Retreating to my quarters, I read the missive again.

Lucas,

Collins and I are departing tomorrow at first light. If you are able to bid us farewell, meet us at my mews by the 7ᵗʰ hour. The following is what I learned about the earl, Lord Webster.

He is facing an insurmountable number of debts. Though he gambled occasionally like many men of the ton, it was a recent failed speculation of a series of merchant ships that were destroyed by the French that put his finances deep in the red. He is facing debtors' prison. I assume the reason he has promised his only daughter to Lord Foxton is to balance his books, but there is talk of other less honorable associations with the man. A scoundrel of the vilest kind, and one I wouldn't let care for my dog, much less my daughter.

HM

One more thing to trouble my mind.

I clasped the bell pull and tugged. Within a minute, Giles was standing before me. "I will be leaving early again tomorrow. Forgive me for yet another unearthly hour."

"It's my duty to serve you, my lord. I have no qualms over what that entails."

I laid a hand on his shoulder. "You are the best of men, Giles. Thank you." I hesitated. "By the way, thank you for suggesting a visit to Greenwich, it has been…" I tried to find the right word—cathartic, transformative, life altering…

"Restorative, sir?" He used the same word from before when he first spoke of the hospital in a way that did not suggest weakness.

I smiled. I'm not so proud a man that I can't accept my limitations, I only bear a great worry to maintain herculean strength for my family and particularly my sisters. "Yes, precisely that."

And in that brief moment, I realized for the first time in months I had not awakened the night before to a grisly, terrifying scene.

"Also, my lord, here is the information you requested on a certain family. The location and a few notes I suspected you might want are included." I glanced over the small parchment. The day after the soiree, I sent Giles out to learn of Eveline Brown's location. Of course, she was now known as Eveline Turner, the wife of Sir Colin Turner.

"Thank you."

As Giles motioned to leave, I stopped him. "Giles, I must tell you something of grave importance and ask that you do as you have always done and keep my confidences on this matter."

He faced me with his full attention.

"This is about Miss Croft. Why she is here and who she really is."

One of his eyebrows arched simultaneously to the beginnings of a grin.

"Not that reason." I chuckled.

Though the utmost propriety had been maintained between Helena and I, there may have been curious chats deliberated below stairs and, while I trusted all of my servants… I trusted Giles with my life.

Chapter Twenty-six

Helena

Sitting at my desk, I fingered the old missive from my Aunt Patricia. The day's events surrounding the moment I had received this letter had swung from highs to lows—from spending time with the sisters to the private conversation in the study, then back to the flower arrangements, and an oddly quiet evening meal, after which I hastily excused myself for the evening.

As expected, the conversation in the study occupied most of my thoughts and attention, so I had not a moment to devote to this letter. While I should have known Lucas would discover my identity soon enough, I had not anticipated his warmth and compassion once he did. This was on the heel of our bristly introduction followed by his relentless teasing. It was as if I viewed him in an entirely different light and, no matter how hard I tried, I could not ignore it. His words... *Please know that my word is sincere. You are safe here,* resonated deep within.

How could one not be swept away by the romanticism of a heroic protector?

I shook my head. But that is all he is... a protector... a guardian like unto his sisters.

Unfolding the parchment, I banished Lucas from my mind and read.

Dearest Helena,

My heart continues to be with you during this most difficult time. I pray with all my might that you might find comfort in the love and friendship of those around you. Your mother's presence will be sorely missed. She was a guiding light for many. I cannot comprehend the things one might do in grief, but please do not blame your father. He is feeling the loss of his soulmate and the love of his life, and his decisions are only made to keep you from feeling the depth of pain. One day, I hope he will see the wisdom in our correspondence.

With love, Aunt Patricia

Her words puzzled me. I read them again and only grew more curious the harder I tried to decipher them. Why would blame fall upon my father? What did he do back then that would warrant forgiveness from me? He certainly didn't kill my mother. She had contracted the fever and there was no doubt about my father's grief. Above all, he and my mother were a love match of the truest kind. Something, sadly, he had tried to rob me of.

A knock on the door brought my mind back to the present.

"Come in," I answered, nearly absentmindedly. Since I had foregone any night revelries, the evening was still young.

"Are you well?" Genevieve inquired. Her countenance shared little insight into her emotions. She came to me and sat in the seat opposite mine. "I am sorry for all that has happened, Helena. I know we had little time to speak of it after Lucas shared with us his discoveries and the dinner bell's chime." She sighed. "I only wanted to confirm what he said. We will not let any harm come to you."

I never doubted her.

Reaching for her hands, I squeezed them over her lap. "I am strengthened because of your kindness. My fears have been comforted and I entrust myself wholly to you and Lucas."

Genevieve's eyes flicked over to the foolscap nearby. "Is this the letter from your aunt?"

I nodded and retrieved it. "Please read it and tell me your thoughts."

The contents were short, so it didn't take her long. Once she finished, she peered over at me, bewildered. "This is the one you received today?"

"Yes, from Eliza. Sally found it in my father's study. It's from my aunt… three years ago."

"So, she wrote to you after your mother's death."

I nodded. "Though I can't understand it. If she wanted nothing to do with me, why write?"

Genevieve handed the letter back to me. "I have a presumption, though, nothing to prove its worth."

I waited for her to continue.

"Since your father was so deeply in love with your mother, the sight of her identical twin sister in your lives could be quite painful." She chewed on her bottom lip. "Do you suppose it was he who refused contact and a possible relationship?"

I let her words sink in. *Could that be the real reason we had lost touch?* It made complete and utter sense. Tears formed in the corners of my eyes as I thought of my father and the torment he must've endured to see a woman who looked so perceptively identical to my mother at the same time he laid his wife to rest. The anguish must've been excruciating.

Genevieve whispered above my thoughts. "This could mean that she would welcome you without hesitation and, now that you have her estate name, there is hope."

Hope.

I dared not allow myself to feel it until now. I wiped my eyes before more tears could break free and jotted my aunt's address on the missive I had already penned. "Will you please see that this is posted in the morning?"

Genevieve reached for the letter, then wrapped her arms around me. "I will do better than that. I will send it with a personal messenger. It could propel a swifter answer."

I then stood up and retrieved my diamond pendant, ruby brooch, and matching earrings from my trunk. "Would you also see if one of the trusted footmen might be able to sell these for me? If I have the funds to travel the moment I receive word, I will no longer be a burden."

Genevieve clasped my hand shut with the jewels inside. "You have never been a burden, Helena, and I hate to see you separated from such personal belongings."

"I want to pay my way. It troubles me to be so dependent on others."

"They are your mother's jewels, are they not?"

I didn't respond.

"I assure you, this is unnecessary."

"Please. Please do this for me," I pleaded.

She reluctantly took the rubies but left the diamond pendant in my hand and kissed me on the cheek before she said goodnight.

After the door closed behind her, I opened my hand and perused the remaining jewel. It was a gift from my parents the last time we were all together, my sixteenth birthday. The ruby earrings and brooch were my mother's and the sorrow from being parted from them was painful, but indeed necessary.

The following morning, I arrived at the breakfast room to a gaggle of giggles. It was such a refreshing change to the dark clouds that had weighed on us heavily the night before.

Once I retrieved my plate and sat down, I realized the sniggers were suspicious.

"Is there something on my cheeks?" I asked as I looked between the sisters, not revealing my relief that it was just us. Although Lucas joined us for dinner the night before, it was apparent that we all had much on our minds and engaged very little.

Josie snickered, and Sariah snorted. They were definitely up to something.

"You cannot keep such delicious secrets to yourselves." I put my piece of bacon down before I took a bite. "Do tell."

"We have decided," Sariah announced with a wide smile, "that we have had quite enough melancholy permeating between these walls."

My eyebrows furrowed. "What precisely does that mean?"

Genevieve joined in, "We have a soiree to attend tonight."

My heart beat faster as I bit my lip. I so missed entertainment of all kinds. "But I cannot leave your house." I wasn't sure how much the younger girls knew of my situation.

Josie could not contain her excitement any longer and blurted out, "We aren't. The soiree is *here*... just the four of us."

I tried to wrap my head around their plans. Soirees were rarely considered soirees with less than a couple dozen attendees.

Sariah added, "Since neither Josie nor I are out in society, we never get to dress for such formal occasions... and with you," she glanced to Genevieve as if she was unsure of what to say. "— with you *confined* within, you haven't been able to enjoy much of the season yourself." She winked. "With Mrs. Parker's help, we have planned a private event here... just us."

Instantly a lightness penetrated the room as if it had been awaiting permission and buoyed us up. "Are you certain it's not too much trouble?"

"Not at all," Genevieve confirmed. "It actually will pale compared to the ones held before our father's death, but it will be lovely all the same."

I had only brought one formal gown with me from home, my favorite. It was a cream-colored dress with a sheer overlay and silver beads stitched on the hem. A lovely green shawl complemented it if we were to go outside... which we were not.

Though Eliza had aired out the gown and placed it in the armoire, there had been no scenario that warranted its use... until now. The very thought of getting dressed up for one night tickled my insides. Then the words Josie spoke struck me. "Only the four of us?" I asked as casually as possible. "Will Lord Lucas be away?" I tried not to let my thoughts of him seep into my tone.

Genevieve glanced at me curiously. Apparently, I had not tried hard enough.

"He left before we could speak of it. Giles said he has many things to attend to today and will most certainly be late. I'm sorry."

"Oh, no, it was only an inquiry. I believe a night with just the four of us is perfect," I blurted out in an effort to shroud my disappointment.

Genevieve leaned closer to me and whispered, "He took your jewelry and the letter and insisted on making the arrangements for the messenger himself."

Of course. The sooner my aunt responds, the sooner he will no longer have to concern himself with me. Then I blanched at my vexation. This was precisely what I wanted, so why did it leave a bitter taste in my mouth?

"That is very kind of him." I smiled sincerely at the girls. "I so look forward to our gathering. What can I do to assist?"

The three sisters smiled in response. "Flowers." They laughed at their simultaneous exclamation.

Genevieve added, "Mrs. Parker will serve dinner at seven and she has agreed to make the meal a grand affair. Afterward, we'll have a short musicale and a dance."

"Dance?" I choked.

"Josie is learning the steps of all the traditional dances," Sariah added. "This might be the only time she can practice in an actual gown. It will be a lark."

Josie pulled a playful face. "It's not like the dress is altogether fitting. They are Genevieve's earlier gowns. Miss Abagale will have to pin them in order for me not to drown in them."

"But regardless," Sariah smiled. "The night will be altogether lovely."

I quite agreed. Dressing up, having my hair done and enjoying one last night with friends; I could not have imagined anything better. I hugged each of the sisters. "Thank you for all you have done and continue to do for me."

Chapter Twenty-seven

Lucas

The news of Lady Helena's success in finding her aunt's whereabouts brought forth mixed emotions—gratitude for her sake, disappointment for my own. A strange unease settled over me as I grappled with her impending departure, and I wasn't entirely sure why.

She was an enigma, this Lady Helena Webster—a captivating puzzle of beauty and intrigue that had ensnared my curiosity. With each passing encounter, a vexing yearning to decipher her complexities had intensified. Vexing, because this was possibly the most inopportune timing in my life to acknowledge any interest for a woman.

Seeing her so vulnerable yesterday in the study brought an assortment of feelings to the surface. The first, *anger*. How could a father do this to his daughter? If I were to ever face such a man, would I be able to control my impulse to plant a facer on him?

Second, *respect*. Lady Helena had shown such strength and fortitude in light of all that she faced. Despite her tears, she bore extraordinary courage. Third, *desire*. But not in the traditional sense. There was no doubt I was attracted to her, but my desire resulted from a desire to protect. I vowed to keep her safe, and it was not just empty words. I fully intend on seeing to her wellbeing and, strangely enough, I didn't want that sense of security to be limited to only the time she remained in my care.

Galloping toward Lord Matthews' mews, I arrived just in time.

Both men were securing their saddlebags while a groom attended a third horse in the stable. It was he, I assumed, who would bring the horses back from the port.

"Walsh! I hoped you might come." Hunter smiled widely.

"Wouldn't have missed it. I nearly packed for the journey myself." I teased, of course, but considering what had recently transpired, the thought had crossed my mind more than once.

Both men chuckled in response.

Approaching Zachary, I rested one hand on his shoulder. "Keep me informed, please." Then I pointed to his hand hidden within the comforts of a fit leather glove. "And know that I am always a listening ear. You can tell me anything."

He clenched his hand into a fist, the absence of his fingers a stark reminder. "I know." He nodded, a sigh escaping him. "Someday..." His words trailed off as Hunter strode closer, gripping the reins of his mighty gray steed, Claymore. The horse, aptly named after the formidable two-handed sword, produced similar power. Facing me, Hunter sobered. "I know you want to join us, Luke, but you are needed far more here than abroad."

I pursed my lips and nodded. Only yesterday, those needs compounded with Helena's welfare. Though I took comfort in the assurance that while she was with us, she was secure. I could never press her to return home and into such a frightening situation.

Matthews leaned forward as though nobody but the three of us could hear. His groom waited a fair distance away. "You don't happen to know where a certain lady has taken refuge, do you?" He arched a brow. "It seems she has simply vanished." His lips twitched, fighting a grin. "And while her father has exhausted his pursuit, it is Lord Foxton who has sent his bloodhounds to flush her out. My source claims they have been unsuccessful thus far."

I exhaled through my nose. "She is safe."

He smiled shrewdly. "But are you?" Then followed up with a deep chuckle.

I shook my head, but the beginnings of a slight smile emerged. Of the four of us, Hunter had this natural ability to find positivity in the least likely scenarios.

He disregarded my silence and slapped my shoulder. "You're a good man, Luke."

"Find Jaxon," I pleaded.

Both men nodded and ascended to their saddles.

"He belongs home whether alive or…" I couldn't finish the sentence. There was no image that deserved acknowledgement where he was not here laughing and raising a glass to our varying life journeys.

"We will," Zachary acknowledged and waved goodbye.

I watched as they raced off to the port.

The reality of the separation sank in. I would not know of their success or failure for weeks, even months, but I could not imagine two men more capable of locating our friend and felt assurance at that.

Steering my horse away from Matthews' townhouse, I reflected on his words. It was no surprise that Helena's father searched for her, and the relief that washed over me at the notion of his pursuit coming to an end brought *some* comfort. But what was the truth? Would he truly shoulder his burdens and seek a solution that didn't hinge upon the sacrifice of his only daughter? Would he dare face debtor's prison? And what of Foxton? Was this a relentless chase born out of pride? He could force practically any connection he wanted. Why pursue one where the lady clearly has no interest? And why send men after her? Bringing a woman back in chains hardly makes for a willing baroness. Regardless, one thing was certain with such a man... with his bottomless coffers, he could effortlessly unleash disorder upon every darkened corner of London while in pursuit. We must tread forward carefully.

My next order of business concluded with a hired messenger well on his way to Northampton to reach Helena's aunt. I would have sent Giles with the letter or one of my own men for such a task if I felt I could spare them, but considering the threats that loomed, I hardly wanted my house to be in short supply of able-bodied men.

Next, I stopped at Stevens Hotel for a bite to eat. Stevens was a place frequented by many uniformed men, mostly officers, but once you've been to war and spent a considerable amount of time with all ranks of men, sharing drinks became one more natural order of things. And there was a contentment found here that could not be found anywhere else—a collective understanding, if you will.

I settled in, preparing to be idle for a few hours since calling upon Eveline this early in the morning would not only be inconsiderate but also improper.

"Lieutenant Walsh?" A man called from the end of my table. As my eyes scanned over the group of three men, a smile filled my cheeks. They were members of my company, having arrived home several months before me and, from the looks of it, appeared happy, hopefully settling into home life and their respective trades with ease.

"Oliver Clark, Arthur Finch, and Hugh Perry," I announced with pride. The men grinned in response.

Hugh raised a hand and called to the waiter. "Round of drinks here. We've got a hero amongst us." The other men in the room raised their glasses to his announcement.

I vehemently protested. "It is I who shall buy this round and every one hereafter," I insisted. "Were it not for you three, I might not be standing here today."

Though my battle charge may have sparked their misguided belief in my heroism, it was these very men who had rescued me from the battlefield before I bled out. I owed them my life.

After an afternoon of reflection and good-natured conversation, it was time I departed for Eveline's, but not without promises of future visits. Though men of the ton rarely associated with men below their standing, I had no qualms about recognizing their worth. They were, by far, three of the greatest men I served with.

Glancing at the note Giles had given me, I led Ace to Eveline's rented rooms located in Lambeth. Not exactly the neighborhood I would have expected for a baron's daughter, but if what Genie told me is true, Evie, her mother, and sister could have fared much worse after the death of Lord Ashton.

Just another thing to fault Justin with.

While we might not have been able to save them from ruin, we could hardly sit back and watch them suffer. Our families had been neighbors for decades.

I knocked on the thick wooden door.

When a heavy-set woman in a simple work dress and pleated mobcap on her head answered, the Brown women's circumstances were further revealed to me. No butler.

"Yes, sir, how can I help you?"

"I'm here to call on the lady of the house, Miss Eveline Brown. Uh, pardon me, Turner." I handed her my calling card.

She nodded and invited me into the foyer to wait. A young woman bearing an uncanny resemblance to Eveline cautiously emerged from a doorway. I observed her with curiosity, and then recognition dawned on me. "April, could it be?" I asked, my voice laced with surprise. She stepped fully into the light. "It's me," I called out. "Your old neighbor, Lucas Walsh."

A radiant smile spread across her face, and as she approached, she dipped into a graceful curtsy. I reached out and pulled her in for a warm embrace. I had known her for her entire fifteen years, minus the two I was away at war. Eveline's younger sister had blossomed into a lovely young woman.

"Lucas!" Eveline came rushing forward from another room and in the most unsuitable manner crashed into me with her arms draped around the both of us. Glancing over her shoulder, I saw the housekeeper freeze at the bottom of the stairs, so stunned she might not have realized her mouth hung ajar. I chuckled. She most likely hadn't seen her mistress behave so informally before. I tightened my hold on them both.

"Oh, Luke." Tears flowed down Eveline's cheeks. "I am so relieved to know you are alive and well."

I kissed her forehead, much like a brother. "I fared better than most."

"It was devastating to hear of your father's death, Luke."

"It is *your* father's death that has brought me the greatest distress. I'm so sorry," I whispered. "I did not know."

Both women composed themselves and led me to a small parlor. Eveline's voice cracked. "It has been difficult, indeed. We miss him so."

Before she stepped inside the room behind us, Eveline turned to the housekeeper, who I assumed had not yet moved. "Please bring tea and send for my mother."

As a perfect hostess, Eveline led me to a sitting area. The room's décor was clean and simple. "I'm sorry we don't have a better parlor to receive you in. We arrived late this season and the better choices had all been let."

"Do not fret, Evie. You know that I have never cared much for ceremony."

"I remember." She squeezed my hand and took a seat across from me. As she and April sat beside one another, they appeared as though they could pass for twins, though seven years separated them. Other than the small lines that appeared around Eveline's eyes, she was just how I remembered her, the picture of beauty and spirit.

Growing up in Hampshire, it was an unusual circumstance that brought the properties of a marquess, an earl, and a baron into touch with one another and, while most of the peerage may have felt threatened by such an occurrence, the friendship that developed between Zachary, Eveline, and I was unparalleled.

I took a deep breath and dove in. "Married, Evie?"

She shifted uncomfortably, her gaze avoiding mine. I prayed she wouldn't compose a reply of half-truths. We were better friends than that. "Yes," she whispered. "For eight months now."

I peered toward the doorway. "Where is this man who has captivated you so? I'd love to meet him."

Her smile was an implausible counterfeit of what I knew of her, and a careful swipe of her hand betrayed her struggle to hold back tears. "He is often away." She stole a deep breath. "But he is good to us."

"What could possibly call him away from his new bride?" I didn't restrain my astonishment. If I were to marry, my wife would have to force me away, for there is nothing I would desire more than to occupy my time with her. Silently, I blanched. I had never considered marriage before now.

"The West Indies, mostly." Her hands fidgeted in her lap. "He tends to his plantations there."

I narrowed my eyes, trying to read beyond her words. "And why are you not with him?"

Her nostrils flared ever so slightly. This was a longstanding tell of simmering frustration. "He has requested we remain here."

I reeled backward. "He's asked his new bride to live without him?"

April stood up. "I'm going to see if Mrs. Donovan needs help."

Although the housekeeper was most certainly capable of retrieving the tea, bless April for giving me the chance to speak frankly with one of my oldest, dearest friends.

"Evie." I scooted toward the edge of my chair and clasped her hands. "Are you happy?"

Tears bubbled on her bottom lashes. "Happiness is different for everyone."

I nudged her hands. "Tell me what happened."

She sighed. "Father, did not make arrangements for us to remain at Ashton Hall, not even in the dower house."

"This goes against everything I know about your father. Are you certain there wasn't a mistake? Another will, perhaps?"

"Oh, there were several wills, but the solicitor said the most recent one did not accommodate us. I have no understanding as to why. I do not recall causing him to be angry with me."

"Of course not. It's all so strange, that's for certain," I consoled.

A lengthy silence passed between us before Eveline spoke up again. "I saw him."

I glanced at her, unsure whether speaking his name brought additional torment.

"Zachary," she mumbled.

"You did? He did not mention this."

"He is cross with me."

I still held her hands but shook them for her to look at me. "He has always cared for you. I'm certain he is more upset at himself than you for leaving you vulnerable and going to war."

She stood up and paced. Irritation was evidenced in every stilted movement. "He never intended to marry at all, Luke. Zach is a lifelong flirt."

"He would have married you if he had known."

She spun around and snapped, "What woman finds pity a choice reason to wed?"

I didn't argue with her. Though I knew Zachary's feelings for Eveline went deeper than pity or even friendship, he kept them hidden from her, for reasons unknown to the both of us.

"Has he taken up residence again in Kensington?"

"Yes." It was the truth. I would not tell her I just bade him goodbye though, it would do neither of them any good. She was now a married woman and, as grievous as it was, it was her reality.

The door opened and the housekeeper reentered holding a tea tray, followed by the baroness and April. I stood to greet them.

"Oh, Lord Lucas Walsh, it is so wonderful to see you." The elder matron clapped in delight.

I reached for her hands and bowed over them. Squeezing her fingers lightly, I smiled. "The pleasure is always all mine, I assure you."

She smiled coyly. "Such a charmer you are."

Once we were all seated again, she poured the tea and we settled into a friendly conversation, catching up on the last two years, pointedly avoiding the more unpleasant topics.

"I saw Genevieve last season," the baroness commented. "She is so lovely, Lucas."

Last year must've been their final season with the status of a baron's family. While I didn't doubt they enjoyed a fair amount of social entertainment being here in Town, their current status most likely limited many engagements.

"Yes," I said with a nod. "She is enchanting. They all are, in fact, and I assure you they will be quite upset with me that I paid you a social call without them. We must rectify that shortly."

"We would love to have you all for dinner, Lucas," she offered.

"It would be the grandest event of the season," I confirmed.

"And Genevieve," Eveline added, "she must be in high demand. She has established prodigious friendships since her come out."

"Yet whoever offers for her will have their hands full." I chuckled. "But yes, from what I heard, her first season was to be envied."

"I saw her once at Gunter's at the beginning of the year."

"She did not address you?" I knew this already from what Genie had told me of Justin's restrictions.

"It is of no bother. She was in the company of Lady Helena. They were being escorted by two handsome gentlemen; she was quite occupied."

"Lady Helena Webster?" I asked, though I was certain that was who she referred to.

"Yes, they both made quite a splash in their come out last year. She and Genevieve became fast friends."

My mind reeled faster than I could control my expression and my smile slipped straightaway into a frown. *If Eveline was aware of their connection, then it was not unrealistic to assume that others were… such as her father or the detestable Lord Foxton.*

"Are you well, Luke?" Eveline touched the sleeve of my coat. I hadn't realized I strayed from the conversation.

"I am, thank you," I said as I forced a grin back on my face. "Only I simply recalled a previous engagement I must attend to." I stood up as each of the women moved to their feet and curtsied.

166

"Forgive me for such an abrupt departure. Please send word when we can visit, and I will bring the girls. They will be delighted." I bowed and hustled out the door.

Once I mounted Ace, I skipped trotting altogether and galloped back to Mayfair. Panic rippled across my chest as I gripped my steed's reins harder and pushed him into as much of a run as was safely possible with the crowded streets. My mind continued to spin. How long before Lord Foxton makes the connection between Helena and Genevieve?

Unless he already had.

The twilight sky above allowed little light to penetrate the shadows, and when I rounded the corner off Arlington Street, a pair of horses were tied to the post near our mews. How odd that Max would not take the guests' horses inside to refresh them in the stable… *lest the guests made their presence unknown.*

I dismounted Ace several meters from the house and tied him to a nearby post. Inch by inch, I approached from the rear. My heart pounded recklessly in my chest as I paused behind the imposing brick wall and risked a glance. My nerves were as taut as a bowstring.

My breath caught the moment I spotted two men skulking near the servant's entrance. One, lithe and agile, shimmied himself onto the windowsill, pressing his face against the glass.

As I unlatched the garden gate, its hinges creaked like a whispered warning. My hand instinctively sought the reassuring weight of my pistol; a constant companion since my return from the peninsula. Though it brought immeasurable comfort, it also provided a stark reminder of the battles I'd survived and the lives I'd taken. I preferred to settle grievances without the use of a firearm, but as an extension of my being, its absence would feel like the loss of a limb.

"Finding anything of interest?" I spoke loud and clear as I placed myself between the men and their escape. They peered over with startled, wide eyes. Neither one appeared to be of gentleman quality, but not so low as from the slums, either.

The man on the sill leaped down, scrambling through a row of newly planted hydrangeas, and hoisted himself up and over the wall effortlessly. It was the second man that drew my attention, a man with an imposing stature. Unlike his nimble counterpart, he exuded an air of unhurried confidence, untouched by a need to flee.

A smirk appeared on his face as he rolled his head and cracked his knuckles, a prelude to an impending confrontation. While Hunter possessed the raw strength of a pugilist, one should never underestimate a man driven to any lengths to safeguard his interests.

Chapter Twenty-eight

Helena

With each step down the main staircase, I felt positively regal. The silken gown molded to my curves and nestled favorably against my skin. It felt like ages since I dressed up for anything other than dinner, and the Walsh sisters' preparations for a private soiree made me realize how much this effort replenished my confidence. The same confidence stripped from me the moment I fled my home.

The warm flames from the foyer sconces swayed to a light draft and tingled the back of my bare neck with delight. Only an hour ago, Eliza artfully twisted my dark waves into an elegant crown dotted with pearls, befitting a grand ball. Beneath my fingertips, the diamond pendant rested comfortably against my collarbone, a shimmering testament to the grandeur that was once my life. Perhaps this would be the jewel's swan song, but the moment demanded its presence.

My pristine new slippers, freshly arrived the day before my departure from home, cushioned my descent with silent grace—a fitting complement to the rare occasion that awaited me. As I took my last step onto the marble floor, a gunshot rang out from the back of the house, followed by unintelligible shouting. I froze and my entire being trembled as Davies ran past me toward the rear entrance. Mrs. Parker flew out of the dining room and Giles reached for a rifle in a closet beneath the stairs. My heart thudded so heavily, I feared it would split open my chest.

Genevieve, Sariah, and Josie rushed out of the drawing room, each with their own spectacular attire and matching frightened faces. Something was happening outside, and I suspected it involved violence.

I remained frozen in place. Everyone had moved toward the doors at the back of the townhouse, but I could not even force my body to respond. *Was Lord Foxton here? My father? Had they come to drag me away, or worse?*

In my peripheral vision, Davies and Giles stepped outside while Mrs. Parker and the three sisters remained just inside the doorway.

"Max!" I heard Lucas yell. "Take this horse to Bow Street straight away. Report that it was used in a crime. Stay there until I arrive, I will be there shortly."

The next few seconds felt like hours until Lucas finally stormed inside. The tear in his fine coat was compounded against his twisted and bloody cravat. Blood trailed effortlessly down the side of his face from a dreadful gash above his eye.

I gasped, my palm pressed weightily against my mouth.

Lucas looked at each of his sisters, then his eyes fell upon me. His gray pupils flickered as he scanned the length of my appearance, yet he remained unreadable.

So, the commotion *did* have something to do with me.

"What has happened?" Genevieve descended on her brother as he replaced what appeared to be a pistol under his jacket.

170

"Did you shoot someone, Luke?" Josie squealed, fear leaking into her voice.

"No, love," he said, forcing a gentleness back into his tone. He held out his arms for her and she slipped into his embrace. Speaking over her head as he held her, he assured them, "It was only a warning shot."

"What happened?" Sariah pressed.

"All is well now." Lucas tried to assure his sisters as they pestered him with additional questions. In between his words, he still struggled to catch his breath.

"I'll fetch the arnica and heat some water, sir," Mrs. Parker said, rushing to the kitchen.

Davies took Lucas' gloves. "My hat is somewhere outside. Will you retrieve it for me?" Then he waved Giles over and leaned in and whispered. Whatever they spoke of was of a most serious nature. Giles gripped the rifle in his hands and stepped back outside.

When Lucas' gaze flashed across the room once more in my direction, a silent understanding passed between us. The gravity of the events unfolding was sensed by the distinct mood engulfing us and merely ascertained our irrevocable connection.

Lucas turned to Genevieve, though he spoke loud enough for me to hear. "I need to speak with you and Lady Helena in the study."

Josie reached for his hand. "But you're injured, brother."

He laid his hand over hers. "It's nothing." Giving a comforting squeeze, he continued. "Josie, will you please placate us with a song at the pianoforte?"

"Now?" she cried.

"Something cheerful, please." It could have been the pleading in his tone that silenced her. When he kissed her on the forehead, he placed her hand in Sariah's, who led her away.

Genevieve came to me and, without a word, linked her arm in mine and escorted me to the study. It's possible I might not have made it on my own without her. When we stepped inside, the cold ambiance reminded me of the last time we had been here, and the reality of my plight. *What was he about to tell me now?* It could not be good news. The heightened state of the household confirmed it.

Lucas arrived and closed the door, and instead of moving to the other side of the desk, he stood before us. I struggled to draw my eyes from his injury which remained raw and inflamed.

"Brother, what has happened?" Genevieve asked again, her voice quivering.

Lucas looked directly at me. "Was your father aware of your friendship with Genevieve?"

My heart sank. "He was, but…" I wiped my forehead. "I—I believed he was so distracted of late that he would not consider her home as a means of protection."

"What about Lord Foxton?"

Genevieve spoke up. "Is this related to the commotion outside?"

"Yes."

I silently replayed every event I had attended in the last year. Genevieve and I spent a considerable amount of time together. My breath caught and I slid into the nearest chair, forcing my trembling hands to my lap. I had brought turmoil and fear to the Walsh family.

Lucas sighed. "I came upon two men outside when I arrived home." He took an extra breath before he finished. This delay confirmed his disinclination to divulge. "I have reason to believe Lord Foxton sent them."

My eyes widened just as Mrs. Parker entered with a bowl of steaming water and a small stack of folded linens, setting it on Lucas' desk then leaving without a word. Genevieve continued talking as if the housekeeper had come and gone without notice. "What occurred… exactly?"

Thank goodness my dear friend had the foresight to think and articulate, something I felt incapable of doing at the moment.

Another sigh from Lucas surfaced as he rubbed the back of his neck. "I only tell you this because you need to know the truth of it. When I arrived home, I discovered two men creeping around the house trying to get eyes on something inside." He stared at me. "I believe it was you they were searching for."

A sheen of moisture blinded me. *Drat these tears.* I removed my formal gloves and retrieved the handkerchief inside to wipe my eyes.

Lucas stepped forward and tenderly cradled my chin, imploring my eyes to meet his. "I vowed to keep you safe, and I intend to keep my promise."

I swallowed hard and looked down, forcing him to let go. "My presence here has jeopardized your household and endangered your sisters. It is best I leave."

He reached for both of my hands and, though this was a highly intimate gesture under any other circumstance, he seemed to know I needed reassurance from him... from *anyone,* honestly.

"Helena." My heart lifted. Hearing his lips speak my Christian name sounded light and natural. He continued, "No man has a right to lay a hand on a woman... especially a father. I will do all in my power to keep you from his reach. Even if it means taking you to Northampton myself."

I gasped. "I cannot ask you to put yourself in harm's way for me."

"You are not asking."

Only then did I become cognizant of our lingering touch, transcending beyond any physical sensation I had ever known. When our eyes locked, a similar recognition flickered in his gaze.

Then, as if the weight of responsibility he bore for my well-being hung heavy, he swiftly disentangled his hands, stepping backward and clasping them behind his back.

Genevieve had remained silent during the exchange. It appeared as if she too, had sensed something. I saw it in her eyes. "What do we do next, brother?" she asked.

"If only Hunter and Zach had not left this morning."

"They're gone?" Genevieve asked. "Where did they go?"

He shifted uncomfortably. "It's of no concern, Genie. Please don't fret."

"What do we do now?" she asked.

"We must carry on." Strength emerged in his voice. "Any change might alert your father or Lord Foxton to our secret."

"But what if he sends more men?" Genevieve squeaked. "You can't stay inside at all times. What if they come when you are gone?"

"I will hire additional footmen." Lucas' expression showed confidence, as if he knew exactly where to find such men.

He looked at me once more and so much was said in that one gaze. There were times I felt so strong, defiant almost, but here at this moment, I felt broken… helpless.

"Do not doubt me, Helena." He commanded my attention with the gentleness of his promise. "I refuse to let anything happen to you."

It was only then that I realized the music had faded from down the hall. Genevieve stood up. "I'll tend to Sariah and Josie," she said, her voice laced with concern.

Lucas' countenance held an air of defeat, the weight of unspoken guilt pressing upon him. My heart ached, recognizing the anguish I had inadvertently inflicted.

When Genevieve departed, she did not close the door behind her but left it cracked open. This allowed me to both maintain a semblance of propriety and remain in the room, for I had no intention of leaving Lucas in this state.

Standing, I moved over to the desk as he leaned up against it. His body stilled, though his eyes tracked my every movement. Retrieving one of the folded linens, I dipped it into the warm water then pressed it against his bloodied brow, my touch, featherlight. He neither winced nor flinched, only his breath momentarily suspended. My thoughts drifted to the unseen wound on his back, a hidden testament to his courage.

"Tell me Lady Helena," he said. "When you are not attending head wounds or reading poetry, what interests you?"

I had never been asked this so directly by a gentleman before and initially the notion caught me unaware. I already knew the answer, of course, since the thought threaded through my very being.

"I wish to make a difference," I mumbled, slightly fearful of what he might think.

For the first time since I had touched his skin, Lucas blanched ever so slightly that it made me wonder if it was from my caress or the answer I gave.

I rinsed the linen in the bowl, its water instantly tinged with a shocking shade of crimson. Wringing the cloth, I returned to him, tracing the path of dried blood from his temple to his cheek. I continued, "I don't want to be remembered for the fashionable gowns I wore or the needlepoint image I'd sewn. I want to teach a child to read, comfort a dying person, or bring a smile to someone's face from an act of kindness on my part."

With another tender brush of his skin, his eyes focused wholly on me. My breath hitched as the light gray turned a darker shade. Heat warmed my cheeks.

"You are extraordinary," he whispered.

My breathing suspended with the final stroke of the cloth. His touch cradled the hand that held it. Whether it was my imagination or the fulfillment of desire, he drew closer, barely a whispered breath away. With this new proximity, I could not deny the palpable intensity between us. His gaze fell to my lips and an unprecedented longing surged within me.

Kiss me.

"Dinner is served." Genevieve's voice rose from the doorway and shook us apart. Though his lips never reached mine, my face blushed as if they had as I quickly stepped backward. There was no doubt in my mind his sister had witnessed whatever it was that transpired between us.

"Yes," Lucas cleared his throat. "Thank you, Genie. Please inform the others to proceed without me. I must change into appropriate attire first and will meet you in the dining room."

Without another word, Lucas lifted my gloves from the chair and handed them to me. The barest of brushes between our fingers left me yearning for more. I curtsied to his nod and met Genevieve at the door, wrapping my arm through hers as we walked silently to the dining room.

Though I felt her eyes upon me, I could not speak. Words would have ruined the nearly perfect moment.

Chapter Twenty-nine

Lucas

I shook my head to clear it as I walked away from the study and up the stairs to my bedchamber.

What just happened?

I almost kissed Helena.

I *would* have kissed her had Genie not arrived at that precise moment.

Tapping my fist against my forehead, I paced. The weight of her wellbeing bore down upon me, a solemn burden I vowed never to exploit. She was a vulnerable miss and in my care. My protection could never be misconstrued as possession.

When I held her hands, the spark that stirred between us sent a jolt of awakening and forced my release. A frail defense against the relentless tug of temptation. But it was when she stood before me, a palm's length away, tenderly cleansing my wound, that my longing to draw her close swelled to insurmountable degrees.

Despite the confrontation with the trespassing miscreants merely an hour ago, I realized the greatest danger I currently faced was the woman in my house… *not of my relation.*

A knock sounded on the door. Giles, to be certain, from his code-like discernable tap.

"Come in."

He entered and placed the rifle against the corner wall. "I searched for the men, my lord, but to no avail."

My jaw tightened. "How dare these men trespass and attempt to violate the privacy of my family and home?"

"I found an empty tuppence box at the gate. From the smell, it was tobacco."

My eyebrows pinched together. "Let me see it." I examined the snuff box carefully. The crafter had etched a scantily clad woman into the lid and, though it was constructed of tin and not a finer material, it still struck me odd that a man not of the peerage would own this. Most working men preferred storing their tobacco in less suitable containers. I set it down on my desk and faced Giles once more.

"Would you help me dress for dinner, then deliver a letter to Bow Street? My sisters are frightened, and I feel that I must remain here. And bring Max back with you."

"How is Lady Helena faring?"

Helena. My mind reverted to the gentleness of her touch, interspersed with the memory of her alluring perfume, the hint of amber confirmed. "She is brave."

"She is fortunate to have a protector in you."

Yes. A protector. I swallowed an unusually large lump in my throat. That is what I am… her protector, and I cannot forget that.

Donned with a pristinely knotted cravat, ocean blue waistcoat, and dark jacket, along with the newest addition to my wardrobe—a small bandage with sticking plaster over my left brow—I joined the others halfway through the evening meal.

I arrived to an uncharacteristic silence that continued throughout the rest of the dinner. The typical gaiety of the girls had disappeared, and everyone ate the roasted duck with its honey glaze and segmented pomegranate with slow and steady bites.

As I surveyed the exquisite dinner spread, I couldn't help but marvel at its splendor. The meal was exceptional, even for a seemingly ordinary evening devoid of guests. I scrutinized the dinnerware, noting our finest china and crystal gracing the table, complemented by remarkably vibrant and aromatic floral arrangements. Surely Helena assisted the girls with this evening's décor.

The notable presentation sparked my curiosity. In fact, upon closer inspection, I realized that amidst the chaos of the evening I had failed to recognize that my sisters appeared to be adorned in attire fit for a grand occasion.

It seemed a shame to let such splendor go to waste. A truly magnificent evening might have unfolded following such a superb repast had the evening not started on a sour note.

Occasionally, I caught an eye in my direction, but it was rare. Josie sighed and groaned the most. Sariah toyed with her minted peas and watercress, while Genevieve studied her punch-filled goblet with unusual attentiveness and... Helena avoided me entirely.

Had I injured her? I am only trying to do the right thing. I could never want someone to love me out of obligation or gratitude.

After several more minutes of complete silence, I stood and bowed to the women. "Forgive me, ladies, but I will forgo the social games for this evening. Please know, your lovely gowns have not gone unnoticed, but I have some urgent letters to write."

"Does this mean our soiree is canceled?" Josie grumbled to her older sisters. Disappointment surfaced in every scrunch of her face.

"Soiree?" I had taken several steps toward the door and swiftly circled back in her direction. "What are you speaking of?"

Genevieve patted her little sister's hand. "We will do it tomorrow, it's only postponed."

"Postponed?" My heart lurched into a panic. "No, nobody is to leave the house." My voice raised a tad.

Sariah wrapped her arm around Josie's shoulder as the youngest fought her tears. Genevieve spoke up. "We weren't leaving the house, Lucas. We only wanted to celebrate at home with just us girls. Sariah suggested it, and everyone agreed we needed something to lift our spirits."

I stole a glance at Helena, who, despite her sadness, looked utterly breathtaking. Her stunning appearance had certainly not been overlooked—not from the moment I saw her at the bottom of the stairs, not from when she stood inches from my arms, and definitely not now. I marveled at her grace and poise for someone facing such heartache, though she didn't return my stare.

Genevieve watched the direction of my gaze. "And you can join us if you like, Lucas." Her lips lifted in a tentative smile.

I cleared my throat. "No, thank you, Genie, I did not accomplish all I needed to today. I suspect I will be gone most of tomorrow." *And tomorrow night, if I can help it.*

As I ascended to the family floor, I had only taken refuge in my room for under an hour when I felt a strong need to reassure my youngest sisters over today's events… much like the older women. They had witnessed a great deal recently without a suitable explanation.

"Come in." Sariah's sweet voice penetrated the door following my knock. I entered to find her still dressed from dinner. She sat at her corner desk, drawing. She had an aptitude for art and, since my return from France, I noticed she found comfort in it as well.

I stood over her shoulder and watched her sketch as a delicate flower emerged. Then I noticed one purple bloom from tonight's bouquets sitting beside the paper on her desk. Her angles were precise, down to the last detail. This astounded me. "You are a gifted artist, Sariah."

She thanked me quietly.

"Might I have a word with you before you ready for bed?"

She nodded and pushed her chair back. I reached for the only other chair in her bedchamber and sat across from her. Gathering her hands in mine, I squeezed.

She looked up at me with sad eyes. "Why have I been kept from your confidences? I am not a child in leading strings."

"I'm quite aware." I sighed heavily.

"Is Helena in danger?" She peered up at me with her soft blue eyes. "Are we all in danger?"

I exhaled again. As a sensible young woman, I should not keep secrets from her. "Helena's father made some foolish choices. Considering his mistakes, he sought to marry his daughter to a man who might have the financial means to pay his debts but will be cruel to his wife."

She gasped. "How awful."

"Yes, it is."

"That is why she is here." She threw her arms around me. "Oh, Lucas! You are such a wonderful brother. You are saving her."

I shook my head. "It won't come without consequences if we are not careful. The law will side with him, which is why we cannot breathe a word of this to anyone."

She nodded vigorously. "I understand and I will not."

"She should not be here. Even the servants could compromise her."

"Oh, they would never," Sariah confirmed. "They've been with the family for decades. They're as loyal as they come."

"I am aware of how long they've been here." I chuckled. "But we are all human and if someone were to offer the right kind of motivation, I fear Helena's discovery could impact your own reputation for the future."

"Lucas." Sariah cupped my face in both her hands. "My reputation carries little importance compared to a woman's life. You have made the right choice to keep her here and keep her safe."

Again, my sweet sister surprised me with her mature words.

"Well, I will leave you to your drawing." I kissed her again. "Don't stay up too late."

I had a surprisingly similar conversation with Josie. Although I kept the details of Helena's father a bit simpler, she was just as generous with her compassion and understanding. I should not have been so astonished. All the Walsh women were merely an extension of our mother, who placed love and kindness above all. How I would find a man worthy of any of them I did not know. It was certain to be an impossible task. That is… if I have any say in the matter.

Chapter Thirty

Helena

Lucas was not at breakfast the morning following our disastrous attempt at the soiree. Though the evening meal and presentation were exceptional, I could not dispense with my growing frustration. It paralleled a labyrinth with no exit. Each turn on this path led me to yet another dead end and another maddening test of my patience.

Though I tried not to be angry with my father, it was he who had started this ridiculous sequence of events, beginning with my introduction to Lord Foxton. If only he had shared with me his concerns like he had in the past. Dozens of times he came to me with perplexing deliberations, though most were related to propriety or decorum and none of a financial nature, I still believed we had the kind of relationship to speak openly. It was only the two of us left. And now it is only I.

"Helena, would you like to help us decorate for tonight once more?" Genevieve pulled me from my musings as she stepped into the library. I had found a Keats book to read and had slipped into the chair I most often occupied for a good read. "Mrs. Parker left the vines and the bouquets in place, but Sariah has instructed me in one of the simplest of delights, fashioning snowflakes out of paper."

"But it's spring," I said with a smile.

"Yes, but it is also our own soiree so we can decorate it however we choose and not find our choices evaluated in the gossip columns." She laughed.

I stood up and placed my ribbon in the book to hold its place. "Did Lucas mention how long it might take for the rider to reach Northampton?"

She wove her arm through mine and led me out into the corridor. "He did not say. He's had so much on his mind, and then the men from last night must've distracted him so." She pulled me close. "But I believe there is someone we can ask." She led me to the nearest bell pull. When Davies arrived, she asked him to send for Giles.

I knew Giles was Lucas' valet, and his batman overseas, but the way he carried the rifle yesterday proved he was a greater part of this household than even the sisters might know.

"Yes, Lady Genevieve, how can I be of assistance to you?" Giles asked upon his arrival.

"Did Lucas happen to say how long the—"

"—Genevieve, come quick!" Josie called. "See what Sariah has done."

Genevieve smiled as giggles floated from the parlor out into the foyer. "Giles, Helena has something to ask of you." She looked at me. "Join us when you're finished."

I had not had an opportunity to speak to this man before, but as he stood before me, his very presence brought an ease to my soul. He appeared to be maybe ten years older than Lucas, strong, capable, and intelligent. As I took in his demeanor, the sides of his mouth twitched as if he was preventing a smile. This told me he also had a sense of humor.

"I was wondering if Lord Lucas had mentioned the time it might take the rider to reach Northampton."

"He did not. He was quite occupied last night with other things on his mind, but I have ridden it myself, milady, and it does not require more than a day with possibly one stop for a fresh horse."

My lips separated. My recollection was that the trip was indeed much longer than one day, however a single rider would certainly be significantly faster than a coach. My heartbeat sped up. My aunt could be holding my missive in her hands as we speak! The thought brought gooseflesh to the surface. I could be gone in a couple of days.

"Will there be anything else, Lady Helena?"

I glanced at him and a volley of questions surfaced. All of which included Lucas and all of which his loyal servant should not disclose. "Might you tell me how Lord Lucas was feeling this morning when he left?"

The man's eyes widened, but he quickly composed himself. He might not have been expecting me to inquire of such a personal nature.

"I only ask because I have brought such undue hardship upon him and this household. I pray that he is much improved by a good night's rest." Taking a breath, I cringed. My words sounded so childish.

Giles' features softened, and he lowered his voice. "You have nothing to worry about, milady. My lord has withstood a great deal more on the continent, but without a doubt he would be pleased to hear of your inquiry."

"Oh, you needn't inform him. I only hoped he would be well, with his injuries and all…" I was rambling. "Th—the one on his brow, and I'm certain the one on his back could not have fared well with the confrontation."

185

His brows furrowed and his head titled sideways. "The one on his back?"

I slapped my hand over my mouth. *Oh, what did I do?* "I—uh, I merely assumed he had many injuries returning from war and they all must've been aggravated recently… oh, excuse me, Giles. I need to see to Genevieve." I dipped into a slight curtsy, though it wasn't necessary for a valet, it helped usher my swift departure.

I did not look back as I rushed toward the parlor, but I could not enter just yet. My cheeks flamed at the memory of the night I saw Lucas for the first time in this house and bore witness to the dreadful scar, and now I had just placed myself in a delicate position.

Would Giles inform his employer of our conversation? I hoped he would not but doubted just the same. I wiped my forehead and cheeks and vowed to bury all thoughts of Lucas Walsh for the rest of the day. It was high time I enjoyed a diverse activity with these remarkable women who had nearly become sisters of my own.

Chapter Thirty-one

Lucas

Like clockwork, I left the house early this morning, prior to breakfast, and with a determined purpose in mind.

I arrived at the Bow Street Magistrates' Court, Covent Garden, the moment they opened for business. "Constable Bailey, please." I asked for the man who Giles spoke with the day before when he brought my missive and what we believed to be the perpetrator's snuffbox.

"I'm Constable Bailey." A tall, balding man with wiry spectacles that could use a thorough cleaning shook my hand. "How might I assist you?"

I introduced myself and reminded him of the missive from the night before. He motioned for me to follow him through a cramped corridor to the back of the bustling building.

"Please have a seat, Lord Lucas."

"Thank you." The tight, dingy space offered one chair and a desk more likely to fit a child in the schoolroom than a man of his height. Stacks of papers spread unsystematically across the top and threatened to slide off the sides at the slightest touch.

The man saw my eyes scan his desk.

"As you can see, we have many cases in which to address." The comment came out snippy, then he quickly apologized. "Forgive me, sir. I do not mean to insinuate that your situation is not a priority."

"I understand."

The constable stopped and studied me. "Are you any relation to Lord Walsh, the Marquess of Granton?"

"Indeed, I am his son."

"His heir?"

"No, that is my brother, Justin."

He nodded and motioned as if he might have more to say but held his tongue.

I glanced at the sole picture on the wall of a young man in uniform. The military insignia represented an earlier war. I curiously wondered if this was a relative or a superior.

"Regarding your case," he cleared his throat. "With so little evidence…" He examined the snuffbox slowly, turning it to view every angle. Pushing some papers aside, he rifled through some others until he found what he was looking for. "Ah, yes." He mulled over the parchment for several seconds. "It seems quite coincidental that two similar items have been located at two different crime scenes."

"Two?"

"Yes, yours would be the second one. The first," he said then paused. "Well, the investigation is ongoing, so I'm unable to disclose the details, but it does make one curious."

"What makes this one unique? There are an inestimable number of snuffboxes and most of them bear vulgar designs."

"Yes, well, that would normally be the case, but only a dozen of these particular snuffboxes were made by a sole ironmonger and only one man purchased all of them."

"Who?"

The constable arched his brows. "Again, my lord, I cannot disclose that information, but we are investigating it."

Over the next several minutes, I relayed what I knew of Lady Helena's situation, her father, the bruise, and when I mentioned Lord Foxton, his attention piqued.

After several minutes of musing over my details with his overly large hand rubbing his neatly trimmed mustache, he finally spoke. "This leans heavily into that of a domestic issue, sir. Business arrangements and contracts require a barrister, not Bow Street." He pulled out a handkerchief and finally wiped his lenses clean. "Although we have a considerable number of runners who are hired for just about anything you can imagine." He sighed. "What is it precisely you are asking of me?"

I wasn't entirely sure, to be honest.

"Keeping my sisters and those under my protection safe in our house is my priority. I can hire additional men, which I fully intend to do, but unless I find out who might be behind this trespass, I fear they may attempt again. Might I have the names of some trustworthy men I could employ to fully investigate?"

"Yes." He stood up. "Got just the men." Then he opened the door and hollered down the corridor. "Talbot, Mitchell. My office." He left the door open and resumed his place behind the desk.

The two men arrived and closed the door behind them. Both men appeared strong and sound, each with broad shoulders and square jaws, much like Mullineaux and Crib squaring off at a boxing bout I witnessed a couple of years before I left for war.

"This is Lord Lucas Walsh. He has something to ask you."

I repeated all that I had shared with Bailey with these two men. Neither questioned the identity of Lord Foxton or how to find him. This told me a great deal. When I presented my pecuniary offer, I sweetened the take for the express purpose to receive swift results. Both men eagerly agreed and immediately excused themselves to set forth. Constable Bailey leaned back in his chair, seemingly pleased with what we had accomplished.

"Is there anything else I can assist you with, my lord?"

I hesitated before I stood up. I had not planned to pursue anything more regarding my father's death, but it never sat right with me.

"You mentioned the marquess earlier. Might you direct me to the constable who oversaw the investigation into my father's murder?"

Bailey took a deep inhale. "It is I."

My eyebrows furrowed. *Why had he not mentioned this?*

He noticed my expression. "My apologies. I'm not pleased with how the investigation has proceeded. We've so little to go on."

"I understand you have a witness," I urged.

"A couple, I'm certain, but only one came forth. And a man deep in his cups is hardly reliable."

"What did he say?"

The constable turned to yet another pile of papers and retrieved a form. Glancing down it, he read, "He claims the horse had an unusual gait, and a highbrow drove the buggy. Now I don't presume to believe he is lying, but not many gentlemen frequent that particular area. Furthermore, how many would deliberately steer their horse toward a man on the side of the road?"

My jaw tightened. "Not to disagree with your reasoning, but my father was a marquess and was *also* found in such a place. It is hardly logical to assume the man who trampled my father could not also be a gentleman or a man of good breeding with a vendetta."

"Did your father have enemies?"

190

"I hardly knew my father. I could not say with an ounce of assurance either way."

"Interesting." The man's frequent mumblings were growing annoying.

"Did you uncover any clues at the scene?" I hoped he would elaborate on what he knew.

"Your father's pocketbook was missing and was later found on the witness."

"So, it can reasonably be believed the incident did not stem from theft."

The constable rubbed his chin. "Have you considered it to be an accident?"

"You are the professional," I pressed. "What does the evidence suggest?"

He breathed loudly through his nose and pushed his spectacles back up onto the bridge of his sweaty nose. "The evidence suggests suspicious activity. The offender would have had to veer quite far off the path to trample your father in the manner it occurred. We also found a fine linen square on the ground covered in blood. The initials point to someone other than your father."

"What were the initials?"

"K.N."

"So, you haven't closed the case."

He shifted nervously. "Theoretically, yes. It's been three months."

Was this a conclusion I could live with? Was there still a chance my father's attacker could face justice? "I imagine most men from Southwark don't carry linen handkerchiefs."

"No, they do not."

"Is it possible the witness told the truth? That a gentleman is involved?"

Bailey stared at me with tired eyes. "Three men worked this case for two months, sir. Nothing more came of it."

We sat in silence for several seconds, though it felt much longer. "Very well." I reached out my hand to shake his. "Thank you for your time and efforts in working this crime. It's most unfortunate that justice did not prevail, but we believe he is at peace with our mother."

He nodded.

"And thank you for introducing me to the runners."

I stepped out of the office at Bow Street and shook my head. I had too much on my mind to carry the added weight of my father's death as an additional burden. The answer was clear: the crime may never be solved, and I needed to be content with that.

With hesitancy, I entered the jewelers. Helena's determination to forge her path to her aunt's estate was admirable, but I remained firm in my plan to offer her our coach the moment we learned of her aunt's acceptance. The shopkeeper approached. "How might I assist you, sir?"

The weight of Helena's jewels pressed upon my conscience as I unfolded the linen and beheld the stunning ruby earrings and brooch. My fingers grazed over their intricate design. These were not mere trinkets to be traded for coin, they were tokens of a mother's love, perhaps Helena's only tangible reminder of her. Carefully refolding the linen, I tucked the jewels back into my pocket with solemn reverence. "Pardon me." I nodded in his direction and departed.

Upon exiting the shop, I headed to my banker. I would retrieve the necessary notes for her but keep the means confidential. One day, when Helena is well established with her aunt, I will give the jewelry to Genevieve to return to its rightful owner. Though I only had a reasonable idea of the value of such jewelry, having never bought any before, I overestimated its worth for her benefit. She would only be led to believe the jeweler was generous in his purchase.

My final destination was Tattersalls on Hyde Park corner, where a fresh shipment of horseflesh awaited auction. Though I lacked a specific need, the relentless urge to both occupy myself and distance myself from home made the acquisition of a new, beautiful stepper an enticing prospect.

After settling upon a handsome chestnut thoroughbred, one I might be encouraged to race one day, I entrusted its delivery to Max at a later hour and headed to Stevens Hotel for a long-awaited repast and the satisfying comfort of ale.

The clock struck nine before I guided Ace into the mews of our townhouse, my day marked by an air of productivity that offered a modicum of reprieve from the burdens weighing upon my mind.

When I entered the house, music rose from the parlor, but it wasn't just the sounds of the pianoforte that drew my attention, but the sound of abounding laughter. It had been days since any lighthearted gaiety surfaced and the sound sailed about so free and unencumbered.

Then I recalled the women's designs to postpone their soiree from last night to tonight and suddenly I remembered my intent to miss the event, which I had now failed at, unless I crept like a common thief up to my bedchamber.

Casting aside my coat and hat, I was drawn to the parlor by a chorus of unrestrained merriment. I leaned against the door frame, observing a spectacle of vibrant delight. Sariah, seated at the pianoforte, dexterously danced her fingers across the keys eliciting a lively minuet. Genevieve and Josie whirled around the room in a graceful ballet, their laughter as infectious as the melody itself. I stifled a chuckle as they nearly collided with a box table and two Bergère chairs.

Once again, the ladies were attired as if they were attending the grandest of parties, each clad in vividly hued gowns, their hair carefully coiffed and adorned with matching jewels. My gaze wandered from one sister to the next until it settled on Helena, diligently turning the pages for Sariah. At the moment our eyes met, my innocent, albeit lingering, gaze was exposed.

193

"Lucas!" Sariah called from the piano.

The two dancers came to a solid stop and swung in my direction.

"Oh, don't let me interrupt." I waved a hand. "I am quite enjoying the display from here."

Josie put her hands on her hips. "You come here this instant," she demanded. "You will partner with me."

I laughed and entered the room. While my attire did not reach the level of formality of the ladies, I was not so far below them I could not behave like a gentleman. I caught Helena's smile only briefly before I stepped over to my youngest sister. Genevieve then retrieved Helena, and both women joined in as well, making the four of us now dancing a quadrille.

For the next set, Genevieve took over at the pianoforte and Sariah took her place at my side. When Helena insisted she play the piano next, a slight discouragement surfaced. I wondered if at any point in this makeshift ball I might have the chance to dance with someone other than a relation, but it seemed it wasn't to be as I shifted from one sister to the next.

As the night drew to a close, Sariah demanded one last dance and took her place at the instrument. Immediately, Genevieve and Josie formed a partnership, leaving Helena and I standing awkwardly beside them. The classical notes of a waltz began.

Though I had seen Helena's dress the previous night, it wasn't until she was standing here before me that I took note of how radiant she appeared. She had claimed previously that her gowns were out of fashion—the foremost reason she could not attend social events with us. If this was one of those dresses, I could not imagine anything else more beautiful.

I bowed in her direction then held my hand out for her. "Would you do me the honor?"

She glanced nervously back over to Genevieve and Josie, then over to Sariah. Genevieve seemed to know something we didn't. "It's alright, Helena," she urged. "It's only us."

I knew the waltz was only becoming more acceptable in recent years, but hoped she would find this small gathering less intimidating.

When her eyes finally met mine, she relaxed and stepped forward.

I reached around and gently placed my hand on Helena's back, she took a graceful step forward. Our hands lightly touched as we moved in a simple yet mesmerizing rhythm: forward, sideways, backward, and repeat.

Within seconds, the room faded away.

Held captive by the trace of amber in her perfume as she moved, I found myself in a blissful state of intimacy I had only experienced in brief spurts in the past week. Though our shared glances could have been uncomfortable, they were not, and neither one of us looked down or away as seconds turned to minutes.

"The dance has ended, Luke." Genevieve's voice gently interjected, bringing us back to the present. Clearing my throat, I stepped back and bowed low, smiling in Helena's direction. With a courteous nod, I excused myself from the room, feeling the lingering warmth of her presence go with me.

I did not even think to say goodnight to my sisters with my thoughts so muddled over Helena. *How had this woman so swiftly burrowed within and taken residence in my mind?*

Upstairs in my quarters, I excused Giles with the intent to undress myself. He hesitated by the door and cleared his throat for my attention. "You might prefer to be made aware of one thing, my lord."

I untied my cravat, waiting for him to speak. "Lady Helena knows of your injury."

I pressed my fingers to my brow. "Of course she does. She helped care for it."

Giles shook his head. "Not that one."

My mouth gaped open. "How?"

"I do not know, sir. She mentioned it today when she inquired of your health."

"You're certain she referred to my back?" I questioned.

"Yes, my lord."

The muscles in my jaw tensed. I turned toward the window as the click of the door closed behind me. *How?* How did she know? My sisters didn't even know. Then my mind whirled back to the night of the nightmare and the pacing on the mezzanine and my belief that I heard a gasp.

It was Helena.

I removed my waistcoat and shirtsleeves and, in my nakedness, a thousand thoughts assaulted me. She has known and kept this secret about me for over a week, yet she never treated me like less of a man. The realization that she knew of my damaged state and still showed interest confounded me.

As I readied for bed, I replayed the day's events over again. The demanding schedule had caused my muscles to ache more than any other day and inflamed my wound, but for the briefest of moments I had forgotten all when I held Helena in my arms. Sitting on the edge of my bed, I reflected on the night... our dance, the touch, and her beauty.

How would it be to have moments like that every night for the rest of my life?

Chapter Thirty-two

Helena

"Miss?"

Eliza knocked at my bedchamber door.

"Yes, come in." I only now realized that I sat at my dressing table for an inordinate amount of time staring at myself through the looking glass. Returning to my bedchamber, I could not help but feel as if my slippers walked on clouds the moment I left the parlor.

Genevieve had assured me that Lucas would not be present tonight, and I had fallen into a comfortability with that knowledge. Then... suddenly he appeared, leaning against the door frame with his arms crossed and a captivating smile spread across his face. That perfect face, marred only by the cut on his brow, reminding me of the lengths he went to protect me and it endeared me to him.

Watching him dance with his sisters so playfully felt as though not one of us had a care in the world. Then, through the subtle machinations of his sisters, the final dance proved to be my reward for such patience…even if it was a waltz. A dance I would not have engaged in with all the eyes of society upon me, but here, it was no less than the most perfect way to end the evening.

The moment he touched my back, it took all my strength to remain upright. Aside from losing myself in his eyes, my only desire was to wilt in his arms and that would never do. While there were moments over the past few days I suspected Lucas might be fond of me, there were other moments when I sensed his restraint.

"Miss?" Eliza closed the door behind her and huffed as if she'd run straight to the upper floors. "I only jus returned. Forgive me." She dipped into a simple curtsy. "I 'ad not meant to stay so late."

After Eliza had helped me dress and styled my hair for the party tonight, I gave her the evening off. Sally invited her to dine with her and, even though we no longer needed Sally to search my father's study, Eliza missed her friend. I was glad they kept up their visits. Even though *I* must remain sequestered in the house, it didn't mean my dear maid must succumb to such restrictions.

"Oh, Eliza," I said as I waved a hand upward. "Do not fret, I can certainly undress myself, I…" My thoughts strayed with the memory of my hand in Lucas'. I wasn't speaking truthfully, this particular gown would have taken me a significant amount of time to remove on my own, but I wasn't entirely focused on my attire.

She stood before me. Her eyes studied me. "Was Lord Lucas present at yer soiree?"

I blinked, then bit my lip, trying to keep my smile from stretching across my face.

"Oh, 'e was, miss!" She giggled then clapped her hands. "And from the color on yer cheeks, I'd say you stood up with 'im."

I clasped her hands. "Oh, Eliza, I feel like I've stepped out of a dream."

Eliza's smile mirrored my own for just a moment, then slowly faded.

I squeezed her hands. "What, pray tell, has you so forlorn all of a sudden?"

"Oh, nothin', miss." She looked down at her hands. I knew she wasn't being truthful. She always worried about Sally and her circumstances. She had the most generous heart. "Let me 'elp you undress." She waved for me to stand up.

"Please, Eliza, tell me what has happened."

Her mouth pinched into a bow. "I 'ave news."

I reached for her hands, aching to hear anything from my father's house. Despite his behavior, I prayed he would find himself right as rain once more.

"Sally says 'alf of the staff 'ave left yer father's employ."

"Half?" I gasped and leaned forward, patting the vacant chair beside the desk. "Come, tell me more."

She did as I asked, but I noticed the slight wringing of her hands. Eliza had never been nervous in my presence before.

"Sally said Jeremy, Mr. Mullens, Mrs. Crandall, and Felicia left. They only remained fer you after yer mother died. Between yer absence 'n the earl's temper... they 'ad no reason ta stay."

"Oh, my, this is dreadful." My palm covered my mouth. "And Sally intends to remain?"

"'er niece 'ad taken ill. She fear'd she couldn't find work ta pay fer the needed medicine."

"Oh, I'm terribly sorry to hear that." I hugged her. "Is there anything I can do to help her?"

She shook her head. "I gave 'er my last shillin'. I don't need it. We've everythin' fer now 'n I'm sure our passage'l be secured once we 'ear from yer aunt."

I frowned. It had only been one day since Lucas sent my letter. Though he tasked a messenger to take it directly there, it was possibly far too early to receive a reply. But even if she received my missive, I had no assurances she would respond or respond favorably.

"You're a saint, Eliza." I hugged her tightly. "Now help me out of this dress before I ruin it."

By midmorning the next day, I still had not seen Lucas. Not at breakfast, not passing in the halls, and not in the parlor. Once again, he must've vanished before sunrise with his many mysterious responsibilities—duties which only piqued my curiosity. Without a doubt, I had been a significant part of his added troubles, but what else occupied his time?

I had mulled this over while I attempted to read a book in the window seat of my bedchamber. Unfortunately, I had read the same sentence a dozen times and still didn't know what it said. Then my hand flew to my mouth. *What if Lucas was courting a woman?* What if I had complicated his ability to see her at social events and other places? Though I believed we shared something special and unique, Lucas would certainly catch the eye of many young ladies, especially those in the beau monde who have more to offer than I do now.

A light rap on the door brought me to my senses. Eliza entered.

"Miss, I, uh, I…" She stumbled over her words and, from her appearance, seemed as though she had not slept a wink.

"Eliza, what's wrong?" I stood up from the window seat.

She fidgeted in place. "I canna do this, miss."

"Do what?" My heart stopped, unsure if I could handle any more bad news.

"Sally told me somethin' last night 'n I—" she shook her head. "I jus can't keep it ta meself."

I reached for her hands, alarm growing in my voice. "Tell me, Eliza."

Her voice quivered. "Yer father…'e's sick as a cushion."

My ears heard her words but somehow the path to my brain did not convey the depth of her statement. I remained silent.

"'e's refusin' ta eat, miss. Won't even let the surgeon in. Sally be thinkin' 'e might pass soon."

My hand flew to my mouth. Never had I imagined my strong and indomitable father would succumb to such frailty.

My mind spun erratically. Regardless of the tumultuous events that unfolded in recent weeks, I couldn't deny that he was my father, and for the better part of my life, he had been a good and loving father.

I held my palm against my forehead and paced before the window. "What should I do?" I stopped and stared at Eliza. She had often served as a confidant and a beacon of wisdom, despite her role as my maid.

She shook her head. "You cannot go to 'im. It'll undo everythin' you've done."

I gazed out the window as a light rain gently caressed the garden. Its shimmer against the stone evoked a chill of solitude. "But he's alone," I murmured.

Eliza scoffed, devoid of sympathy. "'e made choices, miss. Ones that led 'im ta that."

She was right, but that did not bring peace to my soul. I rubbed my forehead now. There had to be a way to see him. Maybe even in a way, he wouldn't know it was me. "What if I dressed as a maid?" I muttered, yet loud enough for Eliza to hear me.

Her mouth fell open.

"If he really is as sick as you say, he won't recognize me, and I could see for myself."

"That's a wretched idea, miss."

"I don't have much of a choice. If I left him to die alone, I couldn't live with the guilt. I couldn't just ignore that he died as a result of my leaving."

"If he died, milady," Eliza stood up and patted my arm, "it'd be 'cause he brought this on 'imself. His risks 'n poor decisions ain't yer fault."

"Change clothes with me."

Her eyes widened. "N—no, miss."

"No?"

"I'm sorry. I don't mean ta disrespect, but I don't think that's safe."

"I need you to get me another dress. Lucas is most likely gone for the day and his sisters are engaged in their daily agenda with their governess. I will leave before tea and be home by dinner, and no one will be the wiser." I pulled several pins from my hair and let my curls fall to my shoulders. "I will need you to tighten my plaits." If I wore one of her hats, no one would suspect it was me if they couldn't see my dark locks.

"What if they ask why yer missin' tea?"

"Inform them I am unwell and choose to remain in my room, and that I do not wish to be disturbed."

"Miss!"

I grabbed both of Eliza's hands. "I need to see him, Eliza. I need to know what has happened. I am not so cruel of a daughter to let a man die alone. Now, please do as I ask and get the clothes for me to wear."

She nodded begrudgingly and stepped over to her connecting room.

I couldn't think fast enough. Thoughts rolled wildly around in my head. I could only pray that I wasn't too late, that my father had not succumbed to his illness overnight as I selfishly pranced around my room dreaming of a future with a certain Lord Lucas Walsh.

I slipped out of my morning dress as Eliza reappeared in my bedchamber holding one of her working dresses. My height exceeded hers a tad, but my half boots would keep my ankles covered.

"I just don't feel right 'bout this," she reiterated. "Ya bein' alone and those men out lookin' fer ya."

Standing in my shift and stays, I reached for her hands. "It is not so far and, with the rain, nobody will glance twice in my direction. I will return before dark. Now help me with my hair."

Eliza remained frozen still.

"Please?"

Chapter Thirty-three

Lucas

For the first time since I had returned home, I sat at a lone table at Brooks's. As I peered around at the empty chairs that were once occupied by Hunter, Zachary, and Jaxon, I sobered. I could surely use their advice at this very moment.

Once more, I left the house at an ungodly hour to avoid the others. While I spent a good part of the night reliving my dance with Helena, I spent the rest of the night scolding myself for allowing my sentiments to soar. Neither of us were in a position to explore those feelings, and the more I attached myself to her, the more difficult it would be to sever it. Besides, other than the undeniable charge that coursed through our touch last night while we danced, I had no belief that I was the right man for her.

Had I abused her trust and wielded my desires in ill-mannered ways?

I spent several hours this morning visiting Pete and Grant at Greenwich Hospital then, through the assistance of Nurse Watkins, I received the locations for a handful of men who had been discharged from the hospital in recent days and were seeking employment. I located three who were more than willing to take up positions in my household and, only minutes into our conversations, I knew they were the right men for the job.

Giving them my address, I sent word ahead for Giles to meet with them and go over the specifics of their duties. Two would keep watch through the night and the other one would defend during the daylight hours. Even once Helena was gone and safely in Northampton, I would keep them on, even take them to my own estate if necessary.

Helena gone.

I swallowed my brandy slowly. Even though it had only been a short time, I could not imagine what the house would be like in her absence. Despite her reasons for being with my family, she brought such a brightness with her that would surely leave a hole when she left… and I knew precisely where that hole would be.

After meeting with the men, I spent the next hour checking in with Talbot and Mitchell at Bow Street. The men informed me they were gathering a great deal of information and should have a substantial amount to share with me in the coming days.

I swirled my brandy before taking another sip then cringed as my one moment of solace was interrupted.

"Lord Lucas Walsh, I presume?" I glanced up to see a man with audacious sartorial choices standing before me. His gold cravat clashed garishly with his orange waist coat, hurling a glare too bold for my shadowy corner of self-pity.

"Indeed," I muttered, my voice barely audible.

The man raised his glass and gestured to an empty chair. "Do you mind?"

While my instincts rebelled, the mantle of gentlemanhood demanded a modicum of civility. "Please," I replied curtly. "And whom do I have the pleasure of addressing?"

The man nodded and settled into the seat. "Lord Foxton, Baron of Castleton, at your service."

Foxton. As my mind raced, I recognized him as the man I had seen with Helena on our first encounter—the uncouth fellow in the barouche. *This is the man she is being sold to?* The very man wreaking havoc in his search for her?

My body tensed. Had I realized who he was before now, I would've fabricated an excuse to escape his company. However, I swallowed my disgust and maintained a façade of composure. Taking a final sip of my half-empty glass, I schooled my features into a fragment of politeness. "I fear you have caught me at the tail end of my social hour. I must bid you good day."

"Oh, please," he insisted. "Do not let me prevent you from getting back to your *sisters.*"

The hair on the back of my neck prickled at the tone in which he spoke. "And what do you know of my sisters? I am not even acquainted with you."

He drained his glass in one swift motion and dabbed his lips with an equally offensive linen handkerchief. His response was measured, his gaze unwavering under my scrutiny.

"Your lovely sister Genevieve, for instance..." he smacked his lips loudly as if wiping away a lingering taste. "She is of marriageable age, is she not?"

My jaw clenched tightly.

A sly smirk curled one corner of his mouth. "I have it on good authority that the newest marquess is in search of a husband for her."

"You're mistaken," I snapped. "She is in mourning." A lie to be sure, for Justin had ended it; but a lie I hoped others would accept, considering our lack of social appearances.

"Oh, I assure you, I'm not. I dispatched an inquiry only yesterday. In two days' time, I ride to Longbriar to confer with the marquess on this very matter."

I looked around and, with considerable confirmation that other's attentions were elsewhere, I reached over and gripped his wrist tightly, turning it in an unnatural twist. He cringed at the pain. I had used this maneuver a couple of times in combat to bring an opponent to his knees. Lord Foxton squirmed uneasily in his seat.

"Are you threatening me?" I whispered tightly.

He took several deep breaths. "I—I am a man of business, Walsh. And a man you would be wise not to cross. Release me at once."

I twisted just a touch harder when the point of a blade poked my leg through my trousers. The man had a knife on me under the table.

"Release me now," he said through gritted teeth.

I did so and leaned back, but he kept the blade on me. Reaching for my revolver would be useless. Straightening his coat cuff, he frowned. "Now I fully intend to be betrothed to a sweet young miss by season's end." He leaned forward and narrowed his eyes. "It will be entirely up to you whether that innocent is Lady Helena Webster or Lady Genevieve Walsh."

My fists tightened, but he pressed the blade a bit closer and I felt it pierce my skin through the fabric. Several scenarios flashed through my mind at lightning speeds.

He mumbled forebodingly, "Don't even consider it."

I stared hard.

"You have two days to decide before I ride to your country estate. If Lady Helena has not returned to her father's home by then, I will assume you have come to terms with me becoming your new brother."

"Never," I hissed.

He chuckled darkly. "We shall see." He lifted his chin haughtily. "Now, you are going to let me stand up and you will remain here and finish your drink."

I seethed long after the putrid smell of that man had departed. *How did he know I was involved?* Had he sent his men to spy on the house again? Had they gained access? Did a servant reveal more than they intended?

I rubbed the spot on my trousers where his knife had pressed. The flesh wound was nothing remotely close to what I had encountered overseas, but it reminded me that he now had the upper hand, both beneath the table and above.

How could I permit a man as repulsive as him to marry our beautiful Genevieve? I couldn't. I would kill him. *Would Justin really consider such a man?* Could he possibly be so intertwined with his marquess responsibilities that he has no logical sense elsewhere?

I fumed in my seat. I refused to oblige Helena's return to her previous state, either. That man deserved to live the last of his days alone in a gutter somewhere.

As Ace led me home, I struggled with what we faced. Baron Foxton gave me two options, but I pledged to find a third, fourth, or even fifth. As many alternatives as I could conceive, but the decision needed to be made together. Genevieve, Helena, and me.

In the meantime, I would send an urgent message to Justin detailing all I knew. He may hold the title, but he needed to understand the depth of his obligation.

I had quietly celebrated our reprieve from Justin's letters, the last having arrived only days before the Drake soiree, but now I worried over his silence and hoped it had nothing to do with entertaining offers from potential husbands for Genevieve.

By the time I arrived home, the dinner hour drew near so I went to my bedchamber and penned the missive to my brother. I did not curb my frustration, hoping my colorful language emphasized his need to know the whole truth of the matter.

While Giles helped me dress for dinner, I divulged the latest news and asked him to hire a messenger to ensure that my letter would be in Justin's hands by morning. Though Giles offered to deliver it himself, I refused. Now that I was certain Foxton knew Helena had taken refuge here, I needed all the men in my employ on high alert. Despite the baron's threats to carry out his actions in two days' time, I didn't trust that he would wait that long if he had the chance to act sooner.

Descending the stairs, I feared my foul mood might make the meal as disastrous as the one two nights ago. I considered my options. If I could get word to Helena and Genevieve without the others noticing my heightened state, we could formulate a solution before dinner took place.

When I entered the parlor, only Josie and Sariah were present. I glanced at the grandfather clock; quarter past the hour. After greeting both with a loving kiss, I paced the room. The other two women would not be considered late for another fifteen minutes.

"Lucas, what is troubling you?"

I spun around to see both sisters facing me.

"Nothing," I said a little too emphatically.

Sariah frowned. "This is precisely how you behave when you are vexed."

"Vexed? Now why would I be vexed?" I smiled and winked for good measure. "I'm about to dine with the most beautiful girls in London."

Josie wrinkled her nose. "It's because Lady Helena is sick, isn't it?"

I tilted my head. This was the first I'd heard of it. "She is ill?"

Josie nodded. "Eliza came down this afternoon and said her mistress sends her regrets and that she will remain in her quarters the rest of today."

I rubbed my clean-shaven jaw. Now this presented a problem. It was imperative I speak with them tonight. Although we had no time to waste, I couldn't very well traipse into the bedchamber of an unattached woman under my roof. The memory of her in her nightclothes the first night we met came to mind and warmed my neck.

"Do you…" Josie eyed me precariously. "Do you love Helena?"

Her comment struck me. "Why would you presume that?"

She shrugged. "Because she is very beautiful."

"Well, you all are very beautiful."

"But you don't look at us the way you look at her."

Sariah smiled and nodded. "It's true."

At a loss for words, I rubbed my cheek and reverted the conversation back to the previous topic. "Is Genevieve ill as well?"

"No, she is not." My sister entered the room with a smile and spoke for herself.

I released a subtle exhale and held out my arm for Genevieve as she slid hers through. Josie and Sariah did the same with each other, and we entered the dining hall together on a much lighter note and far from where the previous conversation was headed.

After dinner, we retired to the parlor. Anxious energy still plagued me over my earlier confrontation. "Sariah will you play for me, and Josie, will you sing?"

"You know I play better than I sing," Josie retorted.

"I think you have an angelic singing voice."

She pulled a face and the two of them walked over to the pianoforte, huddling quietly in their efforts to find the best tune. I took full advantage of the moment and sat beside Genevieve on the couch. "There have been some developments," I whispered.

Her face paled.

"Turn and smile at your sisters. I have no intention of alarming them."

She did as I asked. "What developments?"

"It is something I must speak to you and Helena about as soon as possible."

"She is ill in her room."

210

"I know, and I am truly sorry. I trust she recovers well, but this cannot wait."

"You're scaring me, brother," Genie's voice cracked.

The notes to a Scottish lullaby began, and Josie's tender voice filled the room. I didn't lie about her enchanting voice, although she lacked confidence; therefore, the piano keys generally overshadowed her soft vocals.

"My intention is not to frighten, but we are now facing a grave turn of events and it is imperative that both you and Helena understand the whole of it."

She moved her hands to her lap and tried to hide their trembling. I had frightened her. Perhaps I shouldn't have mentioned it. Regardless, it was cruel for me to keep her ignorant to Baron Foxton or Justin's designs. Maybe between the two of us, we could convince him otherwise.

She whispered, "I will excuse myself after their second song and meet you in the study."

I nodded. Then tried so very hard to let the sweet sound of music envelop me in peace. I only hoped this wasn't the calm before the storm.

I entered the study where I found Genie pacing fretfully between the two box windows. She met me the moment I stepped inside. "Tell me, Lucas. What must I fear for Helena now? Each time we meet in this room, you only have unpleasant news to divulge."

Unfortunately, she spoke the truth. I pursed my lips. I had already decided to pursue this course and I wasn't going to retreat now.

"Genie, love. Sit down." I steered her towards the nearest armchair.

"No," she said as she shook free of me. "I don't want to sit! I have been beside myself worrying over this poor woman and her dreadful circumstances. Did her aunt refuse her? Has her father discovered that she is here with us?"

I shook my head and let it spill out all at once. "Lord Foxton has set his cap for you if we do not send Helena home."

"What?" Her face filled with horror and the color drained from her cheeks. "You jest, brother, please tell me you are jesting!"

"I would never tease over something like this. Foxton heard that Justin is in search of your husband and he has reached out to him and plans to travel there two days hence."

Tears exploded on her cheeks, then she wobbled as though she might swoon. "Where are your smelling salts, Genie?"

She fumbled for the bottle in her pocket and struggled to open the cap. I moved her to the closest chair and held the bottle underneath her nose. "Maybe I should not have told you after all."

Her eyebrows furrowed. "You would keep such a thing from me?"

"On the contrary. Not with good conscience. You must believe I will never let a betrothal happen between that man and anyone I am acquainted with… including Helena."

Her tears started again. "I am so blessed to have a brother such as you."

"I promise I will do all that is humanly possible, but it is Justin we must convince."

She nodded and brushed a handkerchief over her eyes. "Thank you for not sacrificing Helena for me."

"That man will have the devil to pay if he tries to force himself on either one of you."

"Does she know?"

"Helena?"

She nodded.

"No." I ran a hand through my hair. "I only learned of this at my club this afternoon."

"From whom?"

"The blackguard himself."

She squeaked then began crying again.

"I have been thinking incessantly of a way we might avoid this, but we must move quickly."

Genevieve stood up. "I will go to Helena's bedchamber and insist we speak. I am positive she would want to know of this post haste." She marched toward the door. I resisted my desire to follow her, if anything, I wanted to make sure that Helena *was* okay, and that this illness she faced was not serious. She would need to be at the peak of health to travel. The sooner I had both women in a different location, the better.

"I will wait here. If she feels so inclined to join us, we can discuss this together."

I strode to the sideboard and poured myself a generous measure of port. It burned a warm path down my throat, momentarily subduing the gnawing anxiety that clawed at my insides. I wasn't a man for excessive libations, but tonight, the solace of a drink was a welcome respite from the storm brewing within. I poured another. Minutes stretched into an agonizing eternity. Five. Ten. Fifteen. My worry for Helena mounted with each pressing moment. Might her illness be graver than we were led to believe?

The door burst open, and Genevieve stormed in, her cheeks flushed as if she sprinted the length of the house. Behind her trailed Helena's lady's maid, Eliza, her head bowed in a telltale sign of guilt. My heart pounded against my ribs, a frantic drumbeat echoing my building dread. I didn't dare voice the dark thoughts that swirled in my mind, yet my silence felt like a betrayal of my own fears.

Genevieve gestured imperiously. "Tell my brother what you told me."

Eliza's eyes widened, her entire form trembling like a leaf. "I—I shouldn't," she whispered, her voice barely audible.

"Shouldn't tell me what?" I set my glass down and stalked over to the women.

"P—pardon, m'lord."

"Pardon what?" I struggled to subdue the irritation in my tone.

Then her words spilled out with little control. "I told 'er it was a wretch'd idea, I tried ta tell'er not to go. I told 'er. I told 'er."

I reached for both her arms and steadied her. "Who? Who did you tell?"

"M—milady."

"Helena?" I questioned.

She nodded, her eyes tightly closed.

"Where did she go?" My voice rose an octave.

"Home."

The word paralleled a single lightning strike. Precise and painful. One word. One strike. I let Eliza go and ran both of my hands down my face. "What was she thinking?" I turned back to her lady's maid. "Why? Why did she go?"

"She learnt that 'er father took ill. That 'e be on 'is deathbed or somethin'. She didn't want 'im ta die knowin' she didn't say goodbye."

"Who told her he was ill?"

"I—I d—did."

"Who told you?" I tried to keep my voice from rising, but frustration engulfed me.

"Sally. The earl's maid o' all work. She told me."

"Bloody hell," I yelled and whipped around, turning my back to the women. When I faced them again, both offered varying degrees of shock. "Forgive me," I muttered, having never used such coarse language in front of a woman.

"What are we going to do, Lucas?" Genevieve came to me with pleading in her eyes.

I threw my hands up trying to quell the storm of anger that raged within me. Another irritation I struggled to keep buried since my return from the continent, though I worked tirelessly to keep it under control. "What can we do?" I snapped. "She left of her own accord. I would have helped her had she but confided in me."

Genevieve started crying again.

With a heavy heart, I pulled my sister in for a long embrace. "Please don't cry. I apologize for lashing out."

She sniffled against my chest, soaking through my shirt. "You worry because you are good, the very best of men. It's a testament to your kind and generous nature."

"I worry because I'm a fool," I mumbled, turning my gaze to Eliza. "Did she intend to return here tonight?"

"Yes."

Genevieve's sniffling intensified. "Perhaps you should go there, Lucas." Her voice choked with emotion. "Maybe you can intercept her before she arrives."

My eyes flashed back to Eliza. "When did she leave? How did she travel?" I pressed with urgency.

Eliza's voice trembled. "She left three 'ours ago 'n borrowed one of yer 'orses." Her words hung heavy in the air, casting a pall of dread over the room.

"Damn that stubborn woman!" I didn't apologize this time. Exasperation seared through my veins.

Eliza lowered her head again. "She only wanted ta see 'er father one last time—"

I cut her off. "—But it may have cost her freedom." I inhaled slowly and whispered, "It could have very well been a trap."

Horror covered both women's faces. I opened the study door and stepped into the corridor, calling for Davies. "Have Max prepare Ace. I must leave at once."

Giles met me in the foyer with my coat, hat, and gloves. "Have Colborne or Howe arrived?" I asked, referencing the two men who were to begin their shifts tonight.

"Colbourne is here." Giles pointed to a man standing nearby. I retrieved two rifles from the closet underneath the stairs and handed them both to Giles. "Guard this house."

He nodded.

I glanced back to see all three of my sisters sitting on the bottom step now. "Guard them with your lives," I added.

He nodded as I raced out of the house.

Chapter Thirty-four

Helena

The late afternoon chill from the rain cut through the light shawl Eliza had offered me. I could not risk wearing anything of mine, regardless of the warmth my pelisse would have provided.

Rubbing my arms to get feeling again, I dismounted the horse I borrowed from Genevieve's family and tied it to a stall in my own mews.

Only thirty minutes ago I had managed to watch and wait for the Walshes groom to leave before I lifted the smallest saddle onto the smallest horse, which also forced me to ride astride. Thank goodness the simple dress Eliza lent me allowed for such an act. Though readying the horse was not an easy feat, time spent riding at our family estate meant I was not unaccustomed to the task.

Now, standing at the back of the townhouse, I felt oddly distant seeing the structure again since my absence. It almost felt as if *I* was the stranger looking in—a feeling that proved altogether unsettling.

Patting the horse's mane, I praised her for her obedience, though I didn't know her name. Having been sequestered in the house, I never had the chance to visit the Walshes mews and meet the residents there.

I had taken a monumental risk leaving the Walsh home. My intent was to attract less attention dressed as a servant than a lady of standing would and, though I knew the area well enough to ride without direction, I had never once been entirely alone. Although panic threatened to rise, I had little time to allow it a foothold. I had an important undertaking and intended to see it through.

Glancing about, darkness shrouded the property. A sole firelight lit the alley just enough for me to proceed through my neglected garden that bordered the house and maneuver toward our servant's entrance.

Taking a breath, my hand rested on the handle. I hadn't had time to send word to any of the servants, so I prayed they left the door unlocked, as it typically remained for late deliveries.

I turned the lever. It moved, and I breathed a sigh of relief. Had this not worked, my entire journey would have been for naught. I quickly stepped in and closed the door behind me.

"Well bless my soul," Mrs. Morton, our cook, clapped her hands together. "My little peach is here."

Apparently, my disguise really didn't obscure my identity as much as I had hoped.

I ran to her open arms and the motherly woman embraced me tightly. "Now, Sally said you were safe." She kissed my cheek. "I've been prayin' night and day that be the case."

"Yes, I am safe and well."

She pulled me back to assess that comment for herself. When her eyes took in my attire they widened. "Why you wearin' that ole rag of a garment?" Then she looked to the doorway "And why are you 'ere?"

I looked down at my dress. It wasn't as decrepit as she suggested, but it did have a few holes. "How is he?" I whispered.

She shook her head and mumbled something most likely laced with profanity of some sort.

I patted her hands with my own. "I needed to know for myself. Is he... still alive?"

When she nodded her head vehemently, her chin wiggled. "Oh Lord, child, he is still breathin' but you stay away. He could very well have the fever and that jobbernowl be raisin' the breeze not lettin' the surgeon anywhere near 'im." She picked up her wooden spoon and shook it at me. "The man's got a death wish, I tell ya, and 'e's gonna go jus like yer mama did."

I gasped as my heart slammed against my ribs. "I must see him. I can't leave things... the way we parted."

She exhaled loudly through her nostrils. "Very well, doll." She called for Sally, who came running immediately. She slowed to near a crawl when she saw me.

Mrs. Morton waved her forward. "Take the miss to see her papa but stay with 'er."

She nodded and led the way as if I didn't know where to find my father's bedchamber. Along the way, a nippy breeze chilled me. "Why aren't the hearths lit, Sally?"

"No blunt, ma'am. The earl, he be tight-lipped 'bout the coffers and we can't git nothin' on terms no more." She held a single candle in her hand. As we took the first set of stairs, movement caught my attention as a man slid back into the dark.

"Is Jeffries here?"

"No, ma'am 'e left a few days after you did."

"Penny?"

"Nope, she's gone too."

"Lud, who is here besides you and the cook?"

"This new bloke's named Reginald. He showed up after you left. 'e's up to havey-cavey business that one, sneakin' around. I don't trust 'im, but yer father, 'e don't give a tinker's damn."

We started on the second set of stairs leading to the family rooms. "When did Papa fall ill?"

"You know 'e ain't look right fer long time, but after you left 'e didn't eat or get outta bed some days. That man... the one who called on you... Lord Foxton, 'e showed twice and rang a fine peal. I feared 'e wud take yer papa's life right then and there."

My body tensed at the mention of Lord Foxton.

"Has he been back since?"

"No, not that I know of."

Maybe he had finally given up and the matter was over. Well, maybe *that* matter, anyway. Sally pushed the door open to my father's private quarters and the smell in the room struck me hard. I peered over at her, horrified. "When was the last time he had clean sheets or a bath?"

She shrugged. "'e 'fuses to let anyone near 'im, 'e fights us."

I stood at the side of his bed and peered over at the frail man before me. His labored breaths proved he lived, but his face had aged a decade since the last time my eyes beheld him. Though I could not forget everything about our last confrontation, my heart wilted at the sight before me. He no longer appeared as the stoic figure of my memory. Broken and battered, he suffered, and life had dealt him a cruel hand between the loss of my mother, his investments, and now me. I'm certain he had little to live for.

I reached for his hand that felt icy cold between mine and leaned down and kissed it.

He stirred. Licking his dry lips, he moaned. I retrieved the glass of brandy beside his bed and lifted it to his lips.

"Th—thank you, S—" He stopped when his eyes fluttered open and gazed upon me. Confusion flickered across his pupils, then recognition dawned. "Helena," he whispered, then his body shook with sobs. All the pain and anger I harbored within melted away. Replacing the glass on the table, I reached for both his hands again and kissed them.

"Oh, Papa," I cried.

His weak hands struggled to reach me, but when one did, he gently patted my cheek. "Forgive m—me, love. F—forgive me."

I kneeled beside his bed and nestled my head into the hollow of his neck. We remained motionless and content for several moments. When I drew back, I panicked over his continued stillness, but placing my fingers over his mouth, I confirmed he only slept.

"Sally." I stood up. "Get me clean sheets and send for that man Reginald. Tell him to start a fire in here at once. We'll use anything that can burn."

Sally stared at me with wide eyes.

"Now!"

After father had been cleaned up and changed into fresh nightclothes and linens, I sat beside him and waited for him to wake again. Though Reginald obeyed and got a fire stoking, he said nothing while he did it, then disappeared again.

"Helena," Father's whisper came so softly I had to lean in. "Are you w—well?"

"Yes, Papa. I have been well cared for."

"Who?" he croaked out.

I wondered if I should say. While this was not the same man who struck me, I still felt a need to protect the Walsh family.

Father stretched out his hand and I met it. "I will n—never lay a hand on you a—again." It took everything for him to speak.

"Rest Papa." I ran a hand through his hair and he closed his eyes again, then I placed a cool cloth on his heated forehead.

"Where?" he whispered. "Where d—did you go?"

I squeezed his hand. "Don't trouble yourself. I am safe. A kind family has taken me in."

"I m—must th—thank them."

"You must rest. When you are well, I will introduce you to the Walshes."

Father's hand stiffened in mine and his face paled even more than I believed was possible. "Th—the Marquess of Gra—"

"Calm yourself Papa, you need to get strong. Yes, it is the marquess' family, but the elder Lord Walsh has passed away. His heir is in the country and his younger son only recently returned from the war against France. You remember my friend Genevieve, do you not?"

When Lucas asked if my father was the one who made the connection between me and his family, Father's current state of mind confirmed to me it was not his doing. It had to be the baron.

Sally stepped inside the room with a warm bowl of soup and a crust of bread and set it down on the table next to the bed. The powerful aroma of onion and celery rose along with the steam. "Maybe 'e'll eat fer you."

"Thank you, Sally."

I lifted the bowl up and spooned the broth, blowing on it slightly to cool it down. "Father, please take a sip."

He looked at me with sad eyes but opened his mouth to receive the soup. After several bites, I set it down and wiped his mouth with a linen napkin.

"I n—need to tell you something," he strained out.

"Nothing could be more important than your health right now."

He clasped my wrist in a way that drew my attention. Not the same way he had frightened me previously, just with a sense of urgency. I studied him. Tears were leaking out of his eyes. "It's about th—the marquess."

Something in my father's eyes reminded me of the uncertainty I had felt when I fled. Only this time, I wasn't frightened of him or feared what he might do... only what he might say.

"I was th—there."

"You were where?" I whispered, bringing the glass to his lips. "Have some brandy, Father."

He tilted his head forward and took a small sip. "There when the marquess d—died."

My heart skipped a beat. This news could bring answers. Genevieve had shared with me the mystery surrounding his death and how they grieved over the unknown. "Might you ease their pain and tell them what happened?"

He shook his head, growing more and more agitated by the second. "Listen to m—me, Helena. I—I know *how* he died."

I took a deep breath. "Father, calm down. You needn't speak of this now."

"Yes, yes, I d—do!" he yelled, albeit weakly. "If I g—go to your mother, I want my conscience to b—be clean."

A terrible dread washed over me like I imagined a wave at the sea. Crashing relentlessly against the rocks, threatening to pull them under.

We stared at each other for several minutes until I found the courage to speak. "H—how do you know how he died?" Then I closed my eyes, willing the words not to reach me.

"Because... I... k—killed him."

A sob caught in my throat as I pressed my palm against my mouth. "No," I squeaked out.

"I m—must tell you."

I could not believe my ears. I wanted to turn back time, reverse the steps I took leading him to such a confession. My ears burned as he continued to mumble, but everything grew hazy.

"We h—had drinks." He coughed several times.

I had to force my hand to reach for the glass. Though my eyes welled with tears, I studied him. *What manner of man lay before me?* My hand shook as I lifted the drink to help soothe his throat, despite the temptation to let him suffer.

He sipped noisily, then let out a rather loud exhale. "Drinks and doxies in Southwark, at Foxton's Pleasure Gar..." he stopped as if he only now realized he addressed his daughter. "The four of us." He took another deep breath. "Foxton, Walsh, Nicholson, and me."

I placed my hands over my ears. I didn't want to know.

"We were foxed. I—I should not have been driving. Walsh and Nicholson walked... I can't recall why."

In my head, I screamed for him to stop talking. *Don't tell me. Don't tell me.* Lucas' face appeared... his half smile, his words of comfort, his gentle touch... and the longer my father spoke, the more he faded away.

"It w—was an ac—cident."

"No!" I snapped. "I don't want to hear this."

"The t—trace broke and the h—horse swerved."

"Please, God, no," I whimpered, glancing upward, pleading for a different outcome.

"I tried to s—save him."

Tears now streamed down my flushed cheeks. "But it was *you* who ran him over."

"I t—tried to...save..." he sobbed.

My heart felt as if a knife plunged dead center, then if that was not enough, sliced again and again with each word out of his mouth.

"Foxton forced m—me to leave. He threatened..."

I stood up and stiffly paced. "So, to keep him from divulging your dastardly secret," I exhaled, "you offered *me* as the token of silence?" Every word surfaced with a spiteful bite.

"He d—demanded."

I glanced over at the man who lay in this bed, for he wasn't my father… just the shell of a man who used to be good, loving, and kind. How could he have fallen so far, so fast? I walked to the window; the rain had stopped with the sun's descent. I could only hope that the Walshes believed Eliza since I had now been gone several hours.

The Walshes. The fatherless Walshes.

I walked back to my father and pressed my hand against his forehead. He no longer had a fever. Could he possibly be saved if he allowed a physician to treat him?

Did he deserve to be saved?

Anger seared like venom through my veins. I wondered if his death should be the penance for his reprehensible deeds. Maybe this was God's punishment. An eye for an eye.

As difficult as it was to proceed, I knew what needed to be done. We may be family, but we were not the same… and I was not about to let someone die if I could prevent it. I walked to the bell pull and yanked.

"Miss?" Sally appeared at the doorway.

"Get Reginald. Tell him to bring a doctor here, immediately, tonight."

"Yes, ma'am."

I sat back down and stared at the man who had since fallen asleep again. Why did he have to tell me? I wished I could cut this information out of my brain. Everything I had yearned for, wanted, or desired with Lucas would never be. How could a man even consider the daughter of a father who killed his own?

My father may have believed that by declaring his role in the crime, his soul would be cleansed and he would have peace, but all he managed to do was to bring about the opposite for me. A future with no options—a point non plus.

"Ma'am?" Sally took a few steps into the bedchamber. "Somethin's amiss."

Showing little surprise since everything has been amiss for weeks, I sighed. "Please elaborate on that, Sally."

"Reginald's gone, jus dis'peared. Can't find 'im anywhere."

"Is this behavior normal?"

"No, he be around all the time, listenin', watchin' now 'e's gone."

A chill crept up my spine. Had Reginald been listening to my father's confession? The man arrived after my departure and, now that I had returned, he disappeared. Could that be a coincidence?

"Sally, I'm going to arrange for a doctor to come. Could you please come and sit with my father?"

Wrapping Eliza's shawl around my shoulders, I stepped out into the dark corridor. Aside from the fire in my father's bedchamber and the one in the kitchen, blackness shrouded the interior. I did not fear walking in the dark, I had done it dozens of times as a child, but the silence bothered me.

Each time the heel of my boot slapped against the marble, it echoed deafeningly as if I walked through a mausoleum instead of a grand townhouse in London. Inside the kitchen once more, the slight crackle of a dying fire competed against Mrs. Morton's robust snores as she slept in a corner chair. This small tender mercy brought a warmth to my heart and a recollection of happier days.

Tiptoeing to the back door, I sighed as I opened it cautiously and stepped out. The air was now clear from moisture and smelled of renewal and purification. Much how I myself yearned to feel, for once I located the surgeon and saw to my father's temporal needs, I would never have reason to return.

Chapter Thirty-five

Lucas

After Eliza had instructed me on how to reach the Webster townhouse, I didn't waste another minute and raced with all due haste through the darkness. I tried not to imagine what condition I might find Helena in. The very thought tore at my chest and caused a hollowness to settle in. How is it that in such a short time, this woman had put a spell on me… mesmerized and bewitched me?

I only slowed once I reached her street. Dismounting Ace several houses away, I walked him off the road and tied him to a neighbor's gate. When I crept toward the Webster's mews, I slipped inside only to find Nutmeg calmly munching on a thatch of hay. So, Helena borrowed my docile mare. I patted her mane, and she nickered at my touch. I had left in such a hurry I didn't have time to ascertain which of my horses was missing.

Stepping back outside, I noticed the only substantial light in the house came from a window on the third floor. For an earl's

227

townhouse in Mayfair, the ambience felt unusually dark and quiet. A typical household would employ a minimum of ten servants, yet not one noise came from within.

Just then, voices materialized in the alleyway. I stepped through the garden gate and peered around the wall. The profiles of the same two men I had seen loitering around my place were approaching. I flashed back to the windows. *Where was Helena?*

The men stopped at the opening of the stable and one lit a cigarette. They were waiting for someone. In my heart, I wanted to believe it wasn't Helena, but in my head, I knew it was. My frustration with this whole ordeal confounded me. I could not force someone to let me protect them. They must want it. I wished she had come to me first so that I could have escorted her here.

I stepped cautiously through the garden, inching along the wall, knowing full well the men stood just on the other side.

"Think she's still 'bout?"

"Perty sure. Reg says that be her 'orse."

My jaw tightened. They *were* here for Helena. I shook my head and felt for my revolver just to make sure it hadn't shifted in my ride over here. I would not hesitate to use it for more than a warning shot this time.

The light remained in the window that we all seemed to be watching. I grew nervous. I doubted I could take both men on, especially the larger, heftier one. While I got a good punch to his gut the last time, he got me over the eye. I also didn't know if either one carried a dagger or revolver. I might get the best of one, but not the other, then I would be useless to help Helena.

I lingered for a couple of tense minutes. Movement at the servant's door alerted me to someone's presence—someone who vaguely looked like Helena but dressed like the help. If it truly was Helena emerging, as I suspected, I needed those men distracted.

The hinges creaked as the door closed. I snatched up several rocks, hurling them over the wall and down the lane a good ten meters. Their clattering impact resonated sharply. The men cursed in surprise and Helena froze on the steps. Several tense seconds passed before she darted toward the mews. I flew into a position to intercept her.

As she dashed through the garden, I seized her from the path, clamping my hand gently over her mouth and gesturing for silence. The shock of my abrupt appearance left her momentarily stilled in my arms, the pressure of my palm forestalling her cry.

It only took a brief moment for her to recognize me and her eyes flashed from panic to relief.

Pressing her back gently against the side of a thick tree trunk, I faced her as close as one could get without being intimate. Scanning the angles of her face, her efforts to hide her highborn appearance were effective, but she neglected to hide her scent, that enticing fragrance of amber. I tried not to let the sweet aroma distract me from my focus… that and her proximity. I whispered very quietly, "Shhh."

The men's voices grew closer. "Reg said the chit's 'ere. Wasn't that 'er? Lawks, where'd she go?"

"Dunno." A second voice surfaced. "But she ain't gittin' far on foot." The men made little effort to camouflage their boisterous pursuit. We could hear every move they made. When they shifted right, I slid her body left. If they turned left, I slid her right—all the while getting lost in those deep green eyes.

"Boss is gunna be cross if we don't find 'er, 'n I want that tanner fer retrieven 'er."

"Shush it, Lennie. The chit musta slipped past. Go that way, I'll go this'n." The gate squeaked open and, from what we could hear of their footsteps, it put the men back in the alley.

Helena's eyes had grown in size throughout the exchange. Had she really been unaware that her return would raise eyebrows?

I removed my hand, and she blew out a soft breath; one that caught me quite easily with our closeness. My jaw tightened. I had not backed away and wasn't sure I wanted to. Then I came to my senses and remembered why we were in this plight.

"Why did you come here?" My question surfaced in a harsh whisper. We weren't in the clear yet.

A hint of defiance sparked in her eyes. I hadn't intended it, but when my palm moved from her mouth, it went to her waist and fastened there as if to keep her from fleeing.

"I needed to see my father."

"The same man that struck you a mere fortnight ago?"

She closed her eyes and, within seconds, several tears slipped out. I had not meant to hurt her. When she opened them, I foolishly got drawn to them once more and my heart lurched erratically to every blink of her eyelashes.

"I had to," she whispered. "He—he's taken ill. He may never recover."

I exhaled slowly. "Did you see him?"

She nodded.

"Did he recognize you? Was he the reason these men were here?" My tone increased in concern.

"No," she shook her head. "No, he didn't send for them." She sniffled. "He apologized. I'm off to locate a surgeon, he needs medical attention."

"You intend to return?" My eyes widened, awaiting her response, when the men's voices surfaced again.

I motioned for her to be silent once more, only this time I placed both hands on her waist and moved her to the side of the house and pressed her against the wall with my body against hers. Any other time, this would have been one of the greatest pleasures of my life, but at this moment, I only feared for her safety. If either man stepped through the gate and around the tree, it was likely we'd be discovered.

"She couldna gone far."

"Maybe she 'eaded back to the other 'ouse, bet that's where she's goin' and we can cut 'er off."

With her lips against my ear, Helena gasped. Though my heart already pounded from our touch, it sped up over the fact I had now left my sisters alone. If these men worked for Lord Foxton, which I was certain they did, he made it clear he would be pleased with either young woman as his bride. *Did the man really believe kidnapping a woman would be the most logical way to marry?* He risked his throat being slit in the dead of night… at least that's what I suspected Genie would do.

Once I believed the men had vanished, I took a step back. "Pardon me for pressing so close."

Even in the dark, her cheeks blushed. "Thank you for being here… but you should go. Hurry back to your sisters."

I tried to keep the frustration out of my voice. "You must come with me. The threat is not over and you're not safe here."

"My father needs me. He might not even live another day."

I reached for her hand. "I will send for help myself, a doctor and some men to protect him. But please, Helena…" Though we had stepped apart, she remained close with my fingers wrapped around hers. "Please let me keep you safe. Your father may no longer be a threat, but Lord Foxton most certainly is."

She bit her lip and gazed down at our hands. I couldn't read her expression.

"I can explain more of what I've learned about Foxton when we return to the house, but for now, we have to hurry."

She relented, and I led her to the post where I left Ace. Nutmeg remained in the mews and she would be safe there until I could retrieve her later. The plan formulating in my head to race home did

231

not include two horses—if Helena was on the second horse, the chance of us being separated was too high.

"You'll need to ride with me."

Helena stopped in place. "I can ride my own horse." Her eyebrows furrowed defiantly. "The story of me falling off was only to cover for the bruise." She placed her hands on her hips, drawing my attention to her attire. She had tried to camouflage herself as a servant. I held back my smile. *Impossible.*

Ignoring her cheekiness, I clutched her waist. "It's for your safety and my speed. Now, up you go." Without waiting for another argument, I lifted her up and onto Ace, then quickly launched myself up behind her.

Though I heard her breathing accelerate, she said nothing as my hands brushed past her and gripped the reins.

I clucked and whipped the rope, leading my horse into a gallop that should get us to the house before the men if they remained on foot.

"I'm sorry." Helena turned her head so that I could hear her better. This only brought her cheek closer to my lips, which tested every ounce of strength I had to not close the gap. "I'm sorry you've had to protect me in a manner similar to your sisters."

I smiled partway and grumbled my response. "I may be protecting you like my sisters, but I can assure you the reasons are far from similar."

I hadn't expected to be so bold, but the intimacy of the night gave me confidence. I may not be able to act on my desire to kiss her, but it didn't mean it wasn't there.

We arrived at our darkened and seemingly undisturbed house, but it was no different from the last time I had come upon the two cads trespassing. I trotted back to the mews and dismounted. Helena placed her hands on my shoulders and easily slid down. If we weren't in such a hurry, I would have enjoyed the closeness a tad longer.

When we stepped through the gate, Giles met us. It seemed as though he had not moved from this position since the moment I left. I nodded my appreciation and grabbed Helena's hand, leading her inside where Colborne, my newest hire, stood on high alert at the front window where the moonlight offered the only source of light within.

Locating a candlestick, I used flint and tinder to light it. With Helena's hand back in mine, I led her up the stairs, only stopping in the corridor mere steps from my sisters' rooms. The entire ride back to the house, I had been contemplating a plan. "Helena, will you gather my sisters into Genevieve's bedchamber and stay with them?"

"I should help you," she suggested, though her expression showed that she had no idea what that might entail.

"Please," I tenderly caressed her cheek, again allowing myself liberties I wasn't given permission to take, though she didn't refuse. "Please stay with them, so I know you're all safe. I will place a footman outside your door. Do not open it to anyone except me."

She nodded without any argument. It may have been the pleadings or the touch, but I sensed she understood how important it was for me to know they were together.

One by one, she gathered my sisters together. At first, they were frightened, but Helena's calm demeanor soothed them while they went to Genie's room. Once the girls were inside, I heard the door latch closed.

Immediately, I went downstairs and stepped outside to join Giles, updating him on the latest developments.

Though the night seemed relatively quiet, with every turn of the garden and scan of the mews, we made our presence known. While I wouldn't have minded luring the men in and taking them to Bow Street on our own, I refused to risk anything that could put the women in danger.

233

None of us slept during the night. Though I shifted to every sound that surfaced from within and without the house, no one breached the perimeter and, if the men had come, we didn't see them. However, I made sure that anyone who might decide to approach saw the additional footmen and the additional fire power each man carried.

Completely exhausted by first light, I went to Genevieve's room and knocked softly. It took a minute for her to answer the door. Behind her, my two other sisters and Helena huddled on the bed. They had fallen asleep despite their fears.

"Are we safe, Lucas?"

I kissed her on the forehead. "Yes, Genie. Everything is fine."

"Can you tell me what happened? Helena didn't say much."

I peeked another glance in her direction as she slept and asked, "Is she alright?"

Genevieve eyed me carefully, then stepped out into the corridor with me gently closing the door behind her. "What happened last night?"

Reflecting on the night and how close she came to being apprehended by the thugs, I exhaled slowly before I spoke. "She went to see her father. He truly is ill."

"Did you stop her in time?"

"No, but I was able to convince her to return here."

She hesitated, then finally whispered, "You care for her."

I ran a hand down my face. Fatigue settled into my shoulders and neck muscles. "I don't know anything right now, except the sooner Helena gets to her aunt's, the better."

"Is that truly how you feel?"

I groaned inwardly. *No.*

"Yes." My jaw tightened at the mistruth. "Please let her know I've directed the doctor to her father's home and sent men to watch over him." Then I departed without another word.

Chapter Thirty-six

Helena

When I awoke, Josie was draped across my legs and Sariah's hand pressed alongside my back. I had not realized we had fallen asleep and in such unpleasant positions.

Genevieve appeared at the side of the bed and proceeded to wake her sisters.

I yawned. "Was that Lucas' voice I heard?"

She peered over at me, her eyebrows pinched together. "Yes, he was checking on us."

"Is he alright?"

She tilted her head. "That is precisely the same question he asked me about you."

My cheeks flushed with a heat that went beyond the cozy warmth of the room. After the events of the previous night, and Lucas' selfless protection, there was no longer ambiguity about where my affections lay. Yet, an ominous shadow loomed—my father's chilling confession.

One sentence from my father shattered all. *I killed him.*

Unease twisted in my stomach. Still clad in Eliza's simple attire, I cast aside the coverlet, moving to the washbasin. With trembling hands, I filled the bowl with water, dipped a linen square inside and wrung out the excess.

"Why are you dressed in such a manner, Helena?" Josie's voice cut through the silence, her eyes still heavy with sleep.

I cleansed my forehead and cheeks, then turned to meet her gaze. "I went to see my father yesterday."

Josie's face pinched like she tasted something disagreeable. "Why would your attire matter?" Then she slanted her head in confusion. "I thought he caused you harm."

If only they knew how much harm he caused us all.

Genevieve interjected, "Lucas sent the doctor over to your house, Helena."

The Walsh kindness continued to deliver, despite it being more than my father deserved.

"And additional men to watch over him," she finished.

I blew a slow exhale out of my cheeks. Though my anger for my father had not subsided, I was grateful Lucas did as he promised. "Thank you, Genie."

Sariah grumbled as she stretched and sat up. "Why on earth did Lucas require us to remain in one room?" Genevieve and I exchanged looks.

"All is well, Sariah," her older sister continued, "you and Jos may return to your bedchambers, and I will have a bath prepared for each of you."

As the sisters departed, I tarried.

"Genevieve," I called for her attention. "May I ask you something?"

She nodded and gestured for us to sit on her bed.

I had never seen her frown in such a way before. "Are you angry with me?"

She reached for my hands. "No, Helena, I could never be cross with you. But I do worry so." She gnawed on her bottom lip as if she wasn't sure how to formulate her next words. Then she sighed. "I worry about you, your family, your future… all is—"

"—Tarnished," I interrupted and closed my eyes.

"Unknown," she corrected me earnestly.

"And your family is taking a significant risk associating with me." I hung my head, willing away the tears that threatened to fall.

She squeezed my hands tighter. "I have never believed one's friendship should be based on reputation…"

"But marriage should."

Her frown returned. Her silence spoke volumes and, as unpleasant as my situation appeared, I knew it was about to get worse.

She continued, "Lucas cannot only be concerned for himself. Sariah and Josie's futures also rely on him."

"And yours," I added. The one surety amidst the upper-class was an unblemished reputation. My pulse sped up and my cheeks warmed. I had erroneously allowed my heart to wander. I never intended it to drift as far as it did, but I also hadn't made an effort to prevent it.

She hugged me.

I still fought my tears. "I assure you, Genie, you have nothing to fear with me."

She swallowed visibly. "I fear you might have feelings for Lucas."

My heart tore just a little more. "I assure you, my feelings are inconsequential. Nothing could ever come of them."

She studied me, eyeing me pointedly, having seen through my thinly veiled defenses.

"Excuse me, Genevieve, I must go change." I quickly left her room, reminding myself that all will be better the sooner I leave London.

Eliza met me in my bedchamber and waited patiently for me to divulge what I knew. I didn't even want to speak of it and limited my account to a few essential details. Exhaustion spread throughout my body, not only from the uncomfortable sleeping arrangements, but from the culmination of events between yesterday and today.

While there were moments I might never forget—ones etched into my very being—they were destined to be a foregone memory, and that very thought tormented me.

With Eliza's assistance, I slipped into a pale blue morning dress and sat at my dressing table while she styled my hair into a simple chignon. An unfamiliar tenderness smarted my chest—heartbreak. The concept once confined to the pages of novels had now become a tangible reality. Then, as if the hollowness that consumed me wasn't enough, the prospect of revealing the truth to Lucas loomed like a persistent weed, interweaving its tendrils, and causing mayhem on my mind.

I sat down at the corner desk and retrieved my writing materials. After detailing the information my father relayed, including the men involved, I labeled the missive to the Magistrates' Court on Bow Street, but kept the letter anonymous. The constables could unravel the rest. Sardonically, I would be unencumbered from the truth, but realistically, would carry the millstone around my neck for the rest of my life.

"Eliza," I called for her from the connecting room. "Will you please deliver this post haste?"

"Of course, miss." Eliza then pulled a letter from her pocket. "I only jus recv'd this, miss, Davies said it 'rrived fer you last night."

She held it up, but even from the distance, I recognized the handwriting of my Aunt Patricia.

Chapter Thirty-seven

Lucas

"My lord?"

"Yes, Davies."

"There are constables here to see you."

"Constables?" My mind veered toward the Bow Street runners I had hired. Their update would be timely. After the heightened fervor through the night, the day had been relatively quiet. I had yet to see Helena or my sisters since this morning, but admittedly evaded any rooms they might occupy. I knew they would gather shortly for afternoon tea, but there was a suitable reason for my deliberate avoidance… I wasn't quite sure how to put words to my affection yet and, if I laid eyes on Helena, I might muddle everything, skip courtship all together, and propose on the spot.

"And…" Davies handed me a calling card. I glanced at the name—*Lord Foxton.*

"Deuce! What does he want?"

"He arrived with the constables."

I shook my head. "Please advise Mrs. Parker to keep the ladies out of sight. Delay showing the men into the parlor until this is achieved."

He nodded and departed.

"Giles!" I called for my valet.

When he appeared, I informed him of our unwanted guest and asked him to accompany me. Next, I tasked Colbourne with sentry duty disguised as a footman at the front door and Howe at the back. "Keep your revolvers hidden but at the ready."

After several minutes, I stepped into the parlor and was blinded by the peacock of a man. Dressed in a bright array of purples and blues, I wanted to grimace but kept my expression indifferent. Two men stood beside him, the constables I presumed.

"Lord Lucas." Baron Foxton made the motion of a superficial bow. "I apologize for the inconvenience this may cause, but I understand you have something of mine, and I have come to collect it."

My eyes narrowed. Just what *something* was he speaking of? Helena or Genevieve?

"You are mistaken, sir. There is nothing here that belongs to you."

He chuckled to himself and flicked open a small tin snuffbox that appeared quite similar to the one that we had turned over to Bow Street.

My eyes remained attached to the box. Was he the man Constable Bailey referred to who had purchased all of them? He pinched the tobacco between his fingers and inhaled in both nostrils before he pointed to the constables. "Retrieve Lady Helena Webster."

I stepped in front of the men. "This is the home of the Marquess of Granton. You have no permissions here."

One officer stepped forward with a parchment. "I have a signed marriage contract for Lady Helena Webster and Baron Oliver Foxton."

I glanced over the paper, dated a fortnight ago… the day after she left her home.

"Unfortunately, this contract is null and void."

Lord Foxton's eyes narrowed. "How so?"

Just then, Helena appeared at the doorway with Genevieve shortly behind her. *Blast them!* I gritted my teeth. I was expending every last ounce of effort to keep them from harm, and they were not helping.

Lord Foxton's eyes alighted at the sight of both women. His lips curled into the slither of a snake. "You were saying, my lord?"

"The contract is void…" I glanced toward the women, my eyes willing them to accede. "Because Helena is *my* betrothed."

"Preposterous!" the baron bellowed.

Both women's eyes widened, but thankfully they remained silent.

I watched as Lord Foxton's cheeks flamed with anger. His eyes flashed pointedly at Helena and she swiftly looked away.

He gripped the paper and pointed to the bottom. "This is her father's signature. She belongs to me!" he seethed.

Heat coursed through my veins. "She *belongs* to no man."

The baron's face quivered. "I will take what's mine."

I moved in between him and the women. Giles stood at my side. Lord Foxton scowled and reached in his pocket, possibly for his dagger again. Giles took a step closer.

I directed my next sentence to the constables. "Lady Helena's father is being attended to by a physician at this very moment. We will prove that he was not in his right mind to adhere to any contracts while in poor health."

The baron's mouth gaped open. "He was of sound mind when he signed this, I assure you."

"I will prove otherwise." I had kept a clear head thus far but grew more and more frustrated. The constables peered uneasily between us both. They didn't know who to believe.

I dared not look back at Helena. I feared her stubborn pride might say otherwise, but from what we both understood about Foxton, I hoped she recognized I was the better choice.

Lord Foxton's visage grew increasingly dark. A furious shade of plum mirrored his cravat while his sharp finger jabbed in my direction. "I warned you, Walsh. I gave you the opportunity to choose. Now you lose either way. I ride to Longbriar at once."

Helena stepped forward, and from my sidelong glance, I saw panic sweep across her face. "No! Please, leave this family in peace."

I strode toward her, gently entwining my fingers with hers, despite her subtle resistance. Her tear-filled eyes met mine as she said, "I will not sacrifice Genevieve."

"That is quite unnecessary." A booming voice surfaced boldly from the doorway.

Justin.

I held my breath. He had not informed me of a planned arrival, and now I wasn't certain what to expect. Would he offer Genevieve right here and now to this blackguard?

I noticed that Sariah and Josie were now in the foyer. All eyes turned to face our older brother. An attractive woman whom I did not recognize stood beside him.

"My lord," Foxton drawled, bowing low to him. "The timing of your arrival is most fortuitous. Might I speak to you in private?"

"That, too, is quite unnecessary," Justin turned to the side and waved in another man.

Constable Bailey's entrance rippled through the room, now filled with many wide eyes. "Well, isn't this providential?" he remarked, his gaze sweeping over the audience and landing on Lord Foxton. "Precisely the man at the center of our discussion."

Lord Foxton's brows knotted in confusion. "And what discussion would that be?"

Bailey motioned to the two runners who accompanied Foxton. "Your services are no longer required here."

Foxton pinched his cravat as if his valet tied it too tight. "They are my hired runners. What authority do you have to dismiss them?"

"They are *my* runners," Bailey countered. "They answer to me."

Foxton paled.

"I only just informed the marquess that I received a letter this morning that has put events into motion that might be of interest to you all."

Not a sound floated from the room.

"But foremost," he said, facing the baron. "I urge you to join me outside, Lord Foxton." The constable motioned to the door.

The baron jutted his chin like a petulant child in the schoolroom. "Not until my business here has concluded."

Bailey chuckled and let his hand fall to his side. "Very well." He faced the pompous man in a more astute manner. "Lord Oliver Foxton, you are being formally requested to report to the Magistrate's office on Bow Street for questioning concerning your involvement in the death of Lord Walsh, the Marquess of Granton."

A collective gasp swept over the room. Every mouth and eye widened.

"I had nothing to do with that man's death," he hissed. "But I know precisely who the guilty party is." The baron flashed a look in Helena's direction, brief enough for me to catch, before Bailey moved to usher him from the room.

"Unhand me. You have no proof."

"Well, aside from your two hired grunts that are now singing like canaries—"

Foxton scoffed, cutting him off. "—The word of a peasant carries no bearing."

"I wasn't finished," Bailey added. "Aside from them, there is the considerable stack of notes collected regarding your business dealings…" He narrowed his eyes at the baron. "*And* the incriminating statements of several gentlemen."

"Impossible," he sneered.

"Talbot, Mitchell," Bailey called. The very two men I hired appeared. "Remove him." Bailey motioned for them to escort Lord Foxton from the premises. Talbot nodded in my direction as if to say all was accomplished. I nodded my thanks in return.

"And make haste," Bailey instructed. "I'd like to leave this family to their reunion and pleasantries." The constable turned to Justin. "I apologize for disrupting your arrival, my lord. If you might grant me time later in the week, I will update you and your brother on the progress of the case."

"Certainly." Justin appeared as stunned as the rest of us.

Foxton attempted to maintain some dignity during his removal but the derision he directed toward me was not missed. I walked Constable Bailey to the door as he followed the men out. "How did you come to this conclusion?" I whispered.

He leaned in for continued privacy, "We had our suspicions, but the further leg work done by Talbot and Mitchell uncovered connections not previously seen. Then, just this morning, we received an anonymous letter denoting details that tied everything together. It highlighted two more witnesses, and both, mere hours ago, confessed to their contribution."

"An anonymous letter?" I ran a hand down my face. "Received only this morning?" Skepticism seeped through my words.

"Yes," the constable said, pushing his spectacles back up his nose. "Difficult to fathom, I agree, but with enough particulars to warrant immediate action."

Before he departed, I added, "You might also be interested to see the man's snuffbox, currently on his person."

Constable Bailey smiled. "Thank you." He extended his hand to shake mine. "Your assistance as well as your perseverance carry substantive value."

"It was a collective effort," I said.

The overwhelming nature of this conversation nearly made me forget the other surprising news. I swung around to Justin as the constable closed the door behind him.

"You are here?" I said it as both a question and a statement.

He smiled and stole a glance at the woman beside him. "Forgive me for my negligence. My mind was occupied elsewhere."

I glanced between him and the woman, who lifted her gloved hand to her mouth to hide her smile.

"Miss Edith Crowe..." My brother launched into a proper greeting. "I would like you to meet my brother, Lord Lucas Walsh, my sister, Lady Genevieve Walsh, Lady Sariah Walsh, and Lady Josephina Walsh." Josie wrinkled her nose. She despised her given name.

Justin smiled wider than he had in ages. "I would like you all to meet my betrothed, Miss Edith Crowe, niece of the newest Lord Ashton."

"Betrothed?" we cried, simultaneously.

"Lord Ashton?" I gasped, realizing this was a relation to the heir of Eveline's father's barony.

Justin and Miss Crowe exchanged knowing smiles, though I detected a hint of suppressed mirth beneath the lady's smile.

My sisters immediately rushed toward Miss Crowe, who curtsied with an air of regal grace.

I extended my hand to Justin. "Congratulations, brother. This is indeed wonderful news."

He arched an eyebrow. "It seems I should extend my felicitations to you as well. Did I not hear you announce that this charming lady is *your* betrothed?" Justin motioned toward Helena, who stood nervously off to the side.

I glanced in her direction and realized in my flustered state that I had neglected proper introductions as well.

"I—" I began, but Helena interrupted.

"Forgive me, my lord." She addressed Justin. Luc—Lord Lucas' earlier claims were merely a ruse to deter Lord Foxton. We are not, in fact, engaged."

"And who might you be?" he queried.

I had finally found my voice. "May I introduce Lady Helena Webster, daughter of the Earl of Tafney."

Justin reintroduced his fiancée and spoke only briefly to Helena before she abruptly excused herself.

I watched her go.

Justin watched me watch her go.

"Brother," Justin reached out to embrace me. "It is good to have you home and whole." His embrace proved to be another shock.

When we drew apart, he whispered, "I know we have not been close in quite some time, but if I know anything about what is afoot, which I am learning is not much at all… you must go to her."

I looked at the stranger before me and again at his betrothed. If she was the reason for my brother's sudden change of heart, I would be indebted to her for a lifetime. With that, I turned and ran out the parlor door.

I heard Helena's soft footsteps climbing the stairs. If I hurried, I could catch her before she reached her bedchamber. Taking the steps two at a time, I still did not know what I should say.

"Helena," I reached the top of the stairs as she reached her door. "Wait." My desperate plea was disguised as a command.

My approach came with measured caution while her back remained to me. Her hand rested on the lever. "Helena?"

"Please don't say anything, Lucas." Her shoulders trembled lightly.

I wanted to reach for her, to melt her concern beneath my fingertips.

When she circled around to face me, my breath caught in my throat. Her stunning eyes glistened with unshed tears. The sight twisted my heart into a knot of love coupled with fear.

"Thank you for protecting me from Lord Foxton. When you stepped forward to take his place, I—" She swallowed hard without finishing the sentence.

"I didn't do it only to save you."

She bit her bottom lip and my eyes went right to them. Taking another step forward brought me close enough that if I leaned down…

"Lucas." Helena's hand went to my chest to stop me. My heart thumped erratically beneath her touch. "We both know that my reputation will not recover from this." Her voice trembled. "I have no money, no connections. My father will likely be at Newgate soon and I will be living far from here. Your family will only suffer from my association."

I felt as if I had been punched in the gut.

Reaching for her hands, I pulled her to me, wrapping my arms around her. "I don't care what others think." I held her as if I feared once she let go, it might be for good. "I only know what I want."

Helena drew back and, while she tried to hide the pain in her expression, her eyes deceived her. Touching my cheek with the gentlest of caresses, she leaned forward. "Lucas, you are the very best of men." She softly kissed my lips, but I yearned for more. Drawing her in, one of my hands clenched her back, while the other slid up into her hair. My mouth claimed a continuation before she could reconsider.

With a subtle whimper, she detached and quickly fled inside her bedchamber.

I stared at her closed door for several minutes.

What did I do wrong?

I pounded my fist softly against my forehead. I should have answered Justin when he first asked about our betrothal. My hesitation led to her thinking I doubted my feelings. *I did not doubt my feelings for Helena.*

Turning away, I strode to my own room. I needed to release this pent-up energy. I tugged on the bell pull and Giles swiftly arrived.

"Have Max ready Ace."

"Are you well, my lord?"

I gazed at him for a considerable amount of time. How does one answer that with all that had transpired in the last hour—information regarding my father's murder, Justin home... and betrothed. And Helena...

"I need to ride, Giles," I said with frustration. "I need to leave."

"Certainly, sir."

Chapter Thirty-eight

Helena

I leaned against the door and held my breath. Lucas remained in the corridor for a significant amount of time before I finally heard the sound of his boots stomping against the marble in retreat.

I touched my lips, ashamed over my inability to prevent such a glorious, devastating experience. Much like that first night I saw Lucas in his breeches, I knew I would hold every man to that image, and now I would do the same with his kiss.

If only circumstances were different.

If only my father hadn't made such catastrophic choices.

If only I were a woman of circumstance.

If only, if only… but the reality was precisely what Genevieve said. If Lucas tied himself to me, his entire family would suffer for it. Especially now that I knew what my father had done.

Eliza met me several minutes later and, although she didn't let on, I was certain she knew what had just occurred between me and Lucas.

"Might I get ya anythin', miss?" she pleaded. "Anythin'?"

Though I kept my tears at bay, my heart felt enormously heavy. If I refused to let his name slip from my tongue, perhaps I could keep it locked within my heart.

"No thank you, Eliza. I'm going to lie down. I have a megrim. Give my apologies to the family, please."

"Yes, milady." She curtsied and left the room.

Though I laid down, I could not fall asleep. Too many thoughts spun chaotically within. I rose and reread the letter I received this morning from my aunt.

Dearest Helena,

Forgive me for the briefness of this letter, but I insisted my footman get this to you at once. I am preparing to leave myself within the hour and will be in London shortly, two days at the most. I am curious about the name Croft. Have you married? You can tell me all once I arrive. I cannot express how thrilled I was to receive word. I have prayed for this moment for years.

Aunt Patricia

If this letter arrived last night, my aunt would be here by tomorrow. The thought was accompanied with only two emotions—pleasure and pain.

Darkness descended by the time the first knock echoed at my door.

"Helena, it is, Genevieve." Her timid plea came from the other side. "Please speak to me. I fear I have caused you harm."

I didn't answer.

An hour later, Sariah and Josie stopped by. Once again, my voice remained silent to their inquiries.

As bedtime beckoned, Eliza appeared through our connecting door. With my aunt's imminent visit looming, I invited her inside my bedchamber. "Please, Eliza, see that my belongings are packed tonight." With the few possessions I had, the task shouldn't be too arduous.

"If you please, miss," she said, approaching the bed and brushing my loose hair off my cheeks. "The family is troubl'd with yer absence. I didn't say anythin' 'bout the letter, but do ya plan ta see 'em 'fore we depart?"

I exhaled slowly. "I will say goodbye to them in the morning."

She patted my arm softly. "As you wish, milady."

Chapter Thirty-nine

Lucas

I spent much of the evening last night visiting with Justin and his fiancée. I learned that he had been introduced to her while he attended to the affairs of the estate.

This explained not only why there was a decrease in his letters recently, but also a shift in his demeanor. Before I left for war, the similarities between Justin and my father had grown frighteningly comparable. He had become demanding, short-tempered, and impatient. The man who appeared before me was nothing like that.

After Edith had excused herself to retire to her bedchamber, Justin and I tarried, speaking of father's accounts, the tenants, and Longbriar. I was stunned to learn that Father had set a substantial amount aside for the repairs needed at Greenbriar, my inherited estate. And now that Justin was here in London, and with a woman who was more than capable of addressing the propriety needs of our sisters, I intended on seeing to my property as soon as I could manage it, unaware of the extent of neglect.

Despite the friendly conversation and satisfying bottle of port, I could not get my mind off Helena and that kiss. But most importantly, why was she so determined to refuse me?

"Your mind is elsewhere, brother."

"Forgive me, Justin. It has been a long day," I sighed.

"That it has." He chuckled. It had been ages since I heard my brother laugh.

"Remind me to thank Edith."

"For what?" he questioned.

"For bringing you back."

He scoffed, then smiled. "There is no doubt. I see things differently, I feel differently. I am unable to truly put to words the effect she has had on me—" then he stopped and eyed me carefully. "But perhaps you understand more than you dare to admit."

I took a deep breath. "Helena's father made some poor business decisions that were affected by the war and now faces debtors' prison. As you have most likely surmised, he tried to force an unwanted marriage upon her."

"Helena?" He did not hide his surprise at our familiarity. He rubbed his jaw. "So, Lady Helena was being courted by Lord Foxton?"

"Courted is a loose term." I took a sip of my drink and let it slide slowly down my throat. "There is much to share, but the abbreviated account is that Helena feared her father's anger over his failed speculations and fled. When Foxton learned that she sought refuge here, he demanded that I send Helena home or watch him procure Genevieve's hand." Leaning back against the chair, I shook my head. "I was prepared to fight you to keep Foxton's hands off our sister."

Justin chuckled. "You think so little of me, brother."

I arched an eyebrow but kept silent.

"The man is the opposite of all that's good and holy," he said. "After I had received his inquiry of Genevieve, I sent a missive to my

253

man of business here in Town. He uncovered a great deal. On his better days, he was a cad. The worst of days, a devil."

Stunned, I leaned forward. "I thought you were desperate to pawn Genevieve off. I wasn't sure if you were as concerned with whom she wed."

Justin rubbed his forehead. "I may have been hasty in that decision, but Lucas, I would never want to see our sisters fall into harm's way."

I seized a long breath of relief. This was the best of news.

"So, what spurred your swift arrival?" I finished off the last of my drink. "And why did you not send word?"

He chuckled. "I received your rather blunt message and realized it was time we spoke in person. Additionally, I wanted you all to meet Edith."

"She is lovely, Justin. You have my congratulations."

"Thank you."

"But how did you know Lord Foxton was here?"

"I didn't. I just happened to arrive at the same time as Constable Bailey. I assumed that he and his runners came to speak with you. Before we entered the parlor, he mentioned that he had news relating to our father."

"Do you believe they will have a sound case against Foxton?"

"From what my man of business learned, the baron is a wily sort. Most likely someone else will take the fall for him. He has enough affluence to manipulate things in his favor."

"Curiosity is grating on me," I mumbled.

"I imagine we will find out soon enough, but for tonight, what do we do about your situation?"

"What situation?"

"You and a certain Lady Helena Webster. Do I really need to spell it out for you?"

I stood up and paced in a tight circle. "There are many complications."

Justin countered, "Nothing that can't be resolved with money."

I stopped in place. "Justin, would you truly allow a member of your family to marry someone whose family has fallen into dire straits?"

Justin examined his glass intently. "Lucas, listen to me." He narrowed his eyes. "Do not let someone like her slip from your hands. You have the power and influence to make all of this right."

"What do you mean?"

"Offer for her... properly. Go to her father and ask for her hand and offer to clear his debts. You have been granted a substantial income from our father. You can also sell your commission and help Lord Webster avoid debtors' prison. The family will then retain their social status and dignity."

I looked at my brother as if he was a foreign entity. *Who was this man before me?* My voice had completely and utterly failed.

Justin smiled. "Women are powerful creatures, are they not?" It was certain he was thinking of Edith when he said this, but his statement attested to Helena as well.

"Yes." I nodded. "Yes, they are. Thank you, Justin."

"If you need anything from me, just say the word."

We parted late into the night and, with the exhausting day, I should have fallen right to sleep but couldn't. My thoughts only dwelt on Helena and where her sentiments lay. After our shared kiss, she never emerged from her bedchamber. *Am I presuming too much?*

Even if I made the proper arrangements to marry her, did she *want* to marry me, or was I just an alternative to the next scoundrel her father chose? I truly believed she cared for me, but something was holding her back, something significant prevented her from loving with her whole heart.

The next morning, I set out to see the Earl of Tafney earlier than the respectable hour for callers, but I could not wait. I needed to speak with him. I had hoped that in the two days since Helena's visit, he was strong enough for a visitor.

I had received regular updates from Dr. Sawyer through the day and night yesterday. His last correspondence confirmed that, if the staff followed his explicit instructions, the earl should make a full recovery. I also arranged for a substantial supply of provisions to be delivered to the house including firewood, coal, and food. And so that Sally was not overwhelmed, I hired two of the servants who had previously left, increasing all their staff wages. *Justin was correct.* We had the means to make this right and keep Lord Foxton, his money, and his control away.

When I arrived at the Webster townhouse, the men I had placed there to protect the earl told me nothing untoward had occurred in their presence and that Reginald, the devious butler, had not returned.

Sally met me at the door and thanked me profusely for the help before she led me to her employer's bedchamber. "Don't know what we'd done without yer 'elp, my lord. Yer heaven sent, I tell ya."

Though all of it stemmed from my feelings for Helena—her father, this house, and the staff were part of her, and I would do anything for her.

When Sally disappeared inside, she was gone for several minutes before she returned, then showed me in. When I entered, Helena's father was sitting up in his bed. Color I had not expected to see warmed his cheeks. The first report I received from Dr. Sawyer was concerning. The second and third expressed improvement. It wasn't until later last night that his prognosis came with a full recovery upon fulfilled obedience.

"Lord Lucas Walsh." He shifted against the pillows and coughed into his fist. "You must forgive me for not receiving you in the

256

appropriate manner to which gentlemen greet." His words strained to come forth.

I had not forgotten that this was the very man who struck his daughter and, while I allowed the appropriate respect to his station, I had to restrain myself from confronting him. I took a few seconds to measure my own words. "Do not apologize, sir, it is I who should seek your forgiveness for calling on such short notice in these early hours."

"Please, have a seat." He gestured to the chair beside the bed. The same one, I'm certain, Helena occupied while she was here. "I owe you my thanks." He paused to catch a breath. "... for allowing my daughter to spend time in your home."

I tried to control my expression. "You make it sound as if she simply came for a holiday, my lord, a house party, if you will."

The man looked down at his hands.

I continued. "I am glad our involvement doesn't come as a surprise, but I must say with complete honesty that, standing before you, I find it difficult to not reciprocate the harm you brought upon Hel—Lady Helena."

One of his eyebrows arched when he looked up. He studied me, then whispered, "I am profoundly ashamed."

I wasn't entirely sure what I might feel when I came face to face with the man who had struck a woman I care for, but what I saw before me was a very broken man.

"It was only after I discovered Helena missing that my eyes were opened, and I comprehended the depths of my behavior. I sought her out to apologize. You must believe she is the only thing I live for."

"She deserves better. She is..." I stopped myself. I didn't need to defend her against this man. He already knew. He had only forgotten.

"She is what?" he pressed.

I pursed my lips and tried to compress all that Helena is to a simple description. "She is the very sun that rises."

257

The earl's eyes fluttered, and he coughed again. "Will you hand me that box over there, Lord Lucas?"

"Call me Lucas, please." I stood up and retrieved a handmade wooden box. A ballerina's slim and graceful figure was intricately carved into the top.

When I handed it to the earl, he pushed it back into my hands. "This belonged to Helena's mother. Will you see that my daughter gets it?"

I hesitated. "Give it to her yourself."

"I cannot."

"Surely, she will come and see you today. Now that my men are here and Lord Foxton has been detained, she is safe."

"Lord Foxton has been detained?" A sliver of panic rose in his throat.

I nodded.

"For what, precisely?"

I glanced around the bedchamber and thought about the words I was about to say. It brought such a reprieve to say them. "For my father's murder... among other reprehensible things."

Tafney's head fell into his hands, and the forlornness of his action struck me. If he was truthful in his repentance, it should please him such a man no longer had access to his daughter.

The money.

That's right. He needed the money, and I had the power to change it all. I cleared my throat for his attention. "I have come for another matter, my lord." I waited until his eyes met mine once more. "That of Helena's hand in marriage. I'm aware you signed a contract with Lord Foxton, but we can prove that you were not in your right mind at the time and null the agreement."

The earl stared at me intently. When he finally spoke, his mumblings were difficult to hear, but I understood. "Do you love her?"

258

"Yes." *Without a doubt.*

Silence reigned for a considerable amount of time. *Would he truly refuse me?* "The offer includes a substantial amount to clear your debts." I hoped this would help him decide.

"It is not the money, Lucas." An ashen hue spread across his cheeks, and I feared I had exhausted him with a lengthy conversation. He continued, "Did Helena not tell you of what we spoke of when she was here?"

"She said you apologized."

"Nothing more?"

I shook my head. His words were cryptic. I pressed. "What else should I know, my lord?"

He coughed again, and I retrieved the glass from the nearby table and waited for him to take several sips before I replaced it. He licked his lips and spoke again. "Constable Bailey came to my residence yesterday. I am to be detained when my health returns."

My jaw tightened. *Constable Bailey?*

It did not take a brilliant mind to deduce what was being said here. I needed to hear him say the words. "Why, precisely?"

He took another deep inhale. "A heinous act…"

His delay only heightened my anxiousness. "What heinous act?"

"My involvement in your father's death."

I stood up so quickly I knocked the chair to the floor. Heat flushed my cheeks. Turning away, I stormed toward the door.

"Wait, Lucas, please."

I kept my back to him. Both of my fists pumped at my sides, releasing the anger that surged through my body.

Despite my lack of a relationship with my father, nobody deserved to be left for dead on the side of the road like a piece of rubbish.

"Please," he pleaded with a weak voice. "Please allow me to explain. Then you can do whatever you choose. But I must add, if you wish to proceed with a marriage with my daughter…"

I swung around. "A marriage with your daughter?" I choked. "A woman who kept this information from me?"

Tafney found strength in his voice. "If you know my daughter, Lucas," he paused, "and I believe you do, you know she has the purest heart. If she didn't tell you, I am certain she was the very reason the constable came to me. She would not have ignored such a confession, even if it means I will go to prison."

The letter the constable received… the anonymous letter.

My mind spun. Helena must've sent it. Why hadn't she told me? I rubbed the back of my neck. Typical Helena, trying to fix everything on her own.

"Please let me tell you the story in its entirety," the earl implored.

I reluctantly picked the chair off the floor and sat back down. My reasons were more out of curiosity than compliance.

"There were four of us that had invested in a slew of merchant ships. Foxton put up the most capital; but your father, me, and Lord Nicholson, Baron of Jessop, also contributed heavily. We had several successful runs and one night we gathered to celebrate. We met at one of Foxton's dens, The Pleasure Garden in Southwark."

I had heard of the place, a nest of iniquity to be sure.

"Why would men of proper breeding be seen in such a place?"

"It is precisely why we met there, not to be seen by fellow gentlemen. We were reveling in our success. Gambling, drinking and…"

I waved my hand for him to continue. "I don't need to know the lascivious details. Go on."

"We left quite late. Foxton could barely sit upright, so I drove his phaeton and Nicholson and your father walked on the side of the road. They had left their horses a few paces away."

I watched as Lord Webster maintained a faraway look in his eyes as he relayed the events. His voice took on a somewhat perfunctory tone as word after word surfaced.

"Within seconds, Foxton became ill-tempered over me taking the reins and we struggled for control when one trace snapped. The pull on the horse from the left side led us directly toward your father and Lord Nicholson. By the time I got the horse to stop, your father was underneath."

He risked a glance in my direction, but I remained emotionless.

"Lord Nicholson dragged him to the side of the road as I directed the horses to remain still. I jumped out to care for your father against Foxton's wishes. He garbled nonsense while Nicholson and I attempted to aid the marquess."

Once again, the earl's body was wracked by a fit of coughing. This time, it forced him to stop and take another drink. He probably hadn't spoken this much in days.

"I untied your father's cravat to help him breathe easier. Nicholson took out his handkerchief and tried to stop the blood from his head wound, but it gushed in volumes."

Nicholson's handkerchief must've been the one found at the scene with the initials K.N.

"Foxton insisted your father was dead, and we needed to leave at once. When we didn't move fast enough, he threatened. Both Nicholson and I were completely at his mercy. He had the power to ruin us both."

My jaw tightened and sweat pooled in my palms. "So, you weighed the value of money over a man's life?" My head pounded as a profound silence materialized. I wanted to know how Helena became involved. "How did you come to sell your daughter to Foxton?"

The earl blanched at my choice of words though they were true.

"It wasn't until after we received news that the French had sunk our ships—a tragedy mere days before Napoleon abdicated." He reached for a handkerchief and wiped his moist brow. "I owed Foxton a great deal of money and he came to collect."

"How much?"

"Three-thousand pounds."

I gasped. That was indeed a small fortune.

"But then he offered me an alternative. He had seen Helena at a ball the previous night and became fixated on her. He proposed an offer... if I would give him Helena's hand in marriage, he would honor our original payment arrangements and not tell the authorities I killed the marquess."

I stood up again, unable to keep still. "You knew what kind of man he was, and yet you allowed him access to your daughter?"

He held his head in shame. "I was desperate."

What little respect I might have had for the title was gone. Lord Webster may have been good and kind once, like Genevieve told me, but he was nothing of the sort now.

He continued, despite my need to distance myself. "When Helena ran away, the baron demanded payment immediately. I gave what I could, I sold anything that might fetch a price. I even put my country estate up for sale, though I knew that might take months. Still, it was not enough."

I ran a hand through my hair and took a deep breath before I asked, "Where does your relationship with your daughter stand now? Has she forgiven you?"

"If she has, she did not say, and I would not blame her. She deserves a better father."

"Yes, she does."

"She deserves someone who will love her and care for her."

"Yes, she does," I repeated.

"Someone like you," he said.

I circled back around to face him, and my eyes shot to his.

"While I am honored by your offer, Lucas, I don't want your money. I have no right to ask this of you, but if you care for Helena, if you love her, please do what I didn't do. Will you take care of her?"

The fact that he was asking this without a monetary pledge attached helped raise his character just a smidge from before.

"I am going to willingly face the consequences of my actions, but I cannot in good conscience take Helena down with me."

"Her reputation already suffers from your choices."

"Yes, but it doesn't have to suffer from yours." He looked at me pointedly. "I only ask this of you if you love her, which I believe you do. My only concern now is her care."

Had this been his only concern a month ago, we would not even be in this position.

"She has reached out to an aunt in Northampton to take her in."

"Patricia?" he gasped.

I nodded. "Yes, I believe that's her name."

"Oh," he cried again. "I have done nothing but bring sorrow to my dear girl."

I agreed but was not aware of the depth. "I respect you are willing to face whatever consequences may come." My jaw tightened. "I will see that Helena's situation does not parallel yours and that she is taken care of."

The earl buried his face in his hands and wept.

I seized a breath. "Do I have your permission to ask for her hand in marriage?"

He cleared his eyes and, while surprise had flitted across his visage initially, he took a great deal of time to answer. "Only if you have her permission first. I will not force anything upon her ever again."

I nodded and stood to bow. "I wish you good luck with your future, my lord, and may we face one another again under more favorable circumstances."

I turned to leave but before I reached the door, the earl called out. "Thank you, Lucas. Thank you."

Departing the Webster townhouse, I rode directly to my solicitor's office. After Tafney's confession, all the assistance I had planned to offer as part of a wedding contract dissolved in the bitterness of our conversation, then when the man showed some semblance of honor and refused my offer to pay his debts, it changed my mind.

I fully planned to ask for Helena's hand, and with it came an all-inclusive separation from Lord Foxton and his wicked tentacles. Between my solicitor, Justin, and I, we should be able to come up with a way to make that happen, but first I needed to know if the lady would have me.

Chapter Forty

Helena

"Your aunt is ready to depart, Helena." Genevieve stood at the door of my bedchamber as two footmen retrieved my trunk. I had not expected her so early, but with her late arrival to Town last night, she stayed at an inn with the precise purpose to call early and depart swiftly.

Upon her arrival, our greeting remained brief. I had been apprehensive about my reacquaintance with a woman who was essentially a stranger to me, yet when I gazed upon her, I felt as though I faced my mother. Not only from her similar physical attributes but her gentle mannerisms as well. This brought forth a great deal of relief.

Lucas was not present for her arrival, and I had not seen him since our encounter outside my bedchamber last night. Perhaps he recognized that what transpired between us truly was our final goodbye. But what a moment that was.

Reliving the kiss nearly every second since, I shivered at the recollection—from the simple brush of my lips to him taking me fully and kissing me soundly. Just the thought of it all over again made my heart pound twice as hard.

But how could I face him now?

How could I look into Lucas' eyes and be torn between my heart and my head? It was hard enough facing Genevieve, my dearest friend, knowing it was because of my father that her family had been plunged into such difficult circumstances. And now, she stood before me as I said goodbye to this room that had been my refuge for over a fortnight.

Tears welled up and I fought to keep them from falling as she rushed over to me and embraced me with the goodness that she was. My body trembled in her arms.

"Oh, Helena, you are not going to be away from us for long, your aunt has extended an invitation for our family to visit. As early as a sennight, if we so choose."

I was grateful she presumed my grief was over my departure, which was partly true. But I had grown so close to Sariah and Josie as well, and regardless of my intent not to fall in love with their brother, somehow, I still did.

Eliza stepped through the door, her face pink with exhaustion. I had certainly kept her busy the past two days, and I appreciated her fervent wish to help. The first errand was to deliver the letter to Bow Street yesterday. Then just this morning, I sent a letter to my father's solicitor expressing my desire for him to use my dowry to settle any debts my father incurred to Lord Foxton. I did not know the extent of monies owed, but my dowry was significant at five-thousand pounds.

Now that my dowry was bound, I would no longer have the money to entice a future gentleman's courtship, but I was hardly discouraged. If a man could not consent to marry me for me alone, he wasn't worth having. A life of spinsterhood would not be altogether disappointing if I could continue to pursue my dream of doing good, perhaps teaching, or becoming a nurse to care for all the wounded men still returning from war. I did not need to be married to have worth.

Of course, when the very thought of marriage entered my mind, the only man that accompanied that thought was Lucas. He made me feel safe and loved. But he had seen the worst of us. He had been privy to my father's tyrannical and violent behavior, our pressing financial obligations, and in a not-so-distant future, he would soon learn of the far greater injury—that of my father's involvement in his own father's death. No man of good sense would entangle himself in such a snare, and I didn't blame him.

I could only imagine what gossip had circulated Town by last evening's social events. Foxton detained, my father destined to be once he regained his health, and a ruined daughter left behind to fend for herself. Thank goodness for my aunt. If not for her swift arrival, I would be seeking employment with the other maids from the earl's household, despite the Walshes continued insistence to help. The deeper, darker secret that was about to see the light of day prevented me from being a beneficiary of their generosity any longer.

Picturing Lucas' image, I wished we could go back to the night I tended to his wound. That moment of connection was one of many I would cherish; along with the memory of his arms embracing me so protectively… so intimately.

Genevieve released her hold on me and threaded her arm through mine, guiding me toward the stairs. My aunt had expressed her anxiousness to return to her estate despite the marquess' invitation to remain as guests. Aunt Patricia confessed that she left her home in such a hurry that she abandoned her mother-in-law much longer than she intended, despite her servants' generous care.

"Helena!" A girl's voice sounded from the bottom of the stairs and within seconds, Josie bounded between Genie and I, throwing her arms around me. "Oh, I wish you didn't have to leave." When she released, she handed me a lily from the garden.

"This is lovely, Josie, thank you. I will miss you." I then turned to Sariah, who had walked the final steps to join us with measured grace, unlike that of her sister. "And you too, Sariah."

"You must promise to write," Josie insisted.

"And visit often," Sariah added.

"I will." I hesitated. I would have followed up such a statement with *I promise,* but that was a promise I could not keep. One day when Lucas found his future wife, I could not witness his abounding love showered upon another. It was expected to happen, but I would not wish to see it.

Each sister wrapped an arm through mine, leading me out the door as my aunt stood beside her refined Berline carriage.

I glanced around. The marquess, Miss Crowe his betrothed, Genevieve, Sariah, and Josie surrounded me… but no Lucas. My head darted in the direction of Giles as he stood behind the marquess. He stared back at me, but nothing was said.

My heart was torn between wishing he was here to bid me goodbye and being grateful that his presence did not add another layer of complication and sadness to the moment. *Where was he?* Did he already know of my father and refuse to bid me goodbye? A burning sensation surfaced behind my eyes. I knew this was bound to happen, but I was sadly unprepared. I dipped into a curtsy for the marquess and his bride-to-be, then walked toward the carriage with false strength. Regardless of what lay ahead, I knew I must endure.

When I reached the door, it was Giles who had extended his hand out to assist me inside. Giles leaned in as he guided me forward. "He had business to attend to early this morning, my lady. I can assure you, he did not know of your imminent departure."

His eyes met mine with a silent plea, as if he were asking me to wait. I glanced at my aunt who was already settled in with her small spaniel, Lucy, on her lap. It would be terribly rude of me to ask this of her. And even if I did, what would I say? Even if I waited, I knew that once Lucas discovered the full truth of it all, regardless of where my heart lay, it would change everything.

I squeezed his hand. "Thank you, Giles. And please thank him for all that he has done for me. He is…" I lowered my voice but could not complete the sentence, for it could have ended with a hundred attributes.

Giles nodded. "Yes, milady, he is."

I settled onto the forward-facing bench opposite my aunt and Giles dutifully closed the door.

I glanced down at my hands, unable to force myself to look upon the forlorn faces of the Walsh sisters.

"Are you well, love?" my aunt asked sweetly as she studied me.

I nodded, fearing if I opened my mouth, only sobs would escape.

"You will miss this place." She said more as a statement. *She likely understood more than she revealed.*

Aunt Patricia then tapped her cane on the ceiling and the coach lurched forward shortly after.

Before we pulled entirely away, I turned and waved, biting my bottom lip to keep from crying. I could only wish, one day, our paths might cross again.

Chapter Forty-one

Lucas

When I arrived back at the townhouse, Max met me in the mews. "Jus 'verted the fuss, sir."

"What fuss is that?" I hopped off Ace's mount.

"The lady's aunt, blew through 'ere with her fancy coach 'n footmen 'n left aft a cuppa."

"What?" My mind whirled. *Helena's aunt was here?* "Lady Helena, is she still here?"

"No, sir. Gone with 'er."

I rushed to the rear entrance and nearly bowled Davies over. "Did we have guests this morning?"

"Just one, sir. Lady Helena's aunt."

"And they're already gone?" A rise in my tone betrayed my eagerness. "Why didn't the marquess ask her to stay for the night, at the very least?"

"He did." My brother's voice surfaced from behind Davies. "Where have you been?" he asked with a concern to his words.

"Doing precisely what you recommended."

"You asked for her hand?"

"Yes."

He paused, narrowing his eyes. "And?"

By this time my sisters had all converged into the foyer.

"It's muddled."

"It's not, Luke!" Sariah stood with her hands on her hips. "You love her, she loves you. Now, go after her!"

"Yes!" Josie clapped her hands and sighed. "A chase would be so romantic."

I rolled my eyes but peered over to Justin once more.

"Well, did he acquiesce or not?" he demanded an answer.

I felt my heart rate increase. I could not offer for Helena without Justin's full awareness of the circumstances. Our family would already be facing judgement from the hysteria of the trial, including Lord Webster's involvement. Marrying the daughter of the man facing prosecution for such a crime could prove harmful to all. While my foremost thought was making Helena my wife, I wasn't sure Justin would willingly weather the storm.

"Justin, I must speak with you privately."

"No," Sariah demanded with a stomp of her foot. "We have had enough secrecy to last several seasons." She folded her arms over her chest. "Tell us all, Luke!"

She was right, but this was something that Justin needed to hear and process first.

"I need to speak with Justin first, and then I promise." I looked at all my sisters. "I promise to tell the whole of it shortly thereafter."

Justin was already walking toward his study when I quickly followed suit. Once inside, instead of sitting behind the desk like I fully expected him to do, he sat in one of the wingback chairs and gestured for me to sit in the other. I blanched slightly at this new and improved Justin and, once again, silently sent my thanks to Edith.

I echoed my conversation with Tafney nearly verbatim, proffering time for Justin to fully grasp the gravity of the situation. With all due credit, he remained fully composed. He rose from his seat, approached the sideboard, and poured two glasses of port, offering one to me. Silence reigned for several minutes, broken only by the soft clink of glass against his teeth as he took a sip.

"Thank you for your discretion in front of our sisters."

"They deserve the truth, Justin." I held the glass but did not drink. "And as I have been frequently reminded as of late, they are not children in the nursery. They possess strength and intellect, and much like they abided by our father's wishes, they will follow your direction and wisdom. Their faith in you is steadfast."

He looked at me. "But they love *you*, Lucas."

"They love you, too, and even more so after making Edith a part of their lives. They have attached themselves to her rather quickly."

He smiled over his glass. "There is much to attach to." Clearly the man was besotted, and a small pang of jealousy surfaced. I wanted that same freedom to love Helena. How far would I go to do so?

Justin watched me warily. "You love her?"

"More than you can imagine…"

He arched an eyebrow.

I chuckled. "Well, maybe you understand more than I've given you credit for, but yes, Justin. She is everything."

He blew a heavy breath out of his cheeks and through his lips. "This could potentially affect your sisters."

"Not if you, the Marquess of Granton, showed your undying support for us. Your influence would greatly sway the gossipmongers."

"Where will you live?"

"Greenbriar."

He nodded.

"Then what are you waiting for?" He pointed to the door. "She might be halfway to Northampton by now." Logically, she couldn't be, but I smiled at his jest, something I hadn't seen since we were children. I reached out to grasp his hand then thought better of it and embraced him.

"Thank you, Justin."

As I went rushing back to the foyer, my sisters had not moved from their positions and leaped at my return.

"Tell us now, Luke," Sariah reiterated.

I looked at Davies. "Tell Max to ready Ace. I'm leaving." Giles stepped up to me with my hat and coat. "She will be pleased to see you, sir."

I patted his shoulder. "Let's hope so."

"Lucas, you promised!" Josie yelled. I glanced at Justin as he joined us.

"Go," Justin waved. "I will speak with them."

"Where are you going?" Genevieve asked.

I smiled wide.

Genevieve squeezed her hands together. "Oh!" She ran to me and tugged on my sleeve for my full attention. "Please make sure she knows I adore her and love her as a sister." Genevive had tears in her eyes. "And that I was so very wrong."

"Wrong about what?"

"She will know. Now, hurry, go quickly. They might already be out of London!"

I rushed to the mews and helped Max finish getting Ace ready to leave once more.

I did not know the direction they traveled, only the roads that led northwest. I hoped I would not pass them inadvertently and miss the coach altogether, though it didn't matter, I would ride all the way to Northampton if only to see her.

Once on the road out of the city, Ace was able to pick up speed and, while I didn't get a description of their private carriage before I left, there was only one ahead of me in which the timing matched perfectly.

Chapter Forty-two

Helena

In the short time we were together, I quickly came to learn that Aunt Patricia was the sweetest woman alive outside of my mother and Genevieve. She spoke of our years apart and how difficult it was for her to stay away at my father's request. He thought he was doing me a favor and shielding me from such painful memories, but all the separation did, in the end, was generate more pain... for us both.

Since I had been a child when I was last in her presence, I could not recall the reasons for her widowhood, but now as an adult, I hung onto every word she uttered. I wanted to know everything about her life and, when she spoke, I noticed that the few freckles on her nose, the wrinkle on her bridge, and the dimple by her mouth were shared by the three of us... her, my mother, and me. This thrilled me to no end.

She spoke of her estate and how the townspeople embraced her after Mr. Carver's death twelve years ago. And despite her husband's lack of a title, he was a man of means and left everything to her. Sadly, they had no children. Her only other family was an elderly mother-in-law whom she cared for, and an unmarried sister-in-law in Bath.

Patting my knee, she smiled. "There is a vicar's son who I believe will be quite taken with you, my dear. Once he discovers you are as beautiful on the inside as you are on the outside, he will be smitten."

I smiled with politeness and gazed out the window. Though Lucas' absence at our departure was necessary for us both, I struggled to be content with it. Had we met under different circumstances, a different time, he might have courted me properly.

My fingers danced around my reticule string, each twist a testament to my lingering despair. A phantom happiness that would ever elude me, as long as my mind centered on Lucas, yet I knew he deserved better. Regret gnawed at me for not confessing my father's transgressions before our parting. When the truth emerges, my integrity will surely crumble under his misgivings.

Perhaps this morning's absence was no mere happenstance, but a deliberate move to distance himself from the inevitable.

"Why the tears, my dear?"

My aunt's gentle inquiry startled me from my wool-gathering. I was unaware I'd been crying. "I simply miss my friends." I quickly brushed the moisture aside and replied with a forced smile. "They've been pillars of strength these past weeks."

She smiled ruefully. "And might I add there are tender feelings for a certain gentleman amongst those friends?"

I tilted my head curiously. "How did you know?" My tears came faster.

She glanced out the window beside her rear-facing seat and said with a smile, "Women of my age know things. Perhaps this mysterious man will recognize his sentiments in your absence and act upon them."

One could only hope, but doubt weighed heavily. I shook my head. "Alas, my name is attached to scandal. He won't risk the reputation of his sisters for me." I chewed on my bottom lip. "No man would do that."

Aunt Patricia leaned toward the window again and pulled out her quizzing glass, attempting to view something of interest. When she glanced back at me, her eyes softened as she smiled. "Well, it seems he is just not *any* man."

My brow furrowed in bewilderment as my aunt's gaze darted once more out the carriage window. I leaned forward, craning my neck to follow her line of sight. A horse and rider were rapidly approaching, the rider's posture exuding a familiar strength. Then my eyes fell upon his face.

Lucas.

My heart leaped within my chest.

Facing my aunt, she reached for my hands. "I don't presume to know why he is chasing the carriage, I can only use my many years of wisdom to speculate, but if you care for him as much as he evidently does for you…" She smiled broadly. "Scandal be damned." Then she tapped the ceiling of the coach to bring it to a stop.

I would have liked to believe her words but there was one last piece of truth Lucas was ignorant of and it was the very shard that would do the most damage. I wiped the last of my tears off my face and took a deep breath. I could not let my heart run wild. He could very well have forgotten to relay something of importance or maybe the return of an overlooked item left behind. I refused to give my mind permission to wander or linger on hope. It was too perilous.

Once the carriage stopped, I placed my hand on the door and gave my aunt one last loving look, opened it, and stepped out with the help of her footman.

Lucas slowed his mount and jumped off, striding forward with all the confidence a man of his charismatic presentation demanded. His smile broadened the closer he came. Oh, how I wished that smile would never disappear.

Reaching for my hand he led me away from the carriage and to a small grove of trees nearby.

He took both of my hands in his and faced me directly. I wanted to cherish the delicacy of this moment, this one last image of him and his handsome silhouette to be engraved in a special place in my heart.

"Lucas, I—"

"—you forgot these, Helena," he interrupted, releasing one hand and retrieving a folded square of linen from his pocket. The sunlight filtering through the trees cast a shimmering glow upon my mother's rubies.

A gasp escaped my lips as I instinctively covered my mouth. Genevieve had given me the pounds, how is it that the jewels were in his possession? My heart pounded in my chest. Had he never sold them? Or had he, in some unforeseen turn of events, repurchased them? A surge of hope bloomed within me, only to be swiftly extinguished by doubt. Was returning my jewels the sole reason for his sudden intervention? My lips quivered as I fought to maintain composure.

"Forgive me, Helena."

I found my voice, but it had lost its strength. "What must I forgive *you* for?"

His lips lifted partway in that enchanting smile of his. "For not making sure you knew precisely where my heart lay before you left."

My body wanted to bathe in the warmth of such a declaration, then reality set in, and I peered down to my trembling hands.

"I am only one half of a whole, Helena. I never even knew how incomplete I was until you entered my life. I am positively lost—" He exhaled, looking upward and chuckling. "I am certainly making a muck of myself."

I smiled and shook my head. "You are utterly charming."

His fingers delicately traced my chin, lifting it upward until our eyes locked. I longed to drown myself in their depth and never resurface. With a heavy heart I squeezed my eyes shut as tears slipped through. The brush of his thumb felt like a searing flame as he swept the disloyal tears away.

"My heart belongs to you, Helena."

"I—" I drew a steadying breath, willing my voice not to falter. "I have to tell you something, Lucas. Something that will undeniably crush everything." A sob caught in my throat, threatening to break free.

His palm cradled my jaw, his gaze unwavering. I watched as his chest rose and fell in front of me, his measured breath mirroring my own.

"I know about your father," Lucas whispered. "I know of his involvement in my own father's death."

I gasped and took a step backward. My gloved palm covered my mouth, and I searched his eyes in fear, but he reached out for my hands and tugged me back in. Wrapping his arms around me, he drew me close and whispered in my ear. "Tafney has accepted the consequences of his actions and has given me his blessing."

I could not comprehend any of this. "And you still wish to bind yourself to me?"

"Undoubtedly." He spoke with conviction. "But first, I want to know from your own lips if you would have *me*."

My mouth parted in shock and Lucas' eyes darted right to them. The muscles in his jaw tensed as if it took every ounce of resistance for him not to lean in. "Would you have me?" he repeated. The warmth of his breath stilled on my lips.

"You are asking me what I want?"

He leaned back. "Yes, Helena, I would never force you to do anything against your will."

I bit my bottom lip. "I no longer have a dowry," I whispered.

279

The space of several heart beats passed before Lucas answered, "It is not your dowry I desire."

Oh.

Breathe.

Unhindered with reserve, Lucas' hands gently cupped the nape of my neck, drawing me closer, his touch enacting a symphony upon my skin as our lips met in an enticing dance. My arms encircled his neck, my mouth surrendering to his lead, each kiss seamlessly blending into the next, surpassing every expectation I previously held about kissing Lucas.

When we parted, the lingering taste of what could become my daily ritual clung to my lips.

"I love you, Helena," Lucas murmured, his lips brushing against my temple. "I love everything about you and cannot fathom a life without you."

I smiled, but just for added measure, I had to confirm one last time. "Are you certain, Lucas?" Despite the hope that settled within, he needed to understand the depth of our decision. "I could bring shame to your family name."

"I don't care what others might think."

"But what of your sisters?" A hint of worry lingered in my words.

Without hesitation, he affirmed, "They approve." Then as if he knew reservations had been expressed, he added, "Especially, Genevieve."

I searched for anything in his eyes that might indicate otherwise, and it wasn't to be found.

"I know you, Helena, and I know your heart. We will navigate the tempest together. Besides," he smirked. "We have a marquess on our side."

"I love you too, Lucas." I stood on my tiptoes and kissed him again. The sweetness of our touch sparked chills the length of my body from my head down through my toes. "What do we do now?" I whispered against his lips.

He winked. "I imagine your aunt will want to help you choose a bridal gown."

A wide, sincere smile spread across my face.

"Go to Northampton, love. Spend some time with your aunt. I will make the arrangements here. But promise me, our wedding will not be much longer than the time it takes to have the banns read. I doubt I can wait even that long."

I giggled. "Neither can I."

He took my hand and led me back to the coach, kissing me once more out of sight of the windows. Once he assisted me back inside, Lucas stepped up to the doorway.

"Good afternoon, Mrs. Carver. I'm Lucas Walsh, the younger brother of the Marquess of Granton."

Aunt Patricia glanced in my direction, her mouth twitching as if she wrestled with a smile of her own. I pressed my gloved fingers against my slightly swollen lips and felt my cheeks flush. "Well," she tickled the ears of her lap dog. "It seems we have some shopping to do."

Lucas smiled wide and arched an eyebrow in my direction. "That you do."

He faced me once more and reached for my hand and kissed it. "If you and your aunt are not opposed, I shall visit by week's end."

Aunt Patricia spoke up, "We would be delighted to have you in our home."

Our home. My heart warmed at the sound of that. Though it would not be my home for long, it felt truly wonderful to know she welcomed me as family.

"And thank you, Helena," Lucas squeezed my hand.

"Whatever for?" I whispered.

"For making me whole."

Epilogue

Lucas

October 1814

Lying on my stomach atop our shared bed, Helena's fingertips grazed the edges of my scar with a gentleness I craved. Every morning I awoke with her by my side was a gift from God. Her tender caress as she applied the salve to my scar was only part of the healing taking place in my body and soul. Her agreeing to be my wife was the utmost cure.

Leaning in, she whispered in my ear. "The balm is working, love." Her fingers skimmed the length of my back to my neck and chills ran down my spine as she next ran her fingers through my hair, then leaned in, kissing my neck. She was my solace… everything she did brought comfort.

Surrendering to my temptation, I rolled over and pulled her against me. "*You* are my balm, sweetheart. *You* are the reason I am healing."

I had only experienced two nightmares in the five months since our wedding and she held me and soothed me through both. We opted to stay in London even after the season ended while the repairs to my estate were being managed, and Helena accompanied me to Greenwich every week to visit with the wounded soldiers. But by the end of summer we relished in the seclusion and privacy of the country.

Giles' knock tapped fast, harder than usual.

"Privacy, *most of the time*," I muttered.

Helena moved aside and pulled the covers over her body. I smiled at her sweet bashfulness. "One moment Giles," I said. He generally did not disturb us in the morning.

"I would not have come if it wasn't urgent, my lord" he said through the door.

I glanced at Helena, her face stricken with worry. Her father's sentence was to be read later this week. We had plans to leave for London two days hence.

I answered the door in only my breeches. Giles had seen me in much less. "My lord, this just arrived from your brother." He nodded and departed before I closed the door. Helena was now sitting at the edge of the bed in only her shift and, while that was always a distracting sight, my eyes didn't peel from the missive in my hands. I sat beside her and unfolded it.

Justin was a man of few words but what he wrote was always taken into careful consideration.

Lucas,
His Grace, the Duke of Chilton with whom I associate through the House of Lords shared with me only

yesterday that his son, Josiah, the heir to the dukedom was killed in a duel four days' past. A message was swiftly dispatched across the channel to notify Lord Hunter Matthews of his brother's death, posthaste, but as you are well aware, it could take a considerable amount of time for him to return, or he could be here as early as tomorrow. Considering your close friendship, I assumed you would appreciate the news without delay. I look forward to seeing you and your lovely bride at your earliest convenience.
Justin

Throughout the years, we had all suspected that Hunter's cad of a brother would meet his demise in a situation such as this, but it only suddenly occurred to me that the great responsibility now fell upon Hunter's shoulders as the heir apparent to the powerful Duke of Chilton.

"Love, how long would it take Eliza to pack your trunk?"

"Not long," she rose from the bed. "I will help her."

I reached around her waist and drew her close, inhaling that sweet exotic scent I so loved. Nuzzling my face into her neck, I felt her wilt beneath my touch.

"Much longer if you continue down this course," she whispered breathlessly.

Chuckling, I drew back and kissed her deeply. *I am one exceptionally fortunate man.*

Excerpt from book #2 in the Gentlemen of War series- *Hunter*. July 2024

Gwendolyn

Mother's smile blossomed as the Marquess of Devon entered the parlor. We stood to greet him with our traditional curtsies, but I stifled a gasp behind my gloved hand, for the man who stood before me bore little resemblance to his twin. Josiah could command the very air around him with an expression. Hunter's presence came in the form of his physique, nearly as grand as the room itself. Shoulders that rivaled the breadth of the doorway strained against the fine tailoring of his coat—a garment that, I was certain, had never cut in similar ways on his brother.

With a stride that exuded both power and grace, he crossed the room and bestowed a bow upon my mother's outstretched hand. As he turned his gaze toward me, something flickered within those steely brown depths—a spark of intrigue, maybe—before a veil of control promptly descended upon his features.

Curiosity coursed through my veins as he approached, gently claiming my gloved hand in his. A captivating smile curved his lips as he bowed. This struck me with the force of a tempest, for despite the differences in the brothers' stature, the mystery that hinted within those eyes seemed hauntingly familiar. Hidden depths swirled beneath the surface, secrets shrouded behind a handsome face, much like Josiah. I glanced away, lifting my chin with the barest of protective barriers. I would not let myself fall for such deceptions *ever* again.

"Please, Lord Devon, join us." Mother gestured to the empty seat beside me on the chaise. We took our seats in silence.

As Polly delivered the tea, Mother dispatched her to summon Father from his study. We had but a fleeting window—a mere handful of minutes before the men would retreat into the world of politics, estate management, or some other realm that would exclude me. Not that I was ignorant of those topics, the reason lay solely in Father's refusal to allow me to contribute. If I desired answers before Father's arrival, now was the time.

I raised my teacup with practiced grace, peering over the rim at the marquess with a gaze honed over the years of training in the art of captivating the male species. The man met my look unwaveringly, his dark brown eyes betraying no hint of unease or faltering gentility—a refreshing contrast to the nervous fumbling I often evoked in the men of the *ton*. I admired such assuredness, so long as it didn't stray into superiority. Haughtiness and confidence tread a fine line, and the marquess seemed to navigate it with effortless ease. Then I caught sight of a few injuries marring his perfect face and wondered what misconduct led to such wounds.

Another mystery.

"Tell me, my lord," I began with an alluring whisper, "what kind of man takes his dead brother's betrothed to wife?"

"Gwendolyn!" Mother's teacup clattered against its saucer, the crash echoing in the sudden silence.

The man's lips lifted into a partial grin, completely unruffled by my question. Setting his cup down, he leaned forward. The ardent scents of bergamot and leather wafted over me.

"The type of man who finds honor in his commitments regardless of how taxing said commitment might be."

Smiling inwardly, I kept a smooth outward appearance. I had not anticipated him to be so quick and clever. I let my long eyelashes fan against my cheeks for the space of a second before I continued. "It must cause some vexation to know you were not the first choice."

One of his eyebrows arched. "Could not the same be said about you?"

I nearly dropped *my* teacup this time. Was he referencing me as *his* second choice or Josiah's? Society seemed well aware of the reasons behind Josiah's dueling death. In truth, I believed Josiah never considered me as his third, fourth, or fifth choice, but I had not expected Hunter Matthews to state this so pointedly.

Father entered the room at that precise moment and, if not to interrupt the disastrous conversation, his timing surely saved my mother's delicate constitution from a fit of the vapors.

Order *Hunter* today on Amazon

Author Notes

While most authors strive for accuracy in our historical novels, undoubtedly on occasion, we make mistakes. Please know that these are not deliberate and simply overlooked as words and letters blend together over time. Painstaking research is something I personally take pride in and hope to improve upon with each new book I write. Thank you for your patience and especially for taking the time to read *Lucas*.

The main reason I chose to do a Regency series about men returning from war was because of the men in my life who have returned similarly to these four younger sons. While the era and circumstances vary, all four of the men in my family have either been to war or faced overseas deployments, several of them getting shot at and mortared upon multiple times a day... day after day. The nightmares, irritability, frustration, anger, emotional and physical pain are quite real as well as the profound feeling of displacement. Life went on without them and while they were facing life and death situations in the name of defending the freedoms, we enjoy, so many of us back home continued as if nothing ever changed.

As a big *Lord of the Rings* fan, Frodo's final words as he finishes his memoir resonate deeply- "How do you pick up the threads of an old life? How do you go on, when in your heart you begin to understand, there is no going back? There are things that time cannot mend. Some hurts that go too deep...that have taken hold."

For centuries, the effects of such an outcome were considered to be a normal result of war. That one should man up and deal with it. The images, the tears, the sounds, the smells became a daily struggle to overcome. We now have a name for it, PTSD—Post Traumatic Stress Disorder. The men returning from the Napoleonic Wars were considered lunatics if they admitted to such weaknesses.

PTSD affects many different people from many different circumstances, and I do not in any way consider myself an expert, having only experienced it through the eyes of my loved ones, but as we continue to bring it into the light and speak more openly about its characteristics, support, and resources, the greater chance we have of finding balance, a collective strength, and understanding.

About the Author

Leah Moyes is a wife, a mother, a lifelong student with a background in Anthropology and History, and a celebrated author of a dozen novels including her award-winning Berlin Butterfly Series and its Prequel "The Polish Nurse". Between writing and archaeological digs, the world is her playground. She loves popcorn and seafood (though not together) and is slowly checking off her very long bucket list.

Leah Moyes' Novels

Historical Fiction

The Berlin Butterfly Series-
The Polish Nurse (Prequel)
Ensnare (Book 1)
Deception (Book 2)
Release (Book 3)
Anton (Book 4)
Stefan (Book 5)

Second Survivor

Historical Romance

Charlock Series-
Charlock's Secret (Book 1)
Return to Charlock (Book 2)

Charlock's Curse (Book 3)

Gentlemen of War Series
Lucas (Book 1)
Hunter (Book 2 July 2024)
Zachary (Book 3 December 2024)
Jaxon (Book 4 June 2025)

Contemporary Romance
Rock Pride, Country Prejudice

If you loved this story and want to share your thoughts, I would very much appreciate a rating or review on Amazon, Bookbub, or Goodreads. Thank you again!

Made in the USA
Columbia, SC
07 December 2024

48664588R00174